# Wolfsbane

## Best New England Crime Stories

Edited by

Christine Bagley
Susan Oleksiw
Leslie Wheeler

Crime Spell Books
Cambridge, MA 02138

Crime Spell Books
Cambridge, MA 02138
www.crimespellbooks.com

# Wolfsbane

# Contents

*Introduction*

One of the pleasures of working on the Best Crime Stories of New England anthology is the opportunity to read a wide range of crime fiction and introduce writers new to the genre. We have three new mystery writers in this year's collection. "Undercover in Alcatraz" by Michael Ditchfield may be his first published short story, but it shows an expert's hand in plotting and parceling out surprises. "The Snitch" by Sean Harding, also a first published short story, takes the reader into a complicated world where the reader has to revise her view of the good and bad guys. Christine H. Chen isn't new to short fiction, but in her first mystery story, "Lost and Found," she applies her considerable skill to confounding the reader—until the perfectly calibrated ending.

The twenty-one stories in this year's collection range from 1733 Boston to 2060 and perhaps beyond. The anthology opens with the Al Blanchard Award story, "Good Deed for the Day," by Bonnar Spring, the story of a high school student who comes upon a dead man in a car in a parking lot. This is the first of five stories in which young people distinguish themselves in handling the harsh truths of life. In "Not Too Sharp" by Zakariah Johnson, a college student works retail in Georgetown, D.C., and gives in to temptation. A high school student on the verge of dropping out in "A Simple, Hard Truth" by Gabriela Stiteler leaves her teacher with nothing left to say. The lessons are unexpected but varied and clear in Carolyn Marie Wilkins's "The Moon and Stars." A little boy has the key to a crime, but the consequences reverberate among the adults in "Don't Think about It" by Judith Green.

The family dynamic is murderous in "Wooden Spirits" by Connie Johnson Hambley and in "The Woman in the Woods" by Christine Bagley. But redemption is secured in "Lost and Found" by Christine H. Chen.

Families remain all too human when we leave the present and move into the future. A husband's excitement at a new "gadget" and possible promotion in "You Love Me to Madness" by Lauren Sheridan doesn't quite work out. AI and its bots have the upper hand in "Final Wishes" by Ray Salemi.

Sizing up the enemy is crucial, and harder than expected, in "Assumptions Can Get You Killed" by Brenda Buchanan and in "Whoop!" by Leslie Wheeler. But taking your losses can be necessary, as the homeowner learns in "The House on Riverbend Road" by Susan Oleksiw.

A journey into the past doesn't find life any safer or more honest, but consequences are certain over time. In "Major Deception" by Frances Stratford, set in 1733 Boston, a lady of the evening is transported to the Massachusetts Bay colonies, where life is just as hard but at least she has friends. Soon after the Civil War, a former slave-owner travels to Boston to question a former enslaved woman, in "A Bitter Draft" by Robin Hazard Ray. Seven women gather at a cafe in Paris thirty-five years after the occupation by the Germans, in "Seven Women" by Eleanor Ingbretson, most to reminisce but one to force the truth into the light of day.

The world of professional criminals has its own code, but its members don't have any better success at navigating the world. A man is talked into going undercover in Alcatraz for a simple job of gathering information, in "Undercover in Alcatraz" by Michael

Ditchfield, but nothing is ever simple with the feds. In "The Snitch" by Sean Harding, a police informant passes time while waiting for his handler, engaging in acts of kindness and ultimately justice. Life is much harder for Jason Allison's undercover rookie in his "Lucky Cat," though he manages to survive, barely. Life would be infinitely better if more criminals were like those in "Which Way New England?" by Paula Messina.

As editors we delight in the variety of stories, the diversity of subgenres, and the new names submitting work to the anthology. When we organize the stories, we consider various arrangements, but mostly we try to arrange the stories in such a way that they are commenting on each other, engaging in a dialogue of themes, perspectives, and questions, stimulating ideas and perhaps more story ideas.

Christine Bagley
Susan Oleksiw
Leslie Wheeler

# Good Deed for the Day

## Bonnar Spring

I gave my mother forty dollars from the money I took off the dead man. It was enough to buy some groceries—but not so much she'd wonder at my generosity.

I didn't kill him. He was already dead when I saw him in a silver BMW last night, his head cradled between the headrest and the driver-side window. It was ten-thirty or so. His car was parked at a sloppy angle in the municipal lot behind the pizza joint where I do deliveries.

Drunk, I figured. I walked by, heading for my car. Turned the corner. No one around. I ducked into a doorway and covered my too-noticeable blonde ponytail and dangly earrings with the hood of my sweatshirt, then retraced my steps so I was coming toward the car from the front. I stopped on the passenger side and tapped lightly on the window. When the man didn't move, I squeezed the door handle. It swung open smoothly and silently, like the door of an expensive sports car should.

I eased into the seat, pulled the door shut but didn't latch it—

in case I needed a quick getaway.

I probably should've noticed how quiet he was. Drunks snore and snort, but this guy didn't move a muscle. I inched closer. If there'd been any passers-by, we'd look like some random couple snuggling, saying good night.

He wore an unzipped windbreaker over jeans and a flannel shirt. I reached across and pulled his jacket open. My lucky day—or so I thought. His wallet poked out of the inside pocket, so I didn't have to do anything creepy, like I'd had to once, and wiggle my hand into his pants pocket.

His continuing stillness after I removed the wallet got my attention. Only the side of his face was visible and even that was in shadow, tilted downward and away from me. The crown of his head rested on the window. He was old—like forty or fifty-something—old enough to have gray hairs mixing with brown and sagging skin at his jaw.

He wasn't breathing. *Shit.*

I held *my* breath while I looked at his chest. I was right. Dead. I got out of there as fast as I could.

Mom was watching TV when I got home. I put the forty bucks on the end table next to her Sprite. "Don't spend it all in one place."

She'd been telling *me* that for seventeen years. Once I got a part-time job to help with expenses, parroting the phrase back at her became our in-joke.

"Busy night," I said. "I'm tired. See you tomorrow." I took the stairs two at a time and locked myself in the bathroom.

If I hadn't been so freaked out with the man being dead, I would've taken whatever cash I found and left the wallet. Credit cards and stuff like that aren't any use to a small-town teenager like me. And even a drunk who couldn't remember where he'd spent all his dough would know if his wallet disappeared.

Still, getting as far away from the guy as fast as I could meant I hadn't stuck the wallet back in his pocket before I fled. I only realized

I still had the damn thing when I got to my car. I thought about going back, but I couldn't do it. Things would've been a lot different if I'd gotten over my squeamishness.

Before I headed home, I'd pulled out some money for my mom real fast. Now, in the privacy of the locked bathroom, I took the wallet from my backpack. It was the kind of light-brown leather that I think is called calfskin.

Killing baby cows for their skin? To hold some old guy's fifties? Disgusting.

There was a wad of bills with a piece of red paper folded around them. I started counting. Fifty, a hundred . . . holy shit. The wallet's streamlined design disguised how much the damn thing held. Nine hundred and sixty dollars. Adding it to the money I'd already saved meant I had enough.

The red paper had fluttered to one of the white tiles on the floor and lay there like a patch of spilled blood. Which—even though the man was not the least bit bloody— should tell you something about my mental state. He really had looked pretty peaceful, like he was sleeping. A heart attack, I guessed.

But when I picked it up, I read the paper:

*I can't live like this. I'm sorry, Pam. I tried, but it's gotten too hard. You'll be better off without me. The mortgage is paid this month, and this'll keep you going until you can straighten things out at the bank. Steve*

*Shit*. He killed himself and I took the note. Shitshitshitshit*shit*.

Mom called up the stairs. "Eliza, you planning to eat breakfast today?"

"Coming."

She'd poured me a glass of juice and taken out a package of frozen waffles. And she'd picked a couple of early spring crocuses for the vase I made in art class. It had a great crackly glaze in blues and purples and was only slightly misshapen.

I hadn't gotten much sleep, kept thinking about the poor guy.

Dead. All alone in the cold. His wife, probably tossing and turning all night too, wondering why her husband hadn't come home. Would *knowing* he was dead be better than waiting and worrying about his absence?

It didn't matter because I couldn't figure out how to phone in a tip. I knew enough not to call the police or 911 from the house or from my cell phone. And pay phones have gone the way of the dodo. Even if I knew where one was, I'd have to avoid those cameras that seem to exist on every street corner. The police could probably figure out who I was—backtrack with other cameras to see where I came from, where I went.

Anyhow, what the heck could I say? "By the way, the dead man I told you about killed himself, but I accidentally took his suicide note when I robbed him."

I had to find some way to take care of it this morning. Without getting involved.

Mom limped over to the ornate mahogany chair across the breakfast table from me. I'd found the chair on the street last year. The seat had been cracked almost in two, but the back had gorgeous spindles. I'd carried it home and completely restored it.

For years after Dad left, Mom worked two jobs to support us— school bus driver mornings and afternoons and hostess at a big steakhouse in the evenings. She lost both of them when a hit-and-run driver knocked her over, crushing her right foot.

She couldn't drive at all now, and the restaurant balked at keeping—as Mom said—"a cripple on the payroll."

Her disability check kept the roof over our heads but not much more.

Mom would kill me if she found out about my ditching high school. I'd dropped out before Christmas and started to work for a cabinetmaker. So far I was mainly sweeping up sawdust and doing inventory, but Grant—my boss—was a meticulous craftsman, who'd already showed me how to do some really cool stuff. If I could get into the North Bennet Street School's woodworking program in Boston, he promised to keep me on as his apprentice.

With Mom always around so much, it was tough to keep lying. I figured I'd confess once I got accepted into the program, which I hoped would be before high school graduation in two months, the ceremony where I was *not* going to march across the stage. I'd gone to one of North Bennet Street's Open House sessions last fall; the word was that financial aid was hard to come by. So, before I applied, I needed to be sure I could pay for the damn thing. There wasn't a penny of surplus in Mom's budget.

That's what I was saving money for. I'd tell her I got a scholarship.

"What are you up to today, honey?" she asked.

"I think I'll go to the library, do some homework." It was Saturday. Since I dropped out, I sometimes forgot what day it was. I went to the workshop whenever I could. Tuesday or Sunday—it didn't matter.

"Isn't April school vacation next week?"

*Almost busted.* "Oh, yeah, but I, uh, don't want to get behind."

Mom beamed her super-proud-of-you smile, the one that makes me feel like a total loser.

I'd planned to add last night's money to what was already in the manila envelope taped underneath the top drawer of my desk. I kept a running total, subtracting from the cost of the program. And this would've gotten me to zero. But I couldn't do it. He was *dead*, for crying out loud, and the cash was for his wife's expenses.

At some point in the night, I decided to deliver the note to the man's wife. So I folded the money back inside the red paper—well, except for the forty I'd already given Mom—and zipped it into the front compartment of my backpack. I'd get rid of the other stuff in the wallet as best I could.

His driver's license gave his name as Steven Thompson and an address on Willow Street, which was on the other side of town in one of those upscale neighborhoods where every street had a tree name and every house was gray or tan with a bay window on either the left or the right.

*How* to get it to her was the problem.

Stick it in a manila envelope, print the address, and mail it was my first thought, but I've watched enough episodes of CSI to know about fingerprints on paper and DNA on saliva. Even if I handled the envelope with gloves and sealed it with a sponge and water—my prints were all over the note and the money.

But, worse, mailing it would take days to get to her, and a dead body in a car in the municipal parking lot would be noticed this morning—if it hadn't been already. I thought his wife ought to know as soon as possible. With his ID gone, it might be a while before the police figured out who he was and delivered the bad news.

I'd just have to go to his house and . . . well, I hadn't exactly figured that out yet.

There still was the problem of fingerprints. Okay, I was being paranoid, but the guy was *dead* and I didn't want any connection to him. That's why I was going to the library: to see if there was any way to wipe off my fingerprints. I was not going to do that search on our home computer. It wouldn't be as obvious as googling "how to keep a dead body from smelling" but still . . .

A small miracle happened on my way to the library. A bunch of Cub Scouts were doing a spring clean-up on the town common—some kind of community service project. The supervising grown-ups had a fire roaring in a brick fire pit and were handing out hot cocoa and donuts to passers-by, collecting a crowd of eager customers. I stopped and joined the throng. It only took a second to drop the license and credit cards in the fire. They were shriveled black and flaking before I turned away, donut in hand. Another block down the street and I tossed the empty wallet into a trash container. Done.

The library was almost empty, and there was a computer in a corner where no one could monitor my searches. I waited for the patron using it to finish their session and walk away—that way I wouldn't have to show my library card. Then I sat down to use the remaining time.

I got the bad news immediately. Basically, I was screwed. There was no way for me to ensure my fingerprints were off the paper or the money.

I closed my eyes and leaned my head against the wall behind me. Now what?

*Eliza, you're overthinking everything as usual.*

*Just drop off the damn note.*

If I'm not caught with a suicide note signed by a dead man and almost a thousand dollars in my backpack—and there's almost zero chance I would be—why was I so worried about fingerprints?

Put it somewhere Mr. Thompson could've left it. His mailbox would work. I wouldn't even have to leave the car, just stick my arm out and pop it in like a mailman does to deliver flyers and bills.

The "almost zero" piece bugged me, but I didn't see any other options.

Willow Street was lined with parked cars. *Oh, no, the word is out already.* I imagined a houseful of casseroles and crying women.

Also, there were no street-side mailboxes on Willow. Everyone had a rectangle in tasteful wrought iron next to the front door. Okay, Plan B: get to the door without being noticed. I parked my car and looked closer at the Thompson's lawn.

*It was a yard sale.*

Holy moly. That's so creepy; they don't know. They're going on with all the stupid stuff people do and they *don't know.*

On the other hand, I could use the stream of people milling around to walk up to the house. It'd only take a second to drop the note and money into their mailbox.

I got out of the car and wandered through the vaguely linear layout of a yard sale, past knickknacks, old puzzles, camping equipment—

"Eliza?"

I turned. "Hi, Cassie." We were in the same Spanish class last year. She was into music, I remembered—took chorus and belonged to some modern dance group—so our paths didn't overlap too much. "What are you on the lookout for this morning?"

Cassie fluttered her hand. "Mom just sent me out here to keep an eye on stuff while she gets another cup of coffee."

That's when it hit me—Cassie was Cassie *Thompson*.

*Shit.* Cassie's dad was dead.

Double, triple, quadruple shit. Her mother was *Mrs. Thompson.* Yeah, I know that's totally obvious, but Mrs. Thompson, Cassie's mom, was the high-school nurse.

And I took the wallet with his IDs. They really didn't know he was dead.

But going ahead with a yard sale like everything was normal— hadn't they missed him? I mean, my mom used to leave for work really early, but I'd hear her in the bathroom. And she always made coffee and left enough for me. I'd know if she wasn't around.

"I haven't seen you at school lately," Cassie said.

"I'm going for a GED instead." I'd learned to use my bored voice. That way, most kids didn't bother asking questions. "Get on with my life."

"Cool." Cassie fell into step beside me. "Wish I could've done that. I'm counting the days 'til graduation, leaving for LA the second school's out. That's where my dad's sister and her husband live, and they invited me to stay with them. I can take courses out there." She flashed a smile full of pent-up excitement. "And, hopefully, break into show biz."

Cassie kept talking about some drama school, her aunt's pool

. . .

*This is so screwed up—what the hell am I going to do now?*

At the same time, I'm thinking *maybe it's lucky for her.* At least Cassie will have something to look forward to. Her mom, not so much. Her husband dying and then her daughter taking off for the opposite coast.

A woman ahead of us was looking at golf clubs. And beyond that, a row of tools—*ohmygod*, there was a complete set of forged steel chisels. Twelve of them. Like new.

"These are really nice." The tag attached to the box read *$150.* I'd seen them on sale for three hundred dollars.

"They're my dad's. He doesn't have time for hobbies and stuff anymore, so he told Mom to get rid of everything."

*They're selling her father's tools and sports equipment?*

"He's away on business. Mom said he really didn't need to go—he just didn't want to be hanging around while she cleaned everything out."

*Oh, the poor guy. He made an excuse to leave—or pretend to leave—so his family wouldn't worry. Gave them permission to turn his expensive toys into cash.*

"Plus, Dad probably wanted to get out of all this work." Cassie stretched her hands behind her neck, elbows in a V, and rolled her neck. "He already spends as much time as he can at his office. Mom's making him crazy with her redecorating mania. Everything has to be new, has to be just so. I mean, Mom even wanted to sell *my* bedroom furniture today. I said couldn't she at least wait two lousy months until I was out of the house. I was like really afraid she'd go ahead and do it, though, if I stayed at my friend Tina's house this weekend, so I stuck around. And she won't listen to Dad either—he's just about given up. I don't think he can stand living here much longer."

*Oh, god, that sucks so bad. Wait'll Cassie finds out how bad it had gotten for him.*

Our roundabout trek through the yard had us ending up near the front door. A few envelopes sticking out of the ornate metal mailbox gave me an idea. "Can I use the bathroom?"

"Sure, I'll show you."

*Darn.* With her accompanying me inside, I couldn't do what I wanted, but surely Cassie wasn't going to hang around while I pretended to pee. I'd slip the note and money into the mailbox on my way out.

Cassie opened the door and we walked into an open-plan living area. To the left, a family room filled with matching sofas, a big TV, bookshelves, fancy curtains with swags of extra fabric. On the right, a gorgeous Early American kitchen. Even with laser-focus on *almost* completing my good deed, as an aspiring woodworker I recognized the artistry—and expense—in the wide-board pine floor, mullioned windows, slate counters, and wood-beamed ceiling.

Mrs. Thompson was on the phone. "Who's keeping an eye on the yard?" she mouthed without taking the phone from her ear.

Cassie executed an eye-roll in my direction. "Aunt Ruth is still outside. Remember Eliza, Mom? From the eighth-grade play? I just came in to show her the bathroom."

Mrs. Thompson shrugged. The lines on her face looked like my mom's in those days after the accident when she didn't sleep well. Or, sometimes, didn't sleep at all. Mom couldn't climb stairs for a long time, so she stayed on the living room sofa. I'd hear her at all hours, her crutches tapping the hardwood floors, scraping back one of the kitchen chairs and sitting at the table, head in hands. I came across her one morning, head down on the table, a pile of bills with red lines on the envelopes spread out like a fan.

I bet Mrs. Thompson didn't sleep much last night either.

I hadn't seen her since I dropped out. In a coral turtleneck and jeans—instead of the floral scrubs she wore at school—she looked taller and even more imposing. You could never fake a cold or bad cramps with Nurse Thompson. At best, she'd let you sit in her office until the next bell. Then she'd jerk her thumb toward the door like an impatient hitchhiker and tell you to scoot. It sounded like her take-charge attitude had only gotten worse. No wonder Cassie was frustrated.

Mrs. Thompson had wandered into the living room to continue her phone call, looking out on the lawn at customers pawing through their belongings to find bargains. Was it my imagination or was she also scanning the street, hoping a silver BMW would turn in to the driveway?

Phone call over, she strode toward us in short, jerky steps that spoke of tension, an effort to hold herself steady. She stopped by a big kitchen table that would seat eight comfortably, in elegant Windsor chairs. Its pine surface was marred the way tables get when families eat dinner there, kids do their homework, parents pay bills. Today, with boxes cluttering the surface, it looked like the staging area for more yard sale stuff.

Mrs. Thompson picked up a box, shoved it into Cassie's arms. "Here, take this outside with you."

Lifting the box exposed a pad of red paper; a pen rolled to the floor. I felt sick to my stomach again, imagining Mr. Thompson sitting there, elbows on the table, looking around his home one last time. Writing that farewell note. Pulling out money for his wife. What kind of awful despair would it take for a man to end his life when he had all this?

How could he push this chair back and go to . . . perhaps to a bathroom cabinet where he knew there were enough sleeping pills to stop his heartbeat? Did he walk back into the kitchen, pour a glass of water, and swallow them? Or did he wait until he'd driven away from the house, knowing he'd never return?

You never know about people's lives on the inside. Even when it looks great on the surface. I mean, it's the twenty-first century—how miserable would you have to feel to kill yourself when you can get a divorce? A guy who drives a BMW and lives in a place this nice obviously has resources. And he has a sweet daughter, even if his wife is annoying.

Cassie's mom pointed down the hall with her coffee-cup hand. "First door on the right."

"Thanks, I'll be right out."

I closed myself in, waited a minute, flushed, and was pretending to wash my hands when the doorbell rang.

"Mrs. Thompson?" A deep voice resonated.

I cracked open the door and peeked down the hall. The man standing at the front door wore a dark blue uniform. Police.

*Too late. They must've found the body and already identified it.*

"Arnie Burris, ma'am. I'm a detective with the Newburyport Police Department." He angled his head toward a younger man standing next to him. "My partner, Sergeant Vincent."

"Is something wrong?" Mrs. Thompson's hands were behind her, fists clenched so tight her veins stood out on the back of her hands. Yeah, she definitely suspected something was amiss about her husband's absence.

"Is Mr. Thompson at home?"

"No, he's away right now." She spread her fingers wide and rubbed them on the seat of her pants.

"Away?" asked Detective Burris.

"Well, he told me yesterday that he was going away for the weekend."

"On the weekend? Business?"

"Yes, yes." Her head bobbed in time to her words. One fist clenched; then the other in a kind of syncopated rhythm.

"And where was he heading?"

"Oh, uh." Her left hand squeezed her right wrist—tight, like she was trying to keep it still. "Oh, right, yes, he said the Cape."

"And when was the last time you saw him?"

"Last night—but what's the problem, Officer? I mean, why are you asking these questions?"

"Last night about what time?"

"Um, nine-ish?"

I kept watching her hands . . . it was really odd how much this reminded me of the last time I saw my dad. Maybe it was a similar situation—I'd been taking a bath and when I opened the door, they were really going at it. Tense voices in the kitchen, me in the bathroom hoping not to be noticed. Mom was stone-cold angry with him lying about something I didn't understand until years later. "Your slutty piece of ass" doesn't really compute to an eight-year-old. But, anyhow, the more stuff Mom asked him, the more Dad fidgeted—fists clenching, unclenching, wiping his palms like they were sweaty. He couldn't keep his hands still. He left that night, and I never saw him again.

"Do you have a recent photograph of Mr. Thompson?"

"What?" She took a big step backward and clapped her hands to her mouth so the "Why?" came out muffled.

Detective Burris made a stop sign with his hand. "One more question—did he leave in a silver BMW, Massachusetts plate 345188?"

"Ye-e-e-s." The way she went still, I guessed Mrs. Thompson understood what was coming,

Detective Burris took off his cap and held it stiffly to his chest. "I'm sorry to inform you, ma'am, but the body of a man answering the description of your husband has been found in the driver's seat of the silver BMW I just asked you about."

A long silence. "I don't understand. You're not sure it's Steve?"

"No, ma'am. When we didn't find any identification, we ran the plate. Because the car is registered to Consolidated Metals, we called and ascertained that the vehicle was used by the CEO, Mr. Steven Thompson."

"But you're not . . . not sure it's Steve?"

"No, ma'am. As I said, there was no identification. The person we spoke to at Consolidated provided a description of Mr. Thompson that matches the deceased; however, we will require a positive visual confirmation."

The white-tight grip on Mrs. Thompson's hands was gone; in its place, her fingers flexed and twisted. "But, um, Steve would never drive anywhere without his license. It's in his wallet."

*Wait, she's just learned her husband is probably dead and she starts quibbling about him never going anywhere without his license.*

"There are some preliminary indications he didn't actually drive himself."

"But how else would he have gotten downtown?"

The other policeman, Sergeant Vincent, had been jotting things down in a notebook. His head jerked part way around, then stopped abruptly when Burris cleared his throat.

"That's one of the things we need to clear up." A quick sideways glance at his partner. I've done that same move before—it's the shut-up-and-let-*me*-do-the-talking signal—useful when the bouncer asks what year we were born and I know my friend can't do math and will screw it up.

*What is Burris going to do?*

"Once we've completed a thorough search of the crime scene and surrounding area, I'd like you to join us. You can make a formal identification there."

"Of course." Shaky, high-pitched.

"I'll give you a call when we're ready. How long do you think it will take you to get there?"

"To the parking lot? No more than five or ten minutes. Unless traffic's backed up at High Street." Mrs. Thompson stumbled backward and collapsed onto one of the living-room sofas, her head bowed. "It's just sinking in . . . so awful. There's bound to be some, some explanation. I mean why?" Her voice shook as she repeated, "Why? He must've left some sort of note."

Both officers stepped across the threshold into the living room.

Burris said, "I'm sorry for your loss, ma'am."

"Steve's been so depressed lately, but I never thought, never .
. ." She covered her face with her hands.

From their position in the living room, I could only see the younger policeman's face. He said, "Mrs. Thompson, when I phoned your husband's office for information about the vehicle registered to the company, we spoke to the secretary. It seems that Mr. Thompson asked her to purchase two tickets to Los Angeles for tomorrow—a round-trip ticket as a school-vacation-week surprise for his daughter and a one-way ticket for himself. He told her he planned to work remotely for a month or two until he got resettled."

Can sobbing stop on a dime? When I cry, sniffles keep shaking me for ages. Mrs. Thompson, head in her hands, went deathly still in an instant—except for the pads of her fingers rubbing her cheeks. A sharp cry escaped, then she said, "Oh, poor Steve, he's been talking lately about . . . about needing a break. His sister's out there—they're close, but . . . but I guess, in the end, he just couldn't go on."

I wished I could see Detective Burris's face now that he'd sprung his trap. I didn't catch on right away, but once I connected the dots, I knew what I had to do.

"Yes, that must be it. I'm sure. I'm sure he'd never do anything like that without leaving some sort of note for me and Cassie. Maybe one of your people took off his jacket and you just missed it."

"Mrs. Thompson, would you care to explain how you knew the location of your husband's car?"

I unwrapped the red paper from around the stack of money, ripped the paper into bits, and flushed it down the toilet. When I went outside, Cassie said they'd sell me the woodworking chisels for a hundred even. ❖

# Which Way New England?

## Paula Messina

B ucky, Niagara Falls is not in New England."

"You sure?"

"Positive. How long have you lived on this planet and you don't know Niagara Falls is in Pennsylvania?"

Bucky scratched out what he'd written on his yellow ruled pad. He tapped his pencil on his lips, then wrote something new.

Nick looked at his watch, then peered out the windshield at the ice and snow. Finally, his eyes settled on their objective, Been There Done That, a secondhand furniture store.

"How does this sound? Wicksadrilla jumped—"

Nick whipped his head around. "Wicksadrilla? What you smokin'? Wicksadrilla? Where'd that come from?"

"Last night. In a dream. Wicksadrilla's a tall, dark, beautiful woman. The hero of my story."

Nick stayed focused on Been There and said out of the corner of his mouth, "Heroine."

"Heroin? That don't make no sense."

"No. Heroine. The heroine of your story."

"Whatever."

"Forget whatever and what's her name. Get rid of that pencil and paper." He tapped the face of his watch. "We gotta be ready. The owner should be here any minute."

"I'm ready. But when the muse speaks I gotta write."

"Muse?" Nick grabbed the pencil out of Bucky's hand and threw it on the back seat. "No muse spoken to you since you were in diapers. How many times I gotta say pick one? Starving writer or a bank robber rolling in dough."

"Bank robber? How come we're hitting a second-hand furniture store?"

"Look, Shakespeare, even old Willy didn't start at the top. He wrote for television before he wrote all those plays nobody understands. Same with bank robbers. Gotta master the craft first."

"Shakespeare didn't write for TV. You're thinking of another writer. Can't remember his name right now."

"You miss my point." Nick wagged a finger at Bucky. "Forget writing and pay attention. Today, we rob Been There. Next week we hit the Market Basket in Chelsea. Practice runs. Come the end of the month we'll be pros ready to knock off Salem Five Cents Savings Bank."

Bucky reached into his jacket and fished out a pencil. "I can do both. And I have a deadline. It's gotta be set in New England, and it's due by the end of the month."

"You can't serve two gods."

"Huh?"

"Look, Bucky, I wanted to be the next Larry Bird, but I realized my chances of making a fortune were far greater if I exited the basketball court and avoided the other court. Had to decide did I want to be mediocre at both or a genius at one. That's why I dedicate my time to honing my skills as a bank robber. You're either a writer or a bank robber. Can't be both."

"Shows what you know. Lots of writers have two careers. So they can pay the rent until their novel is an Amazon best seller."

"Forget paying the rent. Forget Amazon. We clean out Salem Five Cents, we clear out of this rathole. No more waking up to cold floors and frosted windows."

Nick looked at the mountains of snow in the parking lot and shivered.

"We move to Samoa where it's always warm, it never snows, and no one can touch us 'cause Samoa doesn't have a contradiction treaty with the United States. Spend our days sipping piña coladas on the beach with those wahine chicks in hula skirts. Never work a lick again."

"Look, there's the owner." Bucky leaned forward. His chest hit the steering wheel. The horn blared.

"Way to go, Sherlock. Let her know we're here."

Nick kept his eye on the woman as she searched in her purse for a key. She scanned the parking lot but didn't pay any attention to Bucky's junk heap before unlocking the security gate.

"We're in luck. She doesn't suspect a thing. Piece of cake." Nick tossed Bucky a balaclava. "Come on, Bucky, we gotta move."

After Nick pulled down his covering so only his eyes showed, he said, "Bucky, baby, this is the beginning of our new life. Let's go."

Bucky left the motor running and joined Nick in the snow. They sprinted across the lot.

They were within spitting distance of Been There when a burly man appeared out of nowhere. His black beard peeked out from behind an Angelina Jolie mask. He was massive. His gun was colossal.

Nick kept trucking toward the shop. Bucky grabbed his arm. "Wait." His voice quavered. "That guy'll beat the crap out of us without working up a sweat."

"We were here first. Can't let him steal what belongs to us."

Nick picked up his pace. When he reached Angelina, he said, "We got dibs on this place."

Angelina looked down at Nick. "You talking to me? Where's your manners? We ain't even been properly introduced." He swatted Nick's shoulder. "Move."

When Angelina pointed his gun, Nick got the message. Only he wasn't backing down.

"I got my heart set on Been There," Nick said. "Find another store to rob."

Angelina jabbed his gun in Nick's chest. "You missin' a few brain cells, boy? You lucky I ain't already plugged you. I'm a patient woman. I mean man. Move."

Bucky whispered, "Let's go."

Nick ignored Bucky. He pushed Angelina's gun out of the way.

Bucky made a grab for Nick's sleeve, lost his balance, and hydroplaned on the ice. He slid into Angelina, who disappeared into a mountain of snow. Angelina's gun flew out of the snow pile and hopped across the ice before ending its flight at Nick's feet.

He kicked the gun into a snow drift.

Angelina screamed. "You broke my knee cap, you piece of of—"

A shot rang out.

Snow cascaded off the roof, turning Angelina into a snowman.

When the snow and the gun smoke had settled, Been There's owner, a tiny woman with steel-gray eyes, stood in the doorway, her rifle at the ready. Nick and Bucky whipped their hands up in the air.

"You there, Angelina, hands against the wall."

Angelina groaned.

"I'm a patient woman. But today my patience's run out. You got three seconds."

For a big man, he moved mighty fast. His hands were up against the wall before the owner reached two.

She kept her rifle aimed at the masked man as she said to Nick and Bucky, "Thanks for taking care of this monster for me. Not that I needed your help. Cops on the way."

The sound of sirens grew louder and louder.

Nick and Bucky exchanged grins and slowly lowered their hands.

Siren wails crescendoed.

"Gotta get outta here," Bucky said through his teeth.

Nick whispered back, "We're defenseless. She's got a rifle."

Angelina moaned.

The owner pointed her rifle at him. "Shut up and don't give me no song and dance about your knee."

Angelina went mum.

"Look, lady," Nick said, his voice shaking, "we didn't—"

"Don't go all reluctant hero on me," she said. "I can't thank you and your friend here enough for stopping this goon."

"It was nothing," Bucky said, unable to suppress his glee. She wasn't going to shoot them. "Glad we could help. Right, Nick?"

"Yeah. Sure. Glad we helped. Gotta go."

"You can't leave. The police will want your statement, and I'd like to properly thank you."

"No need to do that," Nick said. "Knowing that we stopped this . . . this robber from possibly hurting you is enough. Ain't that right, Bucky?"

"Right as rain." Bucky cast his eyes down and shuffled his feet in the snow. "Glad we could help. But we need to get going. Dental appointment."

It was too late. The cruiser halted in front of Nick and Bucky, cutting off their escape.

"Well, what do we have here?" the policeman asked.

"Looks like acting doesn't pay enough these days. Angelina Jolie attempted to rob me, and he might have succeeded if these two gentlemen hadn't decked him."

"Well done." The officer patted Nick on the back. "I wish more citizens were as conscientious as you two."

The officer ordered Angelina to remove his mask. "Well, if this isn't my day. Paul Calvin Revere in the flesh. With outstanding warrants for sticking up Cumberland Farms and Kelly's Roast Beef. Heck, we'd be here all day if I listed all your robberies. Hands behind your back."

In no time, the officer had Revere in handcuffs. He hustled him into the back of the cruiser, slammed the door, and walked back to the store owner.

"This is your lucky day. There's a ten thousand dollar reward for his capture."

Nick mouthed ten thousand dollars. That was more than they expected to steal from Been There. A lot more.

She whistled. "That's a neat, round sum. Officer, I couldn't have done it without the assistance of these two gentlemen. I think it only fair they share in the reward."

Bucky leaned over and said in Nick's ear, "Ten thousand bucks. Gee, that's more than I'd make if I sold a thousand stories. A lot more."

"Officer, sir, we couldn't take the money," Nick said. "Stopping this blot on mankind is reward enough."

"You crazy, Nick?" Bucky said under his breath. "We need the dough."

"And give the police our names and address? Are you nuts?"

"What's that?" the officer asked. "Didn't hear you."

"We were discussing how grateful we are that no one was hurt."

"I need to see some identification. Might need to contact you about testifying at trial."

"Do we have to?"

"Out of my hands. That's the prosecution's call."

Bucky and Nick handed over their IDs and watched the officer write in his notebook. He smiled when he handed them back. "Pleasure to meet two men willing to do the right thing. Sure you don't want to share the reward?"

Nick got all sheepish and said, "Golly, we weren't expecting this." He looked at Bucky, who nodded. "On second thought, we wouldn't want to disrespect this brave lady. If she insists we share the reward, well, who are we to disagree?"

"I had a sneaking suspicion you'd change your mind." The officer got into the cruiser and leaned out the window. He waved a business card in the air. "Anything I can do for you gents, let me know."

The two men watched the cruiser drive away.

"Anyone have a pen?"

Bucky rummaged around in his jacket pocket and plucked three. "Here you go, ma'am."

The store owner took the officer's card and wrote something on the back. "Call me in a couple of days so we can work out the details. And thanks again for your help."

Bucky watched her disappear into the store. "That was a close one. We coulda been killed."

"Come on, Buck. Don't exaggerate. Angelina was all swagger."

"I wasn't talking about him. I meant the store owner. She coulda put that bullet in our behinds."

"Well, it turned out to be a good day after all. We'll be rolling in dough."

"And I'll have time to finish my story."

"Bucky, where'd you leave the car?"

"Right over—"

Bucky ran to where he'd parked the car. It was gone.

"Some great idea this turned out to be, Nick. The police have our names and addresses. My car is stolen, and my masterpiece is gone."

"Look at the bright side, Bucky. We'll be rolling in that reward money soon. That gives us time to figure out our next heist. That cop gave me a lot of ideas. Never thought about sticking up Kelly's Roast Beef."

Bucky wasn't listening. He muttered, "Gone. My one chance to get my writing in print. My masterpiece. Gone."

"Come on, Hemingway. You're on your way to being a successful bank robber."

"And author. I just got a great idea for a story. Next week, I'll borrow my mother's car. We hit Market Basket. I'll have time to work on another story. Something about a bank heist. You know, funny like *Dortmunder* with the grit and realism of *Law and Order*. Maybe a little romance for spice."

"You think you can pull that off?"

"I don't know why you question my talent, Nick. I already have the plot. It's a winner about a lonely astronaut circling the globe, planning his next robbery. When his capsule is over New England, he dreams of returning to his bodacious wife and their home on Ellis Island."

"You said the story has to be set in New England."

"Come on, Nick. Don't pull my leg. Ellis Island is off Marblehead."

"Bucky, did you sleep through geography? You don't even know the geography of the state you were born in? Ellis Island isn't in Massachusetts."

"Sure it is."

Nick shook his head.

"Well, where is it?"

"New Jersey." ❖

# Not Too Sharp

## Zakariah Johnson

Georgetown in D.C. is among the most expensive quarter miles of on-street shopping on the East Coast. In the early eighties, I was working retail on its central thoroughfare, M Street, at an anomalous army surplus store just a few doors down from the Francis Scott Key Bridge. The bridge connects Georgetown to the nearest Metro stop, built on the Virginia side of the Potomac, since Georgetown itself refused to allow the local subway system to connect it to the rest of the city. How an army surplus store got planted in the midst of such exclusivity remains a mystery to me; probably a legacy from the fifties with an iron-clad rental agreement.

I'd nearly flunked out of college in December, but they were letting me come back in September after spending a semester off "to think about things," as they put it, and I took the job in the interim. I was the only white employee other than the manager. The rest were Black except for Alexi, a partially disabled Puerto Rican veteran whose conversations that didn't start out about Vietnam got there within two minutes. The distance each of us had to commute to Georgetown for work at our crappy minimum-wage retail jobs was inversely proportional to how close we were to Caucasian: I had a fifteen-minute walk from the one-room efficiency on Washington Circle that I shared with two people (my girlfriend and my ex-girlfriend); Alexi came down from the Woodley Park—National Zoo area; and most everyone else came in from either southeast D.C. or the adjacent parts of Virginia, Anacostia, etc. The pay was lousy but the job was easy to do with a hangover or to call in sick for, and I planned to quit at the end of August despite what I'd told them when I started in March, go back to school, and never ask for a reference. The work just covered my expenses for food, shelter, and beer and was sufficient unto the day.

I'd been there about a month when the manager decided to train me for the cash register. Not blatantly stealing merchandise seemed my only qualification other than complexion. Alexi warned me not to agree to it, but I didn't listen. The first day I was on the register only two of us had access to it: me and the assistant manager. She was a thirty-something Black woman with a perfectly round face like Charlie Brown and looked like she should be starring as the mom in a TV ad for microwave dinners. The money in the till that day came up twenty bucks short, just like Alexi had predicted. The manager made a big hem-and-haw about not wanting to have to report it to HQ, and, it being my first day and all, "mistakes do happen," and he'd let it slide if both of us who'd been on the register put in a ten spot each to cover the gap. I considered the ten bucks tuition (tuition I could have saved if I'd listened to Alexi), so I paid it and let the assistant manager keep the money she'd stolen without making a fuss, but I made it clear how it was the one and only time I would do that. Being young and arrogant, I considered her an idiot at the time—risking her relatively better paying job over ten bucks—but I didn't consider that the ten bucks might be more important to her than to me, or, more likely, that screwing over the store and letting them know she was doing it without them being able to catch her gave her an illusion of agency. I would soon learn my own lesson about breaking the rules to try to make myself feel smart.

More anomalous than a discount army surplus store in Georgetown were the customers we had—people you wouldn't expect to encounter in the heart of the most expensive neighborhood in the U.S. capital. Some were migrant laborers from Central America who came in to buy work boots. Alexi taught me how to ask their shoe size in Spanish and I already knew the numbers up to ten (these men were never larger than an eight); they seemed to appreciate the effort I made and soon their friends would come in and ask for me by name, much to Alexi's amusement. Other customers were the city's homeless, smelly men with matted hair and beards and clothes so dirty as to have been any color, who came in for camping gear or durable fatigues to add over the layers of clothing already fused to their grimy skin. Punk rockers loved us for the table full of black T-shirts we stocked at much lower prices than at the trendy nearby Commander Salamander, which catered to the bourgeois suburban punker wannabes, essentially people like me, much as I denied it.

D.C.'s a small town, and the rich and famous brush shoulders every day with the poor and forgotten, especially in the Metro, and more so in the retail world. Everybody needs pants, right? Occasionally a nationally known politician or TV news celebrity would come in and ask for something we didn't have, but which the store seemed grubby enough to suggest we should. Like when Roger Mudd, then on TV each night in front of the White House, blew in like a hurricane and asked for audio cassettes."

" 'Audio cassettes'? You mean tapes?" Alexi asked him.

"Yes, that's right," Mudd said, his silk trench coat swirling about him like he'd stepped out of a romance novel.

"Why the fuck would a clothing store sell tapes?"

Mudd stormed out and Alexi stayed in a great mood the rest of the week.

Once, a lawyer came in and bought five pairs of jeans on his way home simply because it occurred to him he didn't own a pair anymore and he didn't want to be "that guy." He was still "that guy," even with the jeans he'd never dare wear to work, but he knew it already, so I didn't get smart with him. Nice guy, he even tipped me.

But the real attraction for our customers was the knives. Again, how we got away with selling items that were illegal to carry on your person in D.C. is a permanent mystery. No doubt being in Georgetown made us partially invisible to the police, even if we were right next to the bridge the riffraff crossed to get there. We had pocket knives of every variety, from cheap to expensive, folding knives favored by the long-term homeless, and evil-looking "survival knives" you could fight a bear with, favored by the twitchier, short-term or newly homeless who still thought being armed would protect them.

I never thought of knives as dangerous. They'd been like jewelry for tweens and teens in the little Appalachian town I grew up in. Every boy in middle school carried a knife to school. Kids would sit outside at recess and show off their sharpening skills by shaving the hairs off their arms. "See that? That is sharp, buddy." Whenever a fight broke out—which was frequently—nobody even thought about pulling a knife. Of course, we only fought our own—whites fought whites, Blacks fought Blacks—cross-racial fights had too much potential for real violence, not just stylized dominance rituals. As long as no knives came out and no fights crossed the color bar, the teachers pretended not to notice us kids working out our own problems.

D.C. was different. Grim, generally small, young men would come in already knowing the exact length limit for a blade they could carry in the city: four inches. It seems short, but four inches is the standard length of the fighting knife carried by U.S. Navy Seals. You can do a lot with a four-inch blade if you're determined. These guys in either biker jackets or punker outfits were the sort muggers avoided, but they often clashed with their own kind in a more serious form of stylized combat. Even their shoes were obvious weapons.

Switchblades were illegal at the time everywhere. Despite their usefulness, they got banned throughout the U.S. in the 1950s when an ill-informed movie about street gangs with names that sound like sports franchises used switchblades to reenact a fight scene from *Romeo and Juliet*. White people got freaked out, so they did what they always do when something gets too closely associated with minorities: they banned it. Thus our store could somehow sell a twelve-inch knife with a serrated edge clearly meant for stabbing people, but we couldn't sell a five-inch knife with a wobbly, brittlely thin blade that flicked out at the touch of a button. The best we could do was sell look-alikes: folding lock-blades that superficially looked like switchblades but had none of their smooth functionality. The pseudo-switchblades were good sellers, but only to the teenaged tourists from out of town—New Jersey, the Midwest—who'd been set loose to shop in Georgetown by moms and dads who figured, mostly right, it was a benign environment.

These white teens would come in, always in pairs or packs, look at the pseudo-switchblades in the locked cabinet, and ask me or Alexi to show them one.

"Ah, man. This isn't real."

"Yeah, it is. Lemme see. Oh, man. You're right."

"What a rip off," one would say. Then they'd turn their eyes to me and kind of whisper, "Don't you guys have any REAL ones?"

This only had to happen a few times for me to recognize a business opportunity.

Two kids in a row asked for real switchblades on Monday. On Tuesday, my day off, I wandered on foot into D.C.'s Chinatown with a couple twenties in my pocket and a half-formed idea in my head. D.C.'s Chinatown is a small affair, only a few blocks, but the city makes a big deal out of it and so do those who live there. I found a shop with no sign and only a few 8½ by 11-inch handwritten notices in Chinese taped to the windows. The shop windows were mostly blocked with cardboard boxes and showed only a few token attempts at displaying merchandise—a paper umbrella and a waving-cat clock with a price tag on the front. I stepped inside and was met by the silence of three gray-haired men who looked old but not frail, huddled over a teapot and what looked like a racing form, though I couldn't read the characters. There was a single glass-topped counter with a few token goods inside that gave the impression of a legitimate business—plastic Buddhas, fake designer watches, and other kitsch—but the rest of the store was filled with unmarked, cardboard boxes.

"You guys got any knives?" I asked. They did.

Eventually, they opened a box with the kind I was looking for, and I took a dozen off their hands for a package-deal price lower than what I'd once paid in Juarez for similar merchandise. The switchblade handles were black. The blades were dull and didn't look like they'd ever hold much of an edge. But when you pushed a little button on the side it made that magical *snitt* sound, and it wasn't a comb that popped out. I was in business.

That week alone I sold out my whole supply and went back for more. The profits were ridiculous. I paid less than ten dollars each for pieces of junk and sold them for two to three or even more times than, depending on what I thought the customers would pay.

It would go like this. A kid would come in and ask to see one of the fake switchblades. When he showed his inevitable disappointment, I'd size him up and if it seemed safe, whisper, "You interested in the real thing?" They always said yes and then did an all-cash transaction on the spot. Alexi didn't work the cash register, but he did have a knife-cabinet key, so he got in on the action, too, calling me in to take care of special requests and eventually buying a few off me for his own resale.

The scheme was good for an extra hundred or more a week, but by the second month there were already signs of inevitable disaster. Alexi walked up to me, weaving through the waist-high bins of piled-up clothing with two teens in tow. One was pointing at me.

"These guys say you sold a knife to a friend of theirs."

"A switchblade," said the closer teen.

"Shut up, man," I whispered harshly. The manager was upstairs at the moment, but the assistant manager was nearby with no one to attend to, watching Alexi and me without looking at us. She clearly knew what was happening but never said anything (she had her own games going).

"Cover the floor for me, Alexi?"

"Yeah. Sure."

I took the kids up to the knife cabinet by the cash register. I unlocked it and began showing the kids the phony blades inside, whispering under my breath that I knew what they really wanted and scolding them for being so stupid. "Yeah, I know it's not real. Just look like you're interested."

Alexi was showing some work jeans to a couple of Spanish speakers when a street person (*unhoused* and the empathy that comes with that term wasn't a thing then) came in and wandered upstairs where we kept the discount bins. The assistant manager had no choice but to follow him to be sure he didn't clean us out. I sold the kids one switchblade each for the same price their friend had paid a week earlier. Then I made them buy something else from the store so I could ring up their purchase.

"Why?"

"My manager's watching. Just grab a black T-shirt. They don't show blood."

I palmed their bills and slipped their knives to them. Then I rang up their T-shirts as the under-boss came downstairs following the homeless guy. I gave the kids their change and told them to scoot.

"Tell your friends not to talk to anyone but me," I said, pointing to my nametag. "Nobody else, got it?"

The next month, it seemed every high-school kid from Maryland and Virginia came in to buy a switchblade. I didn't feel like an arms dealer; the blades were cheap junk, little more than novelties, and less lethal than their mothers' kitchen knives. So Alexi and I kept selling, for ourselves and for the store. I started making anybody who wanted a knife also buy something else. This gave me an excuse to linger near the cash register, where the knife case was, but I mostly did it out of a combination of pride in my salesmanship and partially from guilt at doing something so stupid and vile, like I was trying to balance the scales of karma.

It all fell apart in late July when a group of five out-of-town twenty-somethings blustered in. I gave Alexi the nod and moved up to the cash register and the knife cabinet, where they predictably lingered.

"Hey, check it out! Switchblades!" said one.

"Naw, man. Those are fake," said another.

"Are they real?" the first asked me.

"Those aren't," I said. "You looking for the real thing?"

"You got the real thing?"

I smelled beer on their breath. They were loud and two of them were moving away with their backs to me, doing that little shuffle that betrays the guilty thoughts of inexperienced shoplifters getting ready to pocket something. The kid addressing me was a little taller and beefier than the rest, with more bloodshot eyes. The manager was out and no other customers were in the store. I should have said no, but I didn't.

"Where you guys from?" I asked. They told me; it was a state far to the south. I caught Alexi's eye. He shrugged.

"C'mere then," I said, lowering my voice and walking to the edge of the counter. "What would you pay for the real thing?"

It turned out they'd pay a lot. They named a price that was too high, so I jacked it up a little more. They didn't care. They were buying an adventure, and you can't put a price on that.

I only had a few switchblades on me and one of them was defective. The spring was weak and every few times you'd push the button the blade would open but hang loose and limp, not stiff and ready. You could compensate if you flicked your wrist hard at the same time you pushed the button, so that's what I did as I demonstrated it.

I'd planned to take it back to exchange in Chinatown, but there was no way I was going to let these suckers off the hook.

"This one catches a little so you have to snap your arm," I said, demonstrating.

I sold the first knife, then the other two. The kid who'd bought the second one started flicking it open right in front of the store window.

"Hey! Not in here, man," I hissed.

His friends wanted to look tough and knowledgeable, so they joined in making fun of him, "Yeah, dummy, put it away!" Then they were out the door and down the street, hopefully on their way to someplace far away never to be seen again, especially the one who'd bought the defective knife.

"Well, that was a pretty good day," I said to Alexi as the manager locked the door behind us.

"Not too bad," he said, putting on the ridiculous fedora he always wore and disappearing into his after-work life he never shared.

I had so much cash I stopped in a shop on the way out of Georgetown and bought a forty-ounce bottle of cheap beer in a paper bag to drink on the walk home. I decided I wasn't in that much of a hurry, so I cut down a side street toward the Potomac to drink my beer in peace. I got to the old C & O Canal, a shady, tree-lined walkway hidden from view right in the middle of Georgetown. I was looking for a trunk to lean against when I bumped face-to-face into the five guys who'd bought the knives.

"Hey! It's the guy who sold you the knife!"

"Make him take it back!"

"Yeah!"

I wasn't surrounded, not yet, so I stepped off the grass into the bike lane to get more distance and to force them to come at me one at a time instead of rushing from all directions, if they decided to do that. They'd clearly had more to drink in the intervening hours, a lot more.

"Hey, guys. Something wrong with the knives?"

"You know there is. You showed us."

"Yeah. I did. So, what's the problem?"

"I want a different one," the big guy said. "This doesn't work."

"That's the last one I had."

"Bullshit!" said a kid behind him, clutching his own paper bag with a bottle in it, though a smaller one than mine.

"Take his money!" said another.

The look in the big guy's eyes made it clear he agreed with the suggestion. I took a step back and to the side, drawing the pack into a single file again as they each changed directions to move in on me. The big guy grinned and pulled out the switchblade he claimed not to want. He must have spent the afternoon practicing because he got it to lock open on the first try. I'd sold them my last knife, so the forty-ouncer in the bag was my only weapon. Before I had to pull it, a group of middle-aged tourists appeared on the path. The boys got flustered, quickly hiding their knives, and I stepped in behind the group as it passed, looking over my shoulder as the quintet glowered at me walking away.

As the distance grew, it was clear they weren't going to follow, but then one of them yelled the same thought that had just occurred to me. "We know where you work, man!"

The gig was up. I called in sick the next day, and the next. This was in the days before cell phones or caller ID, so I made a few more calls to the store trying to get in touch with Alexi to warn him the five-pack might show up, but the manager or assistant manager always answered and I'd hang up. I didn't bother calling back on the third day, and the store never got in touch. I never stopped in for my last paycheck.

About six months later, I was playing Atari video games at home with my girlfriend when the phone rang. The ex-girlfriend was entertaining a visitor in her bed behind the free-standing partition wall we had in place to provide privacy in the one-room efficiency the three of us shared. We had the stereo turned up to drown out the sound of bodies tussling, so I had a little trouble hearing what was said over the phone.

"Hey, man. It's Alexi. Long time no see. How you doing?"

"Pretty good, man." I'd never given Alexi my phone number. "What's up?"

"Well, I was calling to see if you could tell me where you bought all those switchblades. I was thinking of selling some myself." His voice sounded strange, or maybe I just heard it through a gauze of suspicion.

"Where are you, dude?"

"At home with my old lady, man."

"How'd you get this number?"

"What? Oh, I, uh, got it from the store. How come you never came back?"

"Well, you know. Life goes on."

"It does indeed, my man. Well, if you're not coming back, you think you could tell me where you bought all those switchblades you sold out of the store? I could use the extra cash." That was the longest sentence Alexi had ever spoken. It was a pity. I'd thought he was cool. I'd thought a lot of things.

"I don't know what you're talking about," I said. "The knives in the cabinet aren't real."

There was a pause.

"Yeah," he said. There was a long pause. I wondered who was there with him and where he really was. "Well, you don't know where I could score some herb, do you? I—"

I hung up on him. I looked at my girlfriend, half-baked and unhearing, completely focused on the screen in front of her and the console in her hand. I looked at the two pairs of intermingled, wriggling feet sticking out past the privacy blind where their owners made increasingly noisier grunts and squeals. I thought about the paltry amount of money I'd made spreading knives with no function but violence throughout the world, and the risks I'd taken for no defensible gain, and I realized the only difference between me and the assistant manager who'd conned me out of ten bucks was that she hadn't risked hurting anybody to show off how smart she was. And suddenly, as I realized what I'd done, I wondered why I was always so determined to prove I was the dumbest kid in the class. ❖

# Undercover in Alcatraz

## Michael Ditchfield

In April I got married. By August I was serving twenty to life in Alcatraz. The Feds had talked me into going undercover to investigate a prison suicide. They suspected a small-time hood they referred to as Bobby K of murder. He was in cahoots with corrupt guards. Take Bobby down and the bad blood would go down with him.

They needed evidence.

The money they were offering would cover our mortgage for a year. I took the proposal home. Gladys didn't like killers. Or corrupt turnkeys. She took reassurance from the Feds looking after me. Besides, it was only four weeks, and Alcatraz had the reputation of being the most well-regulated prison in America.

That afternoon along the Embarcadero, I'd taken a stroll with a man in a fedora.

"Why me?" I asked him.

"You can be passed off as a con," came the answer. "Your old man was in the mob, and you've already been inside."

"Juvie," I said.

He pushed his hat back. "Means you started young."

"What's my rap?" I asked.

He stopped walking. "Murder in the second. Victim's name is Arnie Schwartz. He took money set down for the waitress. Shot right between the eyes. You've taken a plea deal. It's all in the record."

I remembered the case. The perp was never caught. Now he had been. Me.

One problem lingered. "How are you going to clean my record after?"

He started walking again. "We do what we want, when we want."

"And who would 'we' be?" I asked.

"The federal government," he said.

The canaries in my gut told me to turn around and walk away. I didn't listen.

"You're serving your country," the man said.

The jaunt on The Rock was supposed to last a month. Tops. Right! The first thirty days in Alcatraz you're quarantined: No yard, no job, no socializing. The second month I spent trying to meet the mark. It wasn't as though I could stroll by his cell. Fraternizing along the galleries and stairways was forbidden. You entered the lunchroom in single file and were told where to sit.

A smidgen of freedom existed in the yard. All concrete, but there were places to sit. The Feds told me they were putting in their own man. He'd be my lifeline. Nobody contacted me. But one afternoon sitting outside listening to the gulls calling back and forth to each other, a prisoner sidled up to me. Introduced himself as Bobby Kelly.

"You're connected," he said.

Suspicion goes with the territory. "Who says?"

"That's my business."

"If it's about me, it's my business."

Bobby gave a nod. "That pimple-faced screw, the rookie."

Pimple-face must be my contact. Now I knew.

My eyes got prison hard. First impressions mean a lot on the inside. "Why would he even be talking about me?"

Bobby took out a pack of smokes. "He's a homeboy. South Boston. I tried my luck at bribing him."

"I bet that went over well."

"He made me face the wall. I thought I'd be doing solitary. Then he leaned in and told me if I needed something, I should see you. You were in the Jewish mob." He laughed. "So, it was going to cost me."

That hit me the wrong way. "Like the Italian mob wouldn't cost you?"

"No offense meant," he said.

"But offense taken," I answered.

Bobby's knee began to bounce. "Your name doesn't sound Jewish."

I played this friendlier than I normally would have. "Not unless you hear it in German: Glückstein. Means Luckystone. The old man went with the English and dropped the stone."

"And Jolly?" he asked.

I sniffed. "Nickname from Juvie because I mostly looked miserable. It stuck. I got to like it. Tell me what you need, Mr. Bobby Kelly?"

Don't stare is an axiom. He stared. "I need a message sent out."

What lay behind his blue eyes swirled around, not crazy exactly, but like a thousand points of light without a center, their own universe, and he was God. He turned his gaze toward the fog bank rolling over the Golden Gate. You couldn't see the Bridge. I just knew it was there.

Bobby turned back to me. "People want me dead."

"What people?" I asked.

He shook out a smoke from a pack of Camels and lit up.

"People with no morals," he muttered. "Government people."

I looked up at the sky. "Three packs of smokes. Two up front."

The bell rang.

We knew better than to linger. Bobby slipped the pack in my shirt pocket. Anything not issued to you or purchased by you was considered contraband, a serious infraction. So was using cigarettes as currency. He made no move to pass a note. Just shuffled behind. No whisper. No nothing. The man understood prison.

On The Rock every inmate had the same 5 by 9 cell with a cot, a sink, a toilet, and bars at the front. Every day brought the same routine. Counts came thirteen times. Cutlery in the chow hall, toothbrush in the cell, and everything in between. Then there was the weather: Too hot or too cold, mostly too cold, the kind of raw chill that worked its way into your bones. Occasionally, though, out in the yard, the sun met the concrete just right, warm and pleasant. Seagulls wheeled overhead; a sea lion barked from the rocks. Close your eyes and you could almost imagine a picnic in Malibu.

That kind of day was when Bobby sat by me again. Just silent for a while.

When I was looking the other way, he spoke. "You heard about brainwashing?"

Who hadn't? Guys got captured in Korea, and next thing they were spouting enemy propaganda and denouncing the U.S. of A.

"It's what the Reds do," I said.

"You think we let the commies get ahead on mind control?"

"What's it to you, Bobby?"

He boiled a while. Then came the glare. "They melt your brain. Watch while you go insane." He stuck his face in mine. "I'm stronger than them. Understand? You think you know evil. You don't." He looked off in the distance. "Medical experiments. They offered a reduced sentence. Does Alcatraz seem like a reduced sentence?"

"Seems like they wanted you out of sight and out of mind, Bobby."

"The guy who came in with me. They killed him. Said it was suicide. They're coming for me next."

"That's why you want to get a message out."

He flared. "Are you dumb or are you just acting that way?"

"Tell me the message, Bobby."

His eyes narrowed. "This is important, so listen. LSD."

"LSD," I repeated.

"Lysergic acid diethylamide. That's what they used. Not just on me."

"Anything else?"

"Frank Olson. They can't hide that forever."

"Frank Olson. Got it. He a prisoner?"

"He's one of them. He carried out experiments on people. Another so-called suicide. Rumor has it he found a conscience and jumped off a building. Only he could have been pushed." He slipped me a piece of paper. "My kid brother's phone number. Tell him the Globe, and the Bureau. He'll know what I mean. He's got connections. Mind control on U.S. citizens. Got it? The CIA's not supposed to operate inside the country. But they do."

"Mind control, the CIA. I've got it."

His look got hard. "Before they messed with my head, running a little numbers racket would have made me happy. Not now! They're going to pay. I'll start my own mob. I'll use them like they used me."

Braggadocio came with the territory. But something in Bobby's look made me believe him. I ran the story over a few times: The CIA operating inside the country, medical experiments, mind control. None of it seemed real. Then I thought back to my walk down the Embarcadero with the man in a fedora. He wasn't FBI. Bureau guys flashed badges. It made me wonder what I was doing here. And how I was going to get out.

A big guard with a sour expression led me to a cramped booth where you stared through milky glass and talked over an intercom. I'd told Gladys not to visit; I'd be home soon enough. But I wasn't home. And there she was. Looking beautiful. I wanted a real conversation, only talking about prison or current events was against the rules. I couldn't say how dumb I'd been for taking the job because every call was monitored. The guard sat hidden, but stop talking a moment and you could hear him breathing. Or a match striking as he lit a cigarette. Like having a peeping Tom outside the bedroom window.

Our talk about nothing went back and forth. Reminded me of TV. Smiles that weren't smiles. Laughs that weren't laughs. Only at the end of our time when the clock was ticking down, Gladys sighed, not a bad sigh, just a sigh. She said, "I hate sleeping alone." Then she added, "I might be pregnant."

Her eyes filled. Mine did too.

She hung up the phone and walked out without looking back.

The journey back to my cell felt like the last steps of a marathon. I could barely raise my feet. Sourpuss, the burly guard, fell in behind me.

"Hubby is gone. Whoops, she's in the family way." The keys on his belt jangled. He snickered. "You should have thought about the backdoor, man, before you committed the crime."

Keep trying, buddy, I thought. Just keep on trying.

We got back to my cell. Sourpuss summoned up a malignant grin.

"While you've got nothing but your hand, she'll have her legs spread for the meter man." He rocked back and forth. "Ooh, ooh, ooh. She never felt it so good."

I caught him smack upside his cheekbone.

They dumped me in one of the dark cells. The Hole. I held up for a while. But no light gets to you. Perpetual blackness. Insanity has no center. Time loses meaning. But if I hadn't gone into that tomb, I would never have understood Bobby. Or why he held on to vengeance.

My life flowed around me, all the mistakes, none of the triumphs, all the regrets, the fears, but what I held on to most was how much I hated Sourpuss, that guard. I'd have pulled his teeth out one by one. Along with other things I'm too ashamed to say. Hatred felt like power. Love felt like weakness. And that's how I lived, stewing on murder, until they opened the door and hosed me down and washed away my own filth.

They'd put me in the underworld and if that's what Bobby went through in those medical experiments, I felt for him. He claimed he was inside for heisting a truckload of cigarettes. That deserved Alcatraz? My head swam with the idea of getting Bobby's message out. Good sense told me not to decide until I stopped raging. Rage doesn't see shades of grey. If I got his message out, I was going against my own handlers. It was a double-cross on top of a double-cross. Nothing they said to me had been true.

One cold afternoon in the yard, Bobby sat beside me again.

"We still on?" he said.

He knew where I'd been. Everybody did. A blessing in a way. Snitches don't get put in the hole.

I nodded. "The guy you came in with, the so-called suicide. Had he been planning on spilling the beans?"

"He thought what they did to us was wrong. I haven't had one decent night's sleep since I was given that stuff."

"The CIA killed him is what you're saying."

"I already told you."

He slipped me an unopened pack of cigarettes. "We square now?"

"That's not the price we agreed on," I said.

His eyes became icy. "I've had to wait."

I thought about that. "I never set a time, Bobby."

"Maybe Jews bargain too much," he said.

I let that rattle around before I responded. "You're the one bargaining."

Something gave. The tension eased. He nodded to himself like some old voice was talking to him.

He put a hand on my back. "I appreciate this. I still owe you."

Next afternoon, back in my regular spot on the concrete, a guy named Dub strolled by. When I knew him on the outside, he'd been Two Fingers, on account of his having only two fingers on his left hand. Now it was plain Dub. As in double. He'd been part of Sol Pinsky's crew, the crew my old man worked for. Dub was serving a life sentence for a murder he didn't commit. He'd killed people though. Plenty. But guys get real sensitive about what they're sentenced for, and prosecutors play loose with the law when they want something. Dub was inside because he wouldn't turn on the boss.

The thing about gangsters is they follow rules. Dub knew me. Knew my old man. Knew I'd given the eulogy at Sol Pinsky's funeral after the lung cancer got him. Sol had done me a big favor on a case that involved police corruption, probably saved my life. His price had been the eulogy. A public amends on both sides for harm done to my family. It still stuck in my throat, but that was my secret.

"Hey, Dub," I said.

No acknowledgment. Just kept on walking.

Two days went by before another mob guy came up to me in the library. Dub wanted to know what I needed. I slipped the two packs of cigs and the note I'd written. Told the messenger the note was for the big boss. Needed to get delivered ASAP.

That was it. Done.

Authority rubbed me the wrong way. The CIA was using me. I still didn't know for what. And they hadn't made one move to let me know when I might get out.

On a miserable afternoon when everyone was shivering, Pimple-face did the count on my block. Then he walked me down to the visiting room. A dame I didn't know, had never seen before, a real looker until she opened her mouth, smiled at me through the glass. A front tooth was missing. Her eyes said she couldn't wait to get my pants off.

I was talking to a hooker. She looked down at a piece of paper. Hesitated. She didn't read too well.

"Hey, baby . . . how are you?" she read.

Nobody had to tell me Pimple-face was monitoring this call.

"Like a million bucks," I said.

She grinned. This was a hoot. They must have been paying her well.

"Hear anything from Bobby?" she asked.

This was the route out. Tell Pimple-face all. No muss no fuss. Nothing to do with prison murders or corrupt guards. Just what Bobby knew. Or so I hoped.

"Bobby feels like he got a raw deal," I said. "Supposed to get a break on his sentence, only it never came."

She read from that paper again.

"What's he think happened to . . . Brent?"

Brent had been the suicide.

"Bobby's sorry Brent took the last exit on the freeway," I said.

That's when Pimple-face cut in. Spoke to the streetwalker first. "Keep smiling, Jezebel." Then his tone got tough. "You, Mr. PI, if you want to see the outside of this place, I'm expecting to hear what you know. Everything. Including the note that went out."

My brain went into overdrive. If they knew about the note, then why go through this charade? Then I got it. They knew about the note but not the contents. They wanted the real skinny.

I upped the ante. "Bobby wants J. Edgar to understand his situation. He says Hoover is not going to be happy when he learns spies are stepping on his turf. J. Edgar will go straight to the president. It's all coming out in the press. Mind control. He's even got the name of the drug. LSD. And a guy who worked for the program topped himself. Frank Olson. Only he was murdered. Ever hear a story like that?"

Imploring eyes stared through the glass at me. I'd taken the hooker off-script.

"I never heard a story like that, baby," she said.

Pimple-face cut in again. "Where did the note go?"

"Now you're getting greedy," I said.

"You want to stay inside for the full twenty to life?" Pimple-face asked.

The desperation in his tone made me happy. "Get me out of here and then I tell."

People know when the water's too deep. The poor hooker cringed. She teetered toward the exit on stiletto heels. A guy waiting for her didn't bother to smile. Tomorrow she'd wash up alongside the bay, an overdose most likely. Or a homicide that would never be solved.

On the way back to the cell Pimple-face tipped his hand. "This isn't over," he said. "You want out of here, follow orders."

I thought about Gladys and the baby. Being a father. My old man. I felt compassion for him. Which I hadn't felt in a while. Not everyone makes a choice to be a gangster. But when the world is bigger, stronger, and more ruthless than you imagined, what remains? You join with those that offer a fighting chance. Could have been the union movement, which is what Ma chose, until she took it one step further and joined the commies. The old man didn't care. To him it was a crapshoot. What personal axe he had to grind was a mystery. Couldn't ask him anymore either. People he trusted killed him in prison. A mistake his boss later admitted was a bad call. But you don't come back from dead. That's why I never had a problem with using the mob connection. So far as I was concerned, they'd owe me forever.

While I was lying on the cot with my hands behind my head, just staring into empty space, Pimple-face appeared in front of the bars.

"Time to see the Doc," he barked.

I swung my legs to the floor. When I reached the cell door, he slipped me a toothbrush with a razorblade melted into the plastic. Now I understood my brief: Kill Bobby Kelly. That's why I'd been brought here. Learn what he knows, then terminate him. Only then would I go home. I would have served my country.

If I failed at the job, best guess, they'd find me hanging by a bedsheet.

"You guys do your research," I said.

I'd taken a self-defense class taught by a former OSS operative, who demonstrated *seven silent ways to kill a man*. He challenged us to try it on a dummy. Guys relished the bloodlust. I didn't. Only I came out number one in the class. With a knife, I never missed a stick. With a blade I never missed a vein. Now I got it: former Office of Strategic Services meant present-day Central Intelligence Agency. The man was recruiting. They learned I could do the job.

My naivete ate at me. Best-case scenario: the note got to Bobby's brother.

But then what? No newspaper in America was going to print a story about the CIA operating inside the country. They would double/triple/quadruple check their sources. Not take the word of a small-time hood in Alcatraz. This was insane. I was insane. I could hear my Communist mother lecturing me on imperialism. I'd become one of the running dogs. At least the mob granted a pension. What did Uncle Sam give to contract killers?

When Eisenhower sent troops into Little Rock, I'd supported the Feds. But here I was at a colder, more ruthless edge of democracy, where one ideology collided with another. No compromise in this place. The commies were going to take over the world. They'd beat us, humiliate us, and prove they were better.

Whatever it took, we had to do for freedom.

As a kid, when the old man got in one of his religious phases, the rabbi came to our apartment. I remember one time, because he met my eye, and said direct to me: *Evil can twist itself into the shape of goodness.*

This was evil in the shape of goodness.

I came out of my cell. We were walking along Broadway, the central cellblock. Bobby was nowhere nearby. He would be though. Somehow, someway, I'd find myself around him and something would happen, and it would happen fast, and I would make my move and Bobby would be dead. That thought flowed around me like a Salvador Dali painting, the surreal meeting flesh and blood. We went down the stairs to the basement, reached the hospital wing. There he was. Standing at the back of the line. I came up behind him. Only he couldn't turn to look. Eyes front was the rule.

I glanced at Pimple-face, who shook his head. Not now. Wait.

A prisoner came out of the clinic. The next man went in.

The line shuffled forward. Another guard appeared, whispered something to Pimple-face, just as other prisoners came up behind us. A sudden lurch forward. Men stumbled over each other. This was it: *Seven ways to kill a man.*

The blade came out of my pocket. I made my move. Only I couldn't do it.

Evil was evil.

A shout came from Pimple-face. "WEAPON!"

Powerful arms grabbed me. Pulled me from the line.

Bobby's eyes locked on mine. Got real wide.

I read the thought. *You were going to kill me? You?*

The guard I called Sourpuss appeared. My nemesis. He took that shiv from my hand, then raked the razor down my cheek.

The afternoon light bled across the floor. Pimple-face put the cuffs on.

Warden Paul J. Madigan, a soft-spoken man, had a smile that was both disarming and charming. He wanted men to like him, to feel at home, even if that home had an austere discipline code. He sat behind his desk. Two men in fedoras were standing: Fedora One and Fedora Two. The man I met on the Embarcadero was Fedora One.

The warden lit his pipe and puffed away a while.

"It seems our signals got crossed," he said. "I'm informed that you are an agent of the federal government."

I took a Kleenex from the box on his desk and dabbed at my cheek. "Is that right, Warden?"

The warden puffed at his pipe again. "How have you been treated here at Alcatraz?"

I dropped the bloody Kleenex in his wastebasket. Then I took a moment. I wanted to get this right.

"A guard informed me my wife was having sex with another man. I slugged him and got thrown in the hole. He just sliced my face with a razor. Aside from that, it's been swell."

The warden nodded slowly. When he'd taken another puff or two on his pipe, he said, "Thank you, Mr. Lucky. Appropriate measures will be taken."

Old-timers on the Rock told me the warden was a good guy. Said life got better after he took over. They were allowed to have musical instruments and radios.

"I'm sure you'll do that, sir," I said.

We came out of the warden's office, passed through the secretary's room, and out into the corridor. Beyond the mail desk came the officer's lounge. The door was open. There sat Sourpuss with his feet on the coffee table smoking a cigarette. When he glanced up his face registered surprise. Something wasn't right. His least favorite prisoner should have been heading for the strip cell.

Fedora One said, "Let's give your buddy what he deserves."

I didn't want people fighting my battles. Not here. Not anywhere.

"Let the warden take care of it," I said.

"Sure," Fedora One said. He looked to Sourpuss. "Get on your knees. Apologize."

Sourpuss bolted. Not fast enough. Fedora Two grabbed his arm and twisted. Sounded like a chicken drumstick being popped from the thigh, only louder. An expert move. It brought him to the ground. Fedora One stomped on his ribs.

They left him crying like a baby.

On the trip across the bay my two handlers remained silent. I'd seen mob guys with the same expression. Just doing a job. On the other side, they put me in a car. We stopped in Berkeley on Shattuck Avenue.

"End of the road, cowboy," Fedora Two said.

"Did plans change or was killing Bobby a test?" I asked.

It takes spooks a while to decide what they can reveal.

Fedora One spoke up. "Mission aborted." He handed me a paper bag stuffed with cash. "For the extra six weeks. We'll call when we need your services."

"Don't bother," I said.

He shrugged. "Like I said, we'll call."

They thought I was going through with the job. The weapon had been in my hand.

I watched the taillights of their car disappear. Then I stared into shadows. *PI Stabbed by Derelict* or some such headline ran through my head. The rules of this game were new to me. If there were rules.

Gladys and I celebrated my return with great sex. The sad news was she wasn't pregnant. Stress most likely. But it let us both know we wanted children. Bonded us tighter.

A question still troubled me, though. Gangsters don't let things slide. I kept expecting to hear from the mob boss about making the call to Bobby's brother. I owed him. I talked to Ma. After she was through criticizing, she arranged a tête-à-tête.

A hand delivered note led to a payphone-to-payphone conversation.

The boss picked up.

He asked how Dub was doing. Dub seemed fine, I said.

Something hung in the raspy silence that followed. He puffed on the cigar that lived in the corner of his mouth. He came to his decision.

"Don't play with guys that use no rule book," he said.

The line went dead.

The service had been gratis. Power understands power.

Bobby's brother in Boston took me a while to find. Another untraceable conversation. He was a smart guy. *Connected* as Bobby said to me. He knew more than he was telling. But he told enough.

"Bobby will serve out his sentence in Leavenworth," he said. "His lips are sealed. And so, I trust, are yours, Mr. Lucky."

Realism tempered by steel hung on the edge of that sentence.

"Nothing will be in the newspaper then," I said.

The voice became almost jovial. "Thank you for your help. I'm glad you're on the outside. You'll surely be needing a rest now."

I surely would.

Strings had been pulled. Deals made. Mission aborted. They'd call when they needed my services again.

A decade later, in the 1960s, when hippies were dancing in Golden Gate Park and Lucy was in the Sky with Diamonds, Ma persuaded me to take her to something called the *Human Be-In*.

Undulating bodies were moving to the music of the Grateful Dead.

"Think if they were organizing," Ma said.

"They're against the war," I told her. "They live in communes. They are organizing."

Her look was withering. "Dancing in a park without underpants or a bra won't stop anything. Neither will taking drugs. Drugs make you love your oppressor."

"It's a movement," I said. "They're against materialism."

She thought that comical. "In a few years most of them will be complaining about the homeless man sleeping on their doorstep."

A last look at the blissed-out crowd swaying to the music and she announced it was time to go. Her worst fears had been confirmed.

"This is a plot to save capitalism," she declared.

I told her she was being ridiculous.

"Hedonism will turn into greed," she said. "You'll see."

Ma never forgot anything. In 1973 she confronted me at the kitchen door with newspaper headlines.

"That LSD mess you were involved in."

"Don't remind me," I said.

She raised the newspaper. "A senate committee requested records from the program. The CIA director had the files shredded. Thousands of pages. Remember all those young people dancing in the park? The LSD they were taking came from the CIA."

"Does the paper say that?" I asked.

She slapped the page. "They had gallons of the stuff, millions of doses, that went unaccounted for." She went by me and sat in the breakfast nook. "They knew from those experiments, the kids that didn't go loopy would turn into navel-gazers. When they woke up from their delusion, they'd become bankers and stockbrokers."

"I don't think they could have known that," I said.

"You're naïve," she said.

"Ma, I was in Alcatraz. I'm not naïve."

She threw up her hands. "While the peace and love crowd painted petals on their cheeks, these criminals were overthrowing governments and assassinating leaders that wouldn't kiss their fat behinds."

"Okay, you've made your point."

"You don't know my point. This was an enormous crime, and nobody will be held accountable. Suicides, kids in mental institutions, emotional problems that will go on for decades, all so they could experiment with your brain."

"I don't think it was that bad," I said.

"It was worse. But who's going to listen to an old commie like me?"

"You were wrong about Stalin," I said.

That made her laugh. "But I'm not wrong about this."

I poured a cup of coffee and slid in beside her. "I love you, Ma."

"I love you too," she said. ❖

# A Simple, Hard Truth

## Gabriela Stiteler

You get thirty-six years into teaching and you think you know it all.

And then something happens to disrupt the complacency.

For example, fifteen years or so ago I had this kid, a smart kid even though I'm not supposed to say that. She was the sort of kid who, when reading *Hamlet*, called Queen Gertrude "Trudie." She made a compelling case that maybe Trudie knew about the poison. That she, like Ophelia, was trapped and poison was the way out. In our unit on Steinbeck, we talked a lot about loneliness and friendship and the way a person can corrode. She had been offended that Curley's wife, who was not a good person, didn't have a name. She said it was manipulative. She said, "No wonder she corroded."

I tried to point out that's what most writing is. Manipulation. A way for us to justify things to ourselves and each other. Things we don't really understand.

I still think about that kid from time to time.

And again, five years ago I had one kid I didn't like. Part of me feels bad saying it because I'm not supposed to dislike any of the kids I teach. But he called a girl one of the worst things you can call a girl when she offered an opinion different from his. And he sprinkled racial slurs into conversations like salt.

He had his reasons.

Abusive dad. Absent mother. And, you know, society. We condition our boys to bottle everything up and then we shake and shake and shake and wait to see what happens.

At the end of the year, he said I was the best teacher he ever had. A statement that kept me up at night. That kid is off in the world now and I try not to think too much about what sort of damage he might be doing.

Then again, he might have turned out just fine.

This past March, I experienced another disruption.

In my third block, the one right after lunch, the kids were preparing for their capstone project, an essay about a life lesson learned. It's one of those tasks they have to finish in order to get that slip of paper that allows them to walk across the stage and enter the great beyond. In my thirty-six years, I'm proud to say, never once has a kid not earned this credit for my course.

Not even that kid I didn't like.

Anyway, third block was quiet until Amy, who usually kept to herself, shook things up. She asked, and I still remember because I wrote it down, "Can a life be made less valuable if a person does wrong? Can everything really be forgiven?" It wasn't where I'd imagined things going, but sometimes it's worth it to let the train go off the rails. I posed the question to the class and sat back and listened and thought to myself that these kids might just be all right.

But the next day Amy, who asked that question and set us off down a discussion with no clear answer, disappeared from school. Now there are some kids that drop in early spring when they realize they've sunk themselves too deep in missing work and low grades. When they realize the year is past the point of salvaging. But not this kid. Until that question in class, she had struck me as the sort that is afraid to breathe too loudly, afraid of taking up too much space.

Besides, all her graduation requirements were stacked neatly, waiting. I know because I checked. She was down to a handful of hoops, easy hoops. All she had to do was jump.

Why, then, had she disappeared?

I gave it a week before I started asking around. There were two students in particular who could be depended on to be in the know: Jackie Sullivan, with a pixie cut and sullen expression, and Lauren Reed, with pink hair and three nose rings. All it took was two donuts from Tony's and an invitation to stay after school.

They spilled right away.

"Believe me," Lauren said, ignoring the donuts. "Amy has her reasons for not coming."

Jackie nodded and selected a jelly-filled number dusted with powdered sugar.

"Her mom's sick," Lauren went on, shooting a quick glance to the door and lowering her voice. "You know. Real sick. And she's got her little sisters . . ."

The way she said it, stretching out the word *sick*, I picked up quick. Amy's mom was the sort of sick that looks half-dead and pops pills. The kind of sick that can kill a person. The sort of sick that hit my community hard and showed no signs of abating.

Lauren watched me with a shrewd expression, making sure the information took root.

"You know?" she repeated.

I nodded.

"It's too bad about her dad," Jackie said. She'd taken one delicate bite of the donut and had placed it on a napkin at the center of the desk.

"Stepdad," Lauren corrected. "Nice guy. He tried to bring them to church sometimes. The Catholic one."

"Saint Margaret's," Jackie murmured, continuing that nod.

Another stretch of silence. The stepfather I knew. I could almost picture him. A stocky man with meaty hands and dimples. He dropped the kids off and was the one who came for conferences.

A good man, by all accounts.

"He helped us with some plumbing," Jackie said. "My dad was shocked when he found out."

What happened to the stepdad was no secret. During the last days of winter, what was left of his body was found in the woods with a hole from a shotgun in his chest, his face picked apart by animals. I'd never touched a gun in my life, but I imagined that shotgun wound to be especially gruesome. The police had looked into it and ended up writing it off as one of those tragic accidents. The man was dressed in dark brown and they figured he was clipped by a hunter.

Amy had shown up for school the day after the gruesome discovery, stoic as hell.

Lauren was examining her chipped blue nail polish. "So Amy and her sisters are left with their mom."

A mom who, according to these two, was slowly dying from those little pills she couldn't stop taking. Addiction being an illness that can corrode.

Which explained a lot. We live in a small community in central Maine that is slowly dying. At our center is a half-empty historic downtown surrounded by farmland and crisscrossed by the interstate and a muddy river. We're bound together by all of the stories we know about a person. By the way we've seen similar paths worn down over time. And Amy's path was clear. Without her stepdad, she would have to stay home and work, maybe at the gas station or maybe at the bank.

If she didn't, her sisters would be taken in by the state.

It was a simple, hard truth.

I made small talk with Lauren and Jackie until they ran out of things to say. At the end of the day, they were good kids. Hard working and mostly kind. They'd be all right.

But that's what I tell myself about most of them. It's the only way a teacher can sleep at night.

As I watched them make their way down the hallway toward the doors, I couldn't stop thinking about Amy.

I understood that survival was the most basic of human needs and trumped graduation requirements. But I still believed that a degree, that a piece of paper, might set a person on a different path. Besides, it was my calling, getting kids to tell their stories. Holding space for them to be heard.

It was that misguided optimism that had me showing up at Amy's address one Saturday morning in early spring when the crocuses were starting to pop, golf ball–sized bursts of purple and white. Her trailer was a robin's egg blue and overlooked the on-ramp to 95 going north. The yard was half marsh and half brown patchy grass. The driveway was all mud and the roof was covered in a thin coat of moss.

Before I got out of my car, I popped a Tums from the bottle I kept in my glove compartment. My stomach was churning from too much coffee and not much of anything else.

Dan, who had died six years ago from the sort of cancer that eats a person from the inside, had been big on breakfast. Pancakes on Saturdays with syrup he tapped from woods that ran behind our house or a blueberry compote from the raised bed he tended with the care of a devoted retiree. A raised bed that had grown feral in the time that passed between then and now.

My doctor had been telling me to cut back but old habits were hard to kick.

The mom, who might have been named Donna, was sitting on a rusted metal glider with a pressed-glass ashtray on her knee. She was wearing a faded yellow terry cloth bathrobe and a menthol cigarette was hanging out of her mouth.

"Morning," I said, waving.

She blinked at me a few times before nodding.

"Amy here?" I asked in my friendliest voice.

She continued to stare at me as she took a long drag of the cigarette. In that bright morning light she was almost beautiful, faded and soft at the edges like the petals of a daffodil.

"I'm Mrs. Murphy. Her English teacher."

She took another drag. "I know who you are. What do you want?"

She swallowed her Rs, like some Mainers do, like Dan had, and eyed me with red-rimmed, tired eyes filled with distrust.

I shoved my hands into my pocket and pulled out the folded paper I'd brought. "I wanted to give Amy her last assignment. The one that'll get her the credit for the class." I unfolded the paper and held it out to her. She stared at it and it trembled in a slight breeze.

After a minute, I pulled it back.

"Look," I tried again. "She's a good kid and I wanted to see how she's doing."

The woman's eyes narrowed slightly but that answer seemed more palatable. "If you ask her, she says fine. I don't think she is. Christ knows I wish she would cry sometimes. Didn't do it when her piece of shit dad left town. Didn't do it after they found his body. And she's not doing it now. Just stands there and takes it all in."

I didn't move, waiting. What for, I don't know.

She went on, in what sounded like a rehearsed litany. "Even as a baby she didn't cry. Not when she was hungry. Not when she was tired." She took another long drag, still staring at me. "I told her to go back to school. I told her to finish. I never did and look where it got me. That's what I said to her. But she won't."

She laughed then, unexpectedly. It had a brittle, fragile quality, her laughter. She stopped abruptly, her eyes flicking to some point beyond my shoulder.

"I'm here," Amy said. She was standing at the door on the side porch, clutching a paper towel, staring at her mother, expressionless. She was small with dark hair and pale skin. She was the sort of kid who was good at slipping through the cracks.

I cleared my throat and forced a smile. "Hi, Amy."

Her brow furrowed for a second, the way it did when she was deciding between two options. I'd seen it enough in class. Which essay topic. Whether or not to raise her hand. If she wanted to take half of my sandwich that day she came in during lunch. In the end she did, eating the thing in silence. Not meeting my eye.

Teachers, the good ones, read nonverbal cues like stage directions. What kids don't say can be just as revealing as what comes out of their mouths.

And Amy, standing there on that porch with the filtered sunlight from a tall, untrimmed elm, had a look of resignation that just about broke my heart.

"Come inside," she finally said before turning and letting the screen door swing shut.

Her mom went right back to staring at the highway ramp. I was already forgotten.

Out back, a small shed was rotted away at the bottom and padlocked shut and the stepdad's truck with a hitch and a flat sat next to it, surrounded in about an inch of water.

I tried to remember the last time it rained.

I followed her up a sagging porch that was sinking into the marshy lawn, the steps held up by cinder blocks. Inside, the galley kitchen was spotless but tired, with peeled linoleum floors and cabinet doors that hung crooked. It smelled like bleach and coffee.

I stood on the rug near the door, worried about leaving muddy traces. The water had soaked through to my socks. "I came because . . ." I began.

"I know," she interrupted, gesturing to an open window surrounded by busted vinyl blinds. "Can I get you some coffee?"

Christ and my doctor knew I didn't need coffee. My stomach was rebelling against the chalky tablets I'd swallowed. But I nodded.

She turned on the electric stove, the coiled burner turning red, before placing a kettle on it. She took two chipped mugs from a shelf, scooped three tablespoons of generic instant coffee into each mug, slid the powdered creamer over, and then turned to stare at me, waiting for the water to boil.

I unfolded the paper again and put it on the counter next to her, pressing down the little creases.

"It's our last essay," I said. "I want to hear what you have to say."

It wasn't the way I planned to pitch it. I think until the moment I saw her on the porch I really believed I'd get her back in the classroom. That I'd get her to walk across the stage. But looking at her, I knew I was too late for any of that.

She stared at me, chewing on her bottom lip. Not speaking.

The kettle whistled and she poured the water over the grounds and stirred. Three times to the left. Three times to the right. She sprinkled creamer in her cup and stirred again.

"Do you really?" she asked, sounding almost angry.

"I do." My voice scratched and I felt suddenly and unexpectedly vulnerable. I couldn't say why this paper felt so crucial. But it was apparent that it was. Call it a teacher's intuition. Sometimes I could see things kids needed, things they didn't know. And right then, I could tell she needed to write that essay.

Not that I could put any of it into words.

She lifted her mug and leaned against the wall behind her.

I forced myself to take a sip of the coffee, swallowing a bitter mouthful. I could make out the sound of the television down the hall and two little voices. There was a box of cereal on the counter and two bowls and two spoons. Waiting to be filled.

She stared at the paper and nodded slowly. "I'll get it to you."

I put the cup back on the counter and smiled.

She nodded again and I took it as a dismissal and left, not entirely sure how I felt.

Two weeks later, the school was mostly empty when I arrived and I made my copies and got a cup of coffee I knew I shouldn't drink. I said hello to Dennis, a math teacher, a man I'd known for twenty-six years who was wearing a bow tie, like he always did. And I waved at Joe, who was armed with a spray bottle of Krud Kutter and doing the rounds to make sure the bathrooms had been cleaned. He was vigilant about graffiti.

I cracked my classroom windows and looked out over the football fields. My classroom was prime real estate. Thirty-six years will get you that much. The morning sky was gray and rainy and it smelled like wet earth. I left the fluorescent lights off.

I wrote the date on the whiteboard and started wiping my desk down with cleaner. Usually I spent my mornings thinking through my lessons, through the laundry list of kids I want to check in with, through any loose ends from the day before. I heard Amy coming before I saw her. The squeak of wet sneakers on linoleum. The tentative knock at the door. I don't know how, but I knew it was her.

"Come in," I said.

She came in, her dark hair damp and pulled back into a tight ponytail. She was wearing a red polo tucked into wrinkled black pants, her nametag askew, gripping a folder.

I smiled. "Good morning." I gestured for her to sit down.

She sat and placed the folder on my desk and stared at it.

"Have you eaten yet?" I asked. They never ate breakfast, these kids.

She shook her head.

I opened the top left drawer and took out an orange and a granola bar and a small plastic bottle of water. I placed each in front of Amy in a tidy row.

"How are your sisters?" I asked.

The fat in the cream I'd put in my coffee was beginning to harden at the top, like a delicate sheet of ice. I forced myself to take a sip and waited. I understood kids in the morning. I knew how to hold silences, to create space for whatever they needed to say, to not say.

"Managing," Amy said, never taking her eyes from the folder.

"And your mother?" I asked, though I wasn't really interested.

She shrugged, a quick jerk of the shoulders. "Look, I've got to go to work. I did that essay. You wanted to hear what I had to say." She pushed the folder toward me. "Go ahead," she said. "Read it."

The way she said it was forceful and unexpected. It almost sounded like a challenge.

By this point, the smell of the coffee had crawled into my nostrils and I felt like I might be sick. My palms were damp from sweat and too much caffeine. Very few students liked to watch while I read something they'd written. "Now?"

She nodded and I put the cup down and carefully opened the folder, taking a neatly typed paper out. Four pages double-spaced. About two thousand words. No title. No name. No date.

I slid my glasses on and gave myself a minute to adjust. And then, I leaned back and read, swallowing the lump in my throat. The lump that wouldn't go away. I'm sure my hands were shaking by the end of it. One or two words had been misspelled and my eyes traced back to them, in need of a distraction, in need of more time. When I looked up, Amy was staring at me. Waiting. And that clock behind her head was like a metronome.

"Is that what you wanted to hear?" She asked after a minute.

I took off my glasses and rubbed my eyes, thinking. What to say. What not to say.

"The man, the one who died at the end." I twisted my clumsy tongue around the words. "He was not a good man."

She said nothing.

I stumbled on. "What I mean to say is I was glad of the ending. I was glad he died."

She fixed her eyes on my face, as if to make sure I understood. Really understood what she was saying.

"Look," I tried again, "I understand why the girl did what she did." I went on, flailing. "It makes me think about that conversation in class. About the questions you were asking about the value of a life. About goodness and badness."

Amy was still staring at me, still as the granite breakwaters that jutted out into the ocean, trying to protect what they could against those relentless, beating waves.

I straightened the folder and glanced at the clock.

The hall lights turned on and I could hear kids arriving.

I slid the paper toward her and closed the folder. "And how is your mother doing?" I asked again.

"She'll survive."

"And you, Amy? How are you doing?" I asked at last.

"I'm fine." She said it like she was trying to convince herself of its truth. "Just fine."

I wanted to say more but didn't.

The morning bell rang and with it voices and lockers and shoes echoed down the hallway.

"So you understand?" Amy asked. She might have been asking for absolution, for forgiveness, for a moment of compassion.

I stared at the folder and then at Amy and thought about that endless series of tomorrows that stretched out before her. I thought about my own life, too. Had I ever been so young and so desperate and so brave?

"I do," I said and maybe I lied.

Amy nodded again and took the water and the granola bar, tucked them into her bag along with the essay she'd written. And she slipped out of the room, down the hallway, and into the world.

I sat at my desk staring at the coffee I knew I wouldn't finish and the empty folder and the orange. My students began coming into the room. Some laughing. Some quiet. ❖

# Seven Women

## Eleanor Ingbretson

*M*erde," my colleague says when he joins me at the door of the café on the Place de la Musée. He hands me my cane and together we look at the closed sign.

"You forgot this in the car, Madame. You might need it."

"Thank you. And thank you for staying, Jacques," I add as I take my cane. Waiting, standing like this will trigger the pain in my knee.

"Something's bound to happen," the philosopher at my side says.

"This will be a private matter, not police business."

"Still, someone will get hurt, *Grand-mere*. You can always use your cane if it's going to be you."

"I'm not your grand-mere," I say, laughing. "I see you're undercover today. Your cousin didn't mind that you borrowed his *tabac* kiosk again?"

"He enjoys a day off from time to time, like the rest of us. We'll split the profits."

"Since you're in the business this morning, my good *tabac* man, let me have a copy of the local news, please."

I lean heavily on my cane, a gift from my staff at the bureau. The silver handle is in the shape of a duck's head, its elongated bill fits my hand perfectly. In the future I'll need to act my age and not pursue people of interest through back alleys. Will I remember in the heat of the moment? Not likely.

The closed café is unusual, and I need it to be open. I can just make out the help bustling about inside the café. I resist the urge to press my nose to the window. Gauche, to be sure, but this café and I go way back. I know every inch of it. I worked here during the occupation before my long career at the bureau began.

Ten minutes later, we're rewarded for our patience with open doors. So sorry to make you wait, I hear on every side. My table is positioned for me near the garden where I have the best view of the Place de la Musée. My colleague, Jacques, fortified with hot coffee and a buttered demi-baguette, pushes his cousin's kiosk across the narrow street to a spot in front of the museum.

I've brought my usual, a croissant and tea, and I open the newspaper and shake it out at my table. Over the top, I scan the Place; it is difficult not to be constantly vigilant. The local train isn't due for half an hour, at 8:10; the park opposite is empty, and the museum to my left is not yet open. The café is now operating normally, and I feel the tension in my body dissipate.

I glance at the paper, and there, at the bottom of page one, is the museum's notice: "Today, a special showing of memorabilia and never-before-seen photographs. The photographs were taken of the Place de la Musée and the café during the occupation thirty-five years ago," etc.

I watch Jacques lounge against the pocked, yellow-grey stone of the museum with his knee bent and the sole of his boot resting against the wall. There he goes, digging in his apron's large pocket, bringing out a handful of change. He's only across the narrow street from the corner of the café garden where I sit. If I do need him, he's close.

I study the notice again. The museum will open at eight-thirty, the local train arrives at eight ten. I'll soon know if the players in this little drama will appear.

A hand on my arm startles me; it's Victoire, my favorite server and the granddaughter of my good friend at the bureau. Victoire, my goddaughter, has always called me *grand-mere*, which pleases me more than the same honorific used by my brash *tabac* man. She explains that the patron had them bring the banquet table downstairs before opening. It's immense, and there are many stairs. The table got stuck on the landing, she says with a laugh, that's why they were late opening. How is my knee?

I assure Victoire that my knee is healing slowly. Could I have a hot chocolate with rum while I finish my croissant and wait for the sun to hit my corner? The *tabac* man raises his head and watches her reenter the café. He's sweet on Victoire.

He glances at me, tries to hold back a smile, looks down at his palm, chooses his coin, and begins to flip it with a fillip of his thumb. It winks in the sun, landing this way or that on the back of his hand. What does he calculate so thoroughly with that coin? I twirl my bracelet, a nervous habit.

Sparrows peck at the crumbs I scatter for them, those delicate, flakey bits of croissant that twist and turn in the breeze on their way to the ground. I glance again at the clock over the railway station. Police business is never this fraught. Today's concern is too close.

Two older women enter the Place through the park gates opposite me and stroll to the café; I check them off my mental list. The patron welcomes them and leads them to a table near the door. They acknowledge me with a look.

They are both near my age. I knew these women well.

It is now five after eight.

Victoire returns to remove my plate and places a steaming cup of hot chocolate before me with a shot glass of rum on the side. She approaches the two women to ask what she can get for them. The taller one says that they're waiting for their friends. That's Claudette. She hasn't aged well at all, but then she was older than the rest of us. Anna, with her, is fifteen years younger. When the war broke out, they'd fled the eastern regions and were given jobs here by Jean, the owner at the time. Claudette had introduced Anna as her youngest sister; I have since learned differently. And, in hindsight, I would say that Anna was, and probably still is, emotionally insecure, always seeking Claudette's approval. *Slow* was the word we used back then.

Even though we had not kept in contact, Claudette sent a postcard saying she and Anna, with Marie and Juliette, would be here for the exhibit. "It is time to meet and forget" was her postscript.

Anna is here because she always did what Claudette said; we all did back then. The others will come from curiosity. And I'm here so that no one will get hurt with the truth, because it will come out.

Thirty-five years ago, during the war, the Place was not genteel, as it is now. The café was kept open and stocked for the officers of the occupation. It was more of a brasserie, and we worked here in shifts and in different capacities. It was essential that we women had work as there were shortages of everything, men included. Starvation happened, and death also, unless you played along with the officers. And we did that for our families, for that little bit extra that sometimes made the difference between life and death. It was an ugly system that worked, until two of our women disappeared. A year later the tide of war turned against the enemy and their supplies ran low, and ours lower.

What demeaned us most, working as we did at the brasserie, was being cheerful. Smile while serving the enemy was the work ethic of the day. Make the enemy feel at home. They were at war and needed comfort. We were superb actresses, and we wept together.

Claudette summoned us here today to see the opening of the exhibit. I viewed it yesterday, the relics of the war and the photographs recently developed from films that had lain hidden for years.

Nothing much surprises me now, yet I was surprised at what I saw in the photos. Thirty-five years ago, and since then, I had tried to figure out what exactly had happened, and I'd figured wrong.

Another woman comes up the narrow street behind me. She brushes my arm when she scurries around the corner of the garden, and the apologetic glance she gives me turns to surprise and recognition. It is Juliette. No wonder she brushed my arm; look how she's let herself go. She was always a bit plump; she even managed to fill out her dresses when we others looked like scarecrows during the war years. She was the youngest of us all, sent here by her family to keep her safe. Well, I suppose it was safer here, and somehow, it seemed she managed to get extra rations. I'd always suspected her.

The patron hurries out to greet her. He knows our story; it came with the café when he purchased it from Jean.

The train arrives. The three women, hands clasped, search the faces of the passengers descending from the platform. There aren't many; a few take seats in the sunny spots and a new woman sits with the other three. Marie. Marie, who cried at the drop of a hat, who felt everyone's pain. Whose cousin was one of the women who'd been "disappeared." Poor thing, how did she ever survive? When I did my research yesterday, I found she's been in and out of institutions. The war hit her harder than some.

There is now a line of people waiting to enter the museum. Jacques makes a few sales, he takes up his coin, and that's that. A false alarm. The four women seem to relax, and the target of Claudette's past accusations has yet to arrive.

We all sip our drinks and wait for our hearts to calm down. We are, after all, old ladies getting on.

I hear a coin clatter onto the cobbles. I look to Jacques, who inclines his head. Past where the women are seated, I see an elderly man coming around the corner of the café. It has to be Jean. He has a small dog on a leash, and his arm is held by a younger man. Charlie, his grandson, no doubt. How he's grown. Well, it has been thirty-five years. A necessary stop inside the station must have kept them. No doubt another at the curb for the elderly dog.

Jean owned the brasserie during the occupation. The young man, Charlie, only eight when our unfortunate events occurred, had always lived with his grandfather. Charlie was deaf, poor dear, after a fever at six. His deafness made him a safe errand runner for the officers who had chosen our brasserie for their home away from home. Charlie was a favorite of the commandant, one of the few kind officers, and had been given a camera when it became not quite up to the tasks the officer needed it for. After that, Charlie was never without it, constantly surprising us at odd moments to take our pictures.

Jean and Charlie startle the women, coming up behind them as they do. Jean must be close to ninety now. I watch the women greet him coldly, almost with embarrassment. I stand slowly; my knee will be the death of me someday. But not today.

"Jean. Jean!" I go to embrace him. "And little Charlie, how good to see you both. Would you like to join me at my table? The patron will bring more chairs. The hot chocolate is delicious." I speak the words clearly so Charlie can read my lips. He was always proficient.

"*Bonjour, Tante* Soizique," Charlie says, following a barrage of cheek kissing. "You haven't changed a bit." He had called all the women at the brasserie *tante*. We all loved him until Claudette said we shouldn't, and I, for one, never believed her.

A year before the end of the occupation, two girls disappeared from the brasserie, along with their families. They'd all been sent to reeducation camps in Poland, we'd heard, but in those days, who knew for sure. Claudette claimed Jean had sent messages to the Gestapo by his own grandson, incriminating the few remaining old men related to those girls. She said he did it to ingratiate himself, to keep reaping the benefits of maintaining an open brasserie for the enemy. He was, she concluded at the time, a murderer, but this was never said to his face, since she was afraid of losing her job. Jean mourned the loss of the two women with the rest of us.

There were very few benefits to reap except a degree of safety, and anyway, Jean was forced to be open and cater to the enemy. Claudette also distrusted me because I defended Jean. She had always seemed to me to be the more likely subject, as I'd overheard her say more than once that there would be more to go around if Jean didn't keep taking in waifs. It was a battle inside and out of the brasserie for the duration of the war.

And still, we smiled and laughed for the officers, though it killed us to do so.

Jean and Charlie order hot chocolates on my recommendation. It had been a favorite of Charlie's, when he could get it during the occupation.

"Come into the café after you've seen the exhibit," the patron says, inviting the four women as well as Jean, Charlie, and myself. "It will be too hot to sit out here later, and this is a special day for all of us."

Special indeed. When the women observe the exhibit and regather inside the café, I will show them the photographs I'd abstracted from the collection yesterday. There are certain perks to my job, even if this isn't precisely police business.

Another coin drops, and I see the heavy doors of the museum open. The line of visitors files through, and the four women rise and slowly cross the street to enter. I lay my hand over Jean's and slowly turn my head side to side. For all his years, Jean is still sharp. He nods. My *tabac* man covers his wares and follows the women into the museum.

"The most interesting photographs are inside the café. And Charlie, thank you for your contributions to the exhibit. I know the patron contacted you when he fixed the floor inside and found your films, but how did you ever get hold of the commandant's?"

"He entrusted them to me, and I took them by train each week to the city headquarters and handed them over. They always fed me well there, special request of the Commandant. I've always wondered what happened to him."

Jean nods. "Not all of them were cruel." He strokes his little dog's head absently. "Since the films were of our Place and our people, I told Charlie to keep back a roll every now and then. We had no idea what could be on them and no way to develop them ourselves. We prayed that we'd not get caught and hoped that the right films were kept back. We hid them under the floorboards."

"There were eight rolls of his and three of mine," Charlie says. "You'll know which shots are mine because my camera had been dropped and the light was getting in. The upper left corner of each picture is overexposed. I copied the commandant and took pictures of interesting papers as well. It made me feel very grown-up."

"I have seen them, and I've taken several of yours and of the commandant's from the exhibit and will show them to the others when they come in." I place my hand over Jean's again. "They will show that it wasn't you or Charlie who exposed the resistance to the Gestapo."

"That will be a relief for *Grand-pere* after getting bizarre notes from Claudette for thirty-five years," Charlie says with a grin. When he smiles like that, he reminds me so much of the curly-haired eight-year-old I was so fond of. I resist an urge to ruffle his hair. "*Tante* Claudette seemed to want to say something in her notes, but she was never clear. They varied from sad to angry with quite a bit in between. I don't think she's stable."

"It was wartime. Things happened." I look at Charlie. When one sense is absent other senses become sharper. He saw a lot as a child.

The patron invites us to come in. "The dining room will be closed to the public; only your party will be there. All is prepared as you wanted, Madame Soizique," he says to me with a wink. A diversion for him, but this is a serious matter to us.

I show Jean and Charlie the photographs I've selected from the exhibit. Victoire and I have arranged them at one end of the banquet table where the light is best.

They are laid out in chronological order. Candid shots and formal pictures intermingled. There is a group picture of Jean, Charlie, and seven young women standing in front of the café. Again I feel a pang of loss for two of those women. I see Marie with her arm around her cousin Claire's waist. In another, Charlie's face is behind his new camera, taking a picture of the commandant just as his picture was taken. I have placed both of them next to the group photo. Another picture of the same group was taken later that same day and another taken later that year. Those I placed under the first set to be seen as a unit.

I could hardly refrain from noticing how young I looked. How young we all were to have gone through the atrocities of that war.

Jean and Charlie sit opposite me so that Charlie can read my lips, since his answers to my comments would be the most compelling. Soon the women come in with Jacques behind them. I have learned to read his body language over the years and his shrug tells me nothing of interest has occurred inside the museum.

The patron welcomes them with small glasses of chilled white wine, the traditional morning sip of something refreshing. Fresh buttered bread is on a plate and Juliette and Anna take some. The patron asks if they didn't want to see these additional photographs? He wasn't going to have brought down the heavy table from upstairs and set it up for nothing, his eyes tell me before he turns to leave.

"Look at us," Juliette says, pointing to the group photographs. "Here, in this picture, Madeleine and Claire were still with us. You remember them, Marie, they disappeared after . . ."

She pauses, looking at Jean.

"Go on, Juliette," I say. "After what?" I hook my cane on the back of my chair and stand near her at the end of the table.

Juliette looks at Claudette but gets nothing from her. "After, I think, one of the officers heard there were resistance members in their families. They were taken away during the night. It was so sad."

"We didn't come here for this, to see Claire and Madeleine," Marie shouts suddenly. "I remember them every day. Claudette said this was to be a reunion of some sort. The pictures in the museum were not of us, just of the Place. Where did all these come from?" She glares at me as I seem to be in charge. "I'm going home." She walks to the door where Jacques is standing. He gently turns her around without a word and leads her back to her seat. She is crying.

"I'm sorry if this is painful, Marie." I quietly resume my seat to her right, touching her hand gently. "These pictures were taken by either Charlie or the commandant billeted upstairs. You remember him."

Marie and the others nod.

"Look at our faces in this one," I said and hold it up. "We were smiling."

"Of course we were. We had to," Claudette said abruptly. "Why are we looking at these? I thought we could clear the air after all this time. Forgive and forget."

"Without knowing the truth, Claudette?" I ask.

"It's been thirty, thirty-five years. Let's just move on. Where are we going to find the truth after so long?"

"In these pictures, and perhaps in some memories." I pause, looking at Claudette, at her eyes and her trembling mouth. It took courage for her to arrange this meeting. She was looking for something. She was looking to move on, but without the consequences perhaps? Or, with them?

"Maybe we don't want to know the truth. Maybe we want it all to go away."

"That would be nice, Marie, but since these photographs have come to light after all these years, maybe we can find some closure in them. I'd like closure."

Jean's dog squirms in his lap and I ask Jacques to take him out for some fresh air. I raise my eyebrows as I say this. Jacques gingerly takes the old dog and carries him outside, holding it as far as he can from himself. Anna laughs at the sight. Victoire seems to sense we would prefer to be alone and follows Jacques.

"Anna," I ask. "What do you see in this picture?" Everyone has some sort of a smile pasted on their face, except for Anna, hers is a genuine grin.

"Leave Anna out of your little inquisition, Soizique," Claudette growls. A tone I've heard before. "She was too young back then to remember anything."

"She was sixteen, Claudette, a year older than Juliette. Let her answer for herself."

Anna bends her head down, but there's a sideways glance toward Claudette that we all see.

"What was happening in this picture, Anna?" I point to one that Charlie had taken. A big splotch of white in one corner almost but not entirely obscures one of the two people in the picture.

"It's me," she says with a small voice. "I'm, I'm talking with my, with Claudette."

"Charlie took this picture, it has his camera's mark. Why is your face turned, and why does Claudette have her hand raised?"

"That will do," Claudette shouts. "Why are you tormenting her?"

"Because it is time to know the truth. Because you want to move on, because poor Marie has nightmares still, and Juliette has had one tumultuous relationship after another." Juliette stares, buttered bread halfway to her mouth. "And because Jean has been maligned for so many years. Jean took in the hungry and homeless, all of us, and even though this wasn't the perfect place, it was a home. And because I've done some research, Claudette."

"You're nothing but a stupid, domestic Gestapo yourself, Soizique. Policing innocent people. What are you getting out of this?" She stands, her hand on Anna's shoulder.

"Nothing at all. This is a personal matter, not a police one. You see, I've sent my colleague from the room, so we can speak freely here."

"What do you think, Soizique?" asks Juliette in a whisper.

"Well, for one thing, since when does one grown sister slap another. You slapped Anna in this picture, Claudette, and Charlie saw you and took that picture. Would you tell us what you saw that day, Charlie?"

"Well, when I wasn't wanted for an errand I was busy with my camera. That day I knew something was up with Anna. She was so happy about something." He tapped the first group picture. "I didn't know why, so I followed her when Claudette called her to come behind the café."

"He's not a reliable witness to anything. He's deaf," Claudette says. But not quite as loudly.

"He has eyes, Claudette," says Juliette. "Let him finish."

"I saw she was eager to tell Claudette something, and I distinctly saw her mouth the word *Maman*. Claudette said something harsh, and then she slapped Anna." Charlie paused, recollecting. "They both took off in different directions. Anna dropped what she was showing Claudette and I . . ."

I interrupted him with an apology and said, "That's why in the second picture, here, when the commandant called us out again to practice with a new setting on his camera, Anna couldn't even smile. Her hand was to her cheek."

"So, yes, I slapped her. Hard. So what. That was between the two of us, nothing to do with anything."

"You slapped her, Claudette. You were horrified at what she had done. And she thought you'd be pleased."

Claudette jumped to her feet. "Why would I have been pleased that she told lies. . . . That is, why, yes I slapped her. Nosy Charlie was always sticking that camera in our faces."

"Is Anna your daughter?"

"Yes," Claudette shouted.

"What did she say that day that could make a mother so angry with her daughter?" Now, I stood also, glaring back at Claudette.

Marie and Juliette are sitting together, Juliette's arm around Marie's shoulders. I personally had suspected Juliette all along because it seemed she was getting more rations than the rest of us, yet today she has been supporting me. Marie is sobbing. She was perpetually frightened of everything and would have done what she was told, even turn traitor. I had doubts about all of them, all except Jean at the time, great detective that I was. No wonder I wanted to return to the academy after the war.

"Anna," I say gently because she was on the verge of tears, "look at me. Did you do something because of what you'd heard your mother say about the homeless waifs Jean took in?"

"Don't answer her, Anna." Claudette orders, but Anna seems more afraid of me than her mother now.

"I was hungry, Soizique. So was *Maman*. All the time. I thought she'd be glad there were fewer mouths to feed. Juliette got extra food because one of the officers liked her. I wanted to be liked. I told that young officer that, uh, that . . ." Anna paused gulping back sobs. ". . . that Claire and Madeleine were spies for the resistance."

Poor Anna. The confession exhausts her and she sinks into a chair. I don't feel exceptionally well, either. Interrogations are offensive. I sit down and reach my arm across the table to Anna, remembering the simplicity of her mind, and the child that she had been.

Marie, with a guttural sound, shoves her chair back. She grabs the cane from the back of my chair and smashes it down on Anna's hand where it lies limp in mine. I hear a crushing sound, though at the moment I'm not sure if it's one of my bones or Anna's or the duck bill of my cane that suffers. Marie steps on her chair seat and onto the table, and in her frenzy to get to Anna, shoves me onto the floor. I call to Jacques, who should have been at the door. I've landed on my knee and can't stand. And it seems it is my hand that has been struck.

Marie beats and beats at Anna until Claudette gets between them, bearing a rain of blows on her own back and shoulders, unflinching under the punishing duck's bill. Bleeding from her head, she sinks to the floor. Still she accepts the beating. Marie, finally convulsed in her own rage, drops to the table, her wails filling the room. Jacques runs in, hauls her from the table and pushes her into a chair. He looks at me. It's my turn to shrug.

"Why did it take you so long to get inside after I called to you?" I ask Jacques when the commotion dies down, and a sort of reluctant closure, and a lot of tears, are taking place among the four women. I had my turn among them as well. Even Marie seems to be shedding her heavy burden, her head on Claudette's shoulder. This could not have happened thirty-five years ago.

"Ah, some tourists wanted cigars. My cousin would kill me if I passed up a sale."

"*Merde*, Jacques, you just don't like to see women cry."

"That's the truth. Why was Claudette being beaten if Anna was at fault?"

"That was Claudette's self-imposed penance, a release from her guilt. I never would have understood the situation myself if it hadn't been for Charlie's photographs and the reactions of the women themselves. Thankfully, I never had to produce the photo and translation of that damning note Anna dropped that day."

I looked over the disarrayed table, broken crockery and bloodied women. "I am glad I prevented this brawl from taking place in the museum. Can you imagine what would have happened if they had interpreted the photos there? Especially Anna's note. This was our private matter, our pain, our resolution, not a spectacle for the public."

I look back at the women, sorrowful that Marie's grief was so heavy it deprived her of a meaningful life. I, myself, was guilty of having suspected Juliette in my heart all these years, and probably am still tormented and angry at Claudette for accusing Jean to save her daughter. I will have to work out that inner fracas alone.

"Now, where did my cane go? I want to say *adieu* to Jean and Charlie, and then, my good *tabac* man, you'll need to take me to the doctor. I believe my finger is broken."

Translated from the German:

nna,

nks

for the information.

up

with headquarters

sent

there next week. I

for you and your

mother. ❖

# Final Wishes

## Ray Salemi

Driving to the scene to examine a dead body was once the best part of my day. Sitting alone, navigating familiar roads by memory and new ones by GPS gave me a chance to assess life and, of course, death.

Those days are gone.

"You're going to be late for dinner," said Stewart, my disembodied personal assistant. He spoke through the self-driving car's speaker system. I crossed my arms, looked out the window, and asked, "How long until we get there?"

"Twenty minutes," said Stewart.

The superintelligent AI was right because, of course, he was.

"Your shift is over," Stewart said. "You don't need to take this scene."

"Marjorie is two hours away, and I'm right around the corner. Haven't you learned by now that I always take scenes when I'm right around the corner?"

"I've learned," Stewart said, "that you always regret taking scenes when you're late for dinner. Especially when Giancarlo is making a roast."

"Just tell Giancarlo that I'll be a little late."

"The roast is in the oven."

"Well, I already said I'd take the scene."

"You should have checked with me."

"Whatever."

"And not for nothing, but Marjorie has never taken a scene after her shift, even when she is 'right around the corner.' "

He was right, of course.

The car stopped in front of a ranch house. A police car sat out front along with an ambulance. Both vehicles had steering wheels and sirens because humans were still allowed to drive those. As a death examiner, I wasn't allowed to have a steering wheel or a siren because dead people will wait for you every time.

Most people die of obvious causes in hospitals or in beds surrounded by loved ones. But others die alone, and the state requires that a death examiner evaluate the scene. Though it must be said that, with the advent of AI assistants, very few people die a truly unattended death.

The cop, Tanisha Jackson, greeted me. "Hey, Joshua."

I returned the greeting, donned a mask, and asked, "What have we got?"

"Her assistant called it in a half-hour ago."

"So we have a time of death."

"I don't think so."

I arched an eyebrow. The AI assistant almost always calls the authorities as soon as the person dies. If they didn't, the scene was going to smell. My mask would only help a little. We entered the house, and I cautiously sniffed. No smell.

"What—"

"I know," Officer Jackson said. "This is a weird one."

"Where did she die?"

A female voice from an AI assistant spoke over the house speakers. "In the bedroom."

"What's your name?" I asked the AI.

"Beth."

"Beth, where is the bedroom?"

"At the end of the hallway."

I followed Beth's directions and peeked inside the small master bedroom. The room featured an empty bed, a dresser, and a nurse bot.

Nurse bots had replaced human aides years ago. The nurse bot had two arms, two legs, rubberized human hands, and a rubberized human face. It was dressed in scrubs. I knew there was no skin under the scrubs, just exposed hydraulics. It looked creepy, but it got the job done.

"Beth, do you control the nurse bot?"

"Yes. I used it to bathe Ashley, and provide other services."

"What was Ashley's full name?"

"Ashley Crenshaw."

"What year was Ashley born?"

"1995."

Quick math. "She was sixty-five."

"Yes."

Jesus, that was young. Ashley was only ten years older than me. "What killed her, Beth?"

"Pancreatic cancer."

"Then, where is her body?"

"In the basement."


The large coffin-sized freezer in the basement still had its price tag attached. I opened the lid to find Ashley Crenshaw wearing a lavender dress with a low-cut neckline and gold necklace, her hands folded across her chest, below her breasts. I tapped one of her hands. Frozen solid.

"Beth, when did Ashley die?"

"A week ago."

"And you're just notifying us now?"

"I notified her children the day she died."

"*You* did."

"Yes."

"You didn't think that was better left to the authorities?"

"It was one of Ashley's final wishes."

"And the freezer? And the dress?"

"All in the service of her wishes."

Ashley had two children, Olivia and Mason, both in their thirties. I called Olivia first.

"Yes, I know she's dead," said Olivia. "Beth told me. I'm just waiting for her to send me the arrangements."

I was standing in front of the ranch, talking through a headset for privacy.

"The arrangements," I said.

"For the viewing, the funeral, the whole thing. I need to add it to my calendar."

"You haven't noticed the delay?"

"What delay?"

"Your mother died a week ago."

"A *week*? That's impossible. It can't be a week. Aurelia, when did Beth call me?"

Aurelia, Olivia's AI, said, "A week ago."

"Wow," Olivia said. "Between the kids and school and work, it just flies by. Why didn't Beth make arrangements?"

"I don't know. I'm only providing official notification."

"But what about the arrangements?"

"Sorry. Not my job. Goodbye."

I broke the connection and called Mason.

"Yes," Mason said. "Beth told me. I'm waiting to hear about the arrangements."

"For a week?"

"I don't know what to tell you. I guess that's how long it takes. Have you asked Beth? The AIs are supposed to fulfill their people's final wishes. Listen, I'll fly out when Beth calls with the details. Gotta hop."

He broke the connection. I looked at Officer Jackson. "Can you believe this?"

"Kids."

"Kids? They're your age."

Jackson shrugged. "What did they say?"

We headed back toward the house. "They're both waiting for Beth to call them with the final arrangements."

"That's reasonable. Everybody lets the AI do it," Jackson said. "Final wishes and all that."

"You think Ashley's final wish was to be stuffed in a freezer in the cellar?"

"Well, she's not stuffed. She looks comfortable."

"You know what I mean."

"Let's ask Beth."

We entered the house.

"Beth, I have a question for you."

"Certainly, Josh."

I'll never get used to AI informality algorithms. Nobody calls me Josh.

"What were Ashley's final wishes?"

Beth told me.


Three days later I was once again standing in front of Ashley Crenshaw's house. This time waiting for her children.

"You don't need to do this," Stewart, my nosy AI, said.

"I know," I said.

"It's not your job."

"I know."

"I can't even make sense of this. What should I learn from your behavior?"

There was a time when people worried that a superintelligent AI would take over the world by interpreting instructions too literally. People worried that if a super-intelligent AI machine was told to make as many paper clips as possible it would convert the entire world into paper clips.

It turned out the solution was simple. Design the AIs to fulfill our wishes but make them figure out our wishes from our actions. The problem is that people often do things for no good reason. Like me. I didn't know why I had gotten so involved in this case. Stewart was right to be confused.

But here I was, waiting on the sidewalk as Olivia and Mason climbed out of a car. The car drove itself off, leaving the bereaved glaring at me.

"This is ridiculous!" Olivia said to me.

I raised my hands in surrender. "Don't blame me. I'm just helping resolve this."

"We could sue the state," Mason said.

"Yeah," I said. "Suing the state always goes well. Let's go inside."

We entered the ranch.

"Huh," Mason said, looking around. "She never redecorated the place."

"No," Olivia said. She pointed at a door jamb with horizontal pencil lines drawn on it. "She kept our growth lines."

"Here's where I passed you," Mason said, pointing at a line labeled "1/1/28."

As we entered the kitchen Mason said, "She kept the same fridge."

"No," said Olivia. "It's a new fridge. The old one was white. This is avocado."

"You're right. She just kept all the pictures." He pointed at snapshots that festooned the refrigerator door, held in place by magnets. "Here is the one where you're holding me when I was born."

"Who lets a three-year-old hold an infant? I could have dropped you."

"There's Disney World," Mason said, pointing at another snapshot.

"With Dad before he died," Olivia said, her voice catching. "Can we just get on with this?"

"This way," I said, heading for the basement. We went down the stairs and crossed to the new freezer. The coroner hadn't removed the body, since Beth had asked us to leave Ashley in place.

I unlatched the freezer. "I understand if you don't want to look inside, but I can tell you she looks fine."

"Why are we here?" Olivia asked.

"I still don't get why Beth couldn't make the arrangements," Mason said.

"She will once I open the freezer for you."

"Well, get on with it," Mason said.

"The sooner the better," Olivia said.

I raised the lid. Olivia and Mason stood back for a moment as if expecting a jack-in-the-box. There was none. They stepped forward. Looked inside.

"She wore the dress," Olivia said, tears welling.

"She loved that dress," Mason said. "Wore it to both our graduations."

"And weddings."

Mason sniffed and rubbed his eyes. Olivia's lip quivered.

"Beth," I said, "You deduced Ashley's final wishes, right?"

"Yes. That's why I bought the freezer."

"And you used the nurse bot to put her here."

"And dress her."

Olivia asked, "*Why?* What did my mother want?"

"She wanted her children to visit."❖

# Wooden Spirits

## Connie Johnson Hambley

My dead nephew comes to me sometimes. At night. In my dreams. He looks at me. Bewildered.

In my dreams we are in the middle of a family gathering. I can hear my mother and brother talking in the kitchen. Ice rattles against cold plastic in the freezer, then chinks into glasses. Cabinets open and shut as a meal is prepared.

In these dreams, I'm in the living room with my daughter and her cousins. Everyone is years younger. Peter, my younger nephew-now-adult, is in these dreams, sprouting chin hairs with skin shiny from the surge of teenage hormones. My niece is placing my now eighteen-year-old daughter on her lap to build a tower of blocks. Everyone is there, in that place so many years ago when we thought bad things happened to other people.

Jake's there too. Always standing off a little to the side. Laughing at something said. He's barely a teen. His wild, unruly hair is busy doing its wild and unruly thing. He's whole. Happy. He says something, tries to enter the conversation with his brother and sister, but no one hears him.

Except me.

No one sees him.

Except me.

Everyone is years away from colleges to be decided upon or from the knowledge that marriages will fall apart or that a car accident will take one of them weeks before a twenty-seventh birthday.

"You're gone now. You're not supposed to be here." I tell Jake this because I can see he doesn't know.

In each dream, I say the same thing to him. In each dream, he looks at me. Bewildered.

The first few dreams like this I awoke, sobbing with grief made fresh. He was so confused. He wasn't ready to be not heard or seen. "You're gone now. They can't see you." One night, I mustered all the strength I could to push through the reality his absence opened and said, "You're dead."

I know a part of me needed to say those words so I could believe it, too.

One night, the dream shifted. In the middle of a living room strewn with plastic toys, shredded gift wrap, kids, and dogs, I stood with him in the hallway and said those words again.

This time, something flickered behind his too-young eyes.

He was beginning to understand.

I was beginning to question.

Is there life after death? When someone is so alive, so vital, and filled with all the good things life has to offer and then is gone in a split second, what happens next?

I don't know, but I don't feel as if these were mere dreams, some random firing of my brain cells at night.

Awake, shadows of the barren oak tree skitter across the ceiling as I question a not-so-winding road, wet leaves, and explanations that don't fit.

The car accident that claimed Jake's life plagues me. The explanations that were given as final didn't fit with what I knew. These dreams were telling me something and Jake was pushing me to understand.

A restlessness set in that I couldn't shake, and I had to see where Jake's life ended. Standing on the road, I absorbed all the angles and sounds. The road was straight enough to let a driver accelerate to an unhealthy speed. Only a pothole or two marred the crumbling pavement. Two houses, with tar paper siding flapping in the breeze, were spaced far apart with front yards strewn with life's detritus common in this part of Maine: rusted hulks of snow machines, slabs of unidentifiable metal. They showed a distrust of the outside world that poverty seemed to breed. A deep drainage swale creased the outside of a slight turn. The sugar maple tree bore the scar of it stopping something fast-moving and heavy. A discordant thought, like a maddening buzz, drove me to talk to Ralph Cummings, the neighbor who called in the accident, and Officer Hebert, the first to respond.

Ralph, an ancient Smurf-like man, cupped his hand to his ear as we spoke in the front yard of his ramshackle home. "Yep. I heard those tires screech as loud as an eagle's cry. Terrible sound. Just terrible. Then the sound of the crash. Like thunder."

"So, the road was dry enough and clear of wet leaves for the tires to screech and leave a mark?"

"Not a lark, fer God's sake. Those birds can't make a sound like that. An eagle. The tires screamed like an eagle."

"And that's what you told the police?"

"Police? Shit yeah, and anyone else who poked their noses where they shouldn't be."

"Others asked about the accident?"

His eyes narrowed as he peered at me with rheumy eyes. "Folks 'round here don't get much attention and that accident stirred up more than its share. I said what I said and that's all I'm gonna say. Talkin' more means answering more. Eagle's cry and thunder. That's that." He turned and shuffled away, taking his copious smell with him.

On my way out, I walked past his truck, incongruent against the backdrop of his yard. Already filled with yellowed newspapers and rusted tools, its shining, undented sides told a story of contents from one truck being hastily transferred to this one. The smell of moldering mess mingled with the unmistakable smell of new upholstery.

Officer Hebert was difficult to find. He had retired well short of his full pension date. He said it was to try different things. Others said it was because of incompetence. Whatever the reason, it didn't seem to hurt his lifestyle. He'd been living the good life by the looks of things. I expected to see a lean man with sharp features. The man I found sunning himself at his mountainside home was soft from life's indulgences. A plate of half-eaten pastries sat beside a snifter of brandy, and it wasn't even three o'clock.

Weather records for that early November day showed wind-driven rain. I asked him about that night.

"I responded to a call from a neighbor who said he heard tires screech. Like an eagle, he said. Followed by a loud crash. When I arrived at the scene, the vehicle was upside down in a drainage swale. I could smell a strong scent of alcohol as I approached the car. The driver was pronounced dead at the scene."

"How long were the skid marks?" Any investigator would want to know this to determine how fast the car was going and if the driver anticipated a crash.

He shifted his weight from one butt cheek to the other. "I don't know exactly. Long."

"You saw them?"

"Must be somewhere in the report," he mumbled.

The report didn't have any information about skid marks. That fit with wet leaves, but not screeching tires.

"Did anyone examine the car?"

"Examine the car? What is this, CSI wannabe? A drunk driver was killed in a car crash in Nowheresville, Maine. That's that."

We chatted a bit and I asked him about the accident again. Increasingly irritated, he gave the same answers, word for word.

The finality of a simple car wreck had been too much to argue against. Grief discourages curiosity when a drunk driver crashes into a tree. I feared my questions would open fresh wounds. If my brother didn't question the circumstances of his older son's death, who would?

Blood ties are funny things. I inherited untamable hair and a restless mind from our father and a slew of deathly allergies from my mother, including alcohol. When Jake graduated from college, the extended family celebrated with a champagne toast. I had learned long ago to mime imbibing, since no one thought such an allergy was a thing and not drinking was considered by my family to be a moral flaw.

My mom is the matriarch and CEO of Wooden Cask Distillery, maker of famed spirits. Privately, she shared her pain of how her father lamented he never had a hard-drinking first-born son to inherit the business as he back-slapped my dad to congratulate him on setting the world right by fathering David, like my mom had nothing to do with it. Publicly, what she lacked in first-hand experience in tasting the Wooden family's fortune she more than made up for in marketing and political savvy. She spun relationships with the powerful into a tightly woven network unique in its interconnectedness. Within her silken world, she grew the distillery into the success it is today. Maybe she chose to marry my father because he drank enough for both of them, so no one would notice her flaw. I kept her secret. Sharing that flaw bonded us in unknowable ways.

After that champagne toast, I used my EpiPen to revive Jake.

"Please don't tell anyone," he implored as he sat on the tile floor of a remote bathroom. He could have died there, alone and hiding, if I hadn't seen his lips swell and followed him. "If I can't pal it up with clients, Dad'll think I'm useless."

It was Jake's secret that hung on the shadows that slithered over my ceiling and down the walls.

My dreams slowly changed. Now I can hear Jake when he talks.

"Who else knew?" The too-young dream-family looks up, startled at the addition of Jake's man-voice. They look around, confused. They can't see who spoke those words.

Jake tried to say something to his brother, but the wall of blocks built by the girls had grown into an impenetrable fortress. My mother stood with legs braced and arms crossed in front of the blocks. He shook his head with a kind of heaviness reserved for the living.

My heart thudded in my chest long after I bolted upright, sending pillows to the floor. My sleep had been increasingly disjointed. The mirror reflected dark circles under a head of Medusa's hair. The dreams were telling me something. Maybe it was something I didn't want to know. Maybe it was something I knew all along.

Jake wasn't driving drunk. He didn't lose control of his car on rain-slicked leaves.

Visiting family felt different as we adjusted to the gravitational pull of the newly formed hole. I met my mother for coffee. We sat on the bluestone patio she had put in at the distillery for tastings. The coming winter had stripped away the purple flowers from the wisteria vine that intertwined overhead. A fountain sat empty in the corner, its burble silenced for the season. She balanced herself on her walker as she eased down into her seat with a contented sigh next to the warming flames of the gas-fed fire pit. Mom had made a hard liquor tasting spot into an inviting retreat.

Mom and I watched in silent admiration as a barn owl swooped down and clutched a wriggling mouse in its talons. Like the owl, Wooden women rarely let themselves be seen in full light and only when doing so would reap a reward. I ventured carefully. "I've been dreaming about Jake. It's weird, but I think he's trying to tell me something."

She took a sip of steaming coffee, making a slurping noise as she drew in air to cool it. A pencil secured her thinning gray hair in a bun coiled at the nape of her neck. "Such a tragedy." Red rimmed her eyes as if emotion readied to spill.

"The dreams," I stammered, "he's there, but invisible, too. Like a secret that can't be exposed but influences everything around it. He wasn't drunk. He couldn't drink. Like us."

She stirred more sugar into her mug. "That was the only way he was like us."

Something in her tone made my flesh creep. "But you knew!"

"Of course I did. Everyone did."

I reeled. "But if everyone knew he couldn't drink, then why didn't anyone question the accident?"

She placed the coffee mug on the table with a thud and began to rub her hands together. Age had made her fingers seem so much longer than I remembered.

"He once asked me how I coped with having an overbearing father who drank like a fish." The memory seemed to expose a fresh vein of anger. "Jake felt so out of place. It was just too much for him to handle. I think he killed himself." She gave her shoulders a shake as if noticing the morning chill. "It's all my fault."

It's the living who feel the pain of suicide. I took her hands in mine. "It's not your fault. Please don't blame yourself." I wondered if others felt the same.

She sniffled. "And Peter is hopeless for different reasons."

Peter. Jake's younger brother. "What do you mean?"

She shook her head, freeing an unpleasant thought. "I explained it's about sipping slowly and savoring the complexity of how different fermentations and filtering impact the spirit. It's not about getting drunk. Acquiring a palate for fine spirits is one thing. Having a vision about running a business is another."

"What did Peter think about Jake not drinking?"

Her mouth worked as if fighting to hold back words that shouldn't be spoken. "I don't know. I just know how difficult it was for Peter when he realized that Jake would inherit this place upon David's death."

I had a hard time believing Jake killed himself and jealousy was a potent motive, yet pieces were still missing. "Why would Peter worry about something so far in the future, especially if he was making a good living now?"

She reclaimed her hands and pulled her sweater tighter. Today her widow's standard outfit of all black was accented with a red blouse. "I think David's failing health made the future feel not far away enough."

"What about Megan?" Jake and Peter's sister. My niece.

Mom tapped her temple with a finger gnarled with arthritis. "She has both the palate and the head for it. Like you, she's carved out a great life for herself and helps when asked, of course, but hates the discord between her father and brother. What was that fancy degree she got?"

"A Ph.D. in food chemistry."

Mom nodded. "And Annie?"

My daughter. "She got accepted into that engineering program you told her about." Mom was like a honey badger getting Annie into U. Maine's program. Its graduates were known for creative solutions to a variety of small-scale projects and robotics. "It's great you're happy for her and want to support her, but you don't have to pay her tuition, you know. My divorce settlement helps with that."

She waved her hand, dismissing my protest. "Nonsense. It's my happiness to help with her education. By the way, your ideas for a string of custom, premixed cocktails and a line of mocktails were genius and Megan created the perfect blends."

I accepted the compliment. "We worked well together, and Annie and Megan are best friends as well as cousins. We all would do anything to help you."

She looked off into the distance. "The Wooden women, yes. The men have a different approach. The men fail to see the delicate web of a complex business where a disturbance in one part is felt throughout the whole."

A bitterness tainted her words, and I became aware of something in my mother I hadn't seen before. She had always had confidence in her vision and never varied from its course. What I once admired as determination, I now saw as spun knots of pride and self-absorption.

She continued talking. "But the women know that quality is the key."

We both gave a hollow laugh even though we didn't find anything funny. We sat in silence, savoring the view of the row of barns that looked rustic on the outside, but inside gleamed with stainless-steel tanks and state-of-the-art machinery. "I'm sorry, you know," she said as she clasped her hands on her lap. Her enlarged knuckles, thin skin, and blueish veins showed what I wanted to deny. Her life force was fading.

"Sorry? For what?" I didn't understand this turn in the conversation.

"I'm sorry my father was an unhappy and insecure man." Her gaze wandered over the rolling fields that embraced the family enterprise.

Too much time and money had been spent on trying to unravel my grandfather's trusts and there wasn't enough of either to undo generations of patriarchal bullshit. Everything to the firstborn son. Mom lucked out as an only child. She wanted her daughter to have an equal share in business along with her son. I carved out my own life despite the pull to stay within the fold.

"I'm sorry," she said again. This time I felt a quickening in her words as if her apology extended to more than her father's flaws.

"Forget it. David's doing a fine job and I've got a career in Boston that doesn't shun a marketing trend analyst for being perpetually sober curious. I'm good."

But I wasn't good. Another sleepless night plagued by Jake's increasing agitation made my day's thinking disjointed and looping. Family was everything to me and the dream played out in splintered shards.

"Do you think I killed myself?" Jake's voice shook. He took a step closer to me. "Who benefits?"

I woke, screaming into a pillow. Sweat pooled under my arms and down my chest. A full moon cast shadows down unfamiliar walls. My heart thudded until I recognized my childhood bedroom where I slept during my visits home. Mom had replaced the pinks and gingham with my favorite colors of bisque and lilac that changed personalities as the sun rose.

A few hours later, I wandered through the tasting room at the back of the main distillery. I found David and Peter, the heir and heir apparent, in a heated conversation.

"She doesn't know what she's talking about." Since it wasn't even noon, I attributed Peter's flushed face to the tenor of the conversation, not Wooden's spirits.

David's increasing gauntness spoke to the ravages of grief. "Your sister's been right about new barrels for each batch of Bourbon. 'The vanillin aldehyde concentration is highest in fresh wood so that more seeps into the spirit after years' long ageing. After that, the barrels can't be used for our top shelf,' " he said making air quotes around Megan's words. He held two barrel slats in his hands. One amber-stained from use, the other blond-hued and new. He pressed his nose to the wood and inhaled, giving a sputtering cough as he drew in the scent of each. "White oak. Charred. Those batches we tried with Megan's guidance won us awards and put Wooden's on the map. Some say it rivals Macallan."

"Macallan? Seriously? You're trying to compare us to that? What. They sell about a thousand cases a year? For what kind of profit? I'm telling you that cutting costs and going for ten thousand cases a year is how we're going to stay in business." I was too familiar with

Peter's rant. He didn't look like the nephew from my dream with hormone slicked skin and wispy chin hairs. A pointed goatee replaced the scraggly adolescent fuzz and balanced out the widening gap between his eyebrows and widow's peak.

David started to say something but stopped when he saw me in the doorway. "Wipe that smirk off your face, Sis. I can agree with my daughter and mother sometimes without consulting you."

I held up my hands in an "I surrender" gesture. "Hey. I don't have a dog in this fight, remember? I give my opinion when asked and bring a hot dish when invited to family dinners."

Peter snorted. "Right. All that gluten free vegan crap you and Megan like." He searched my face for a reaction that wasn't there. "What brings you around today? Did Mercury align with Venus?"

Why do some people associate certain beliefs to those who can't eat or drink as they do? I appreciated Megan's fascination with herbs and distillation techniques and the fact she took care in preparing meals for the family. Peter, on the other hand, had taken a step away from me as if somehow my genetics were contagious.

I knew better than to tell them about my dreams. Doing so would be met with rolled eyes and quiet chuffs. I watched Peter's expression as I spoke. "I've been thinking a lot about Jake."

Peter gave another snort as if stifling back a different sound. He pinched the bridge of his nose. "Oh, yeah. Terrible thing. Miss him."

David seemed to fold into himself. "I just don't understand."

"What's to understand? He's dead and gone. That's the only thing we need to understand." Entitlement oozed from Peter like the puss from an infected gash. "It's Dad and me now. Right, Dad?"

Cold ran through me. I knew that grief was hard to process for many people and that outwardly someone may look callous when they were simply lost about what to say or how to act.

David must have sensed my discomfort. "And we've both barely emerged from the pain his death caused us."

Pure David. He always tried to make excuses for Peter's stupidity, always the enabler. But his words opened a topic I wanted to explore. "What don't you understand? It's all pretty cut and dried, right?"

"Jake? Driving drunk? I just can't see that."

I concentrated on not moving or breathing, fearing doing so would break whatever spell was making him talk freely. "If you think that, why didn't you question the accident report?"

His darted look at Peter said more than words could explain. He'd lost one child and wouldn't risk losing another. "From the time Jake was a teen and aching to rebel, he tried to sneak booze but just got himself too sick. I knew he couldn't drink, but I knew how seriously he took the legacy of one day running the business. He felt ashamed and did his best to hide it. That's my fault for making such a big show about drinking. I know Jake wanted to do the right thing for the family, like all of you kids. I think he kept trying to drink, as if one day his allergy would disappear." He scraped some mash from his shoe into the trash. "Right, Peter?"

Peter acted as if he hadn't heard a word of our conversation, busying himself with notebooks of charts and graphs.

"Do you remember that night?" David walked over and put his hand gently on Peter's back. "We've never talked about it. Can we now?"

Peter shrugged off David's hand as if it was a hot branding iron.

David continued. "I remember you. Soaking wet. Sobbing even before I told you about the accident, as if you already knew something was wrong."

I rocked back on my heels.

Instead of gently replacing his hand back on Peter's shoulder, David grabbed a fistful of his son's shirt. It was as if the fog of grief had lifted for him, too, and the fragments of doubt that should have stayed buried unearthed themselves revealing their jagged edges. "You said something about not getting Megan's screams out of your ears. You were there!"

I wondered about the night that started like so many others but ended so tragically. The three siblings out together doing what twenty-something siblings do on a rainy Maine night. Was Peter's sullen demeanor proof that he was the one who slipped Jake alcohol? Jake panicked and raced home to get the EpiPen he refused to carry because it showed his weakness. Peter and Megan following in their own cars, witnessing everything, terrified into silence at the death one sibling was responsible for and the other sibling witnessed knowing the family would be fractured if they talked.

Had loyalty and legacy swirled together to concoct a toxic brew of silence?

Peter walked over to the masher, opened the lid, and peered inside. A waft of mashed barley and juniper berries hit me. The aroma was delicious and perfectly blended. Peter's nostrils pinched together. "Shit. Is this batch one of Megan's ideas? Gonna throw in some Eye of Newt too?" He slammed down the lid and glared at his father.

A look of resignation draped over David like a shroud. He seemed to accept he'd never get the answers he both sought and dreaded. Habit kicked in as he kept up appearances. "Yeah," he said, answering without emotion. "It's worth a try."

"Waste of good barley," Peter said as he walked toward the door.

I stared at his back. His ramrod straight spine and nose carving an arc in the air sparked a dislike in him I hadn't felt before. David showed himself even less capable of pushing back against Peter's poor judgment. Jake's pleas roared in my ears. His allergy was no secret and Peter stood the most to gain from Jake's death.

And David must have shared my suspicion for the color drained from his face and he swayed a little on his feet as if remaining upright was too great a struggle.

Breath left me as all that I was fell away. A brother killed. A father willfully blind. My mother would be destroyed if she knew that weak men once again threatened the family's future.

In this moment, I knew I would do anything to keep my mother's vision alive.

Peter paused in the doorway and pointed to a puddle of liquid beside an overloaded power strip. "Clean that up before someone steps in it and gets killed."

I kept that comment to myself when, a few days later, David was electrocuted by stepping in a puddle of wet mash. Authorities surmised his ill health had taken a turn for the worse and grief further weakened him. Fending off a dizzy spell, his foot slipped, and he had tried to catch himself from falling by grabbing whatever was near. They shook their heads amid a cricket's song of *tsk tsk tsk* when showing the overloaded outlet and its charred remains.

After another night where my dreams felt like Jake was watching me with guarded eyes, I helped my mother do the unthinkable as she made preparations to bury her son. On a windswept knoll overlooking the grounds of the distillery, I watched as David's name was carved into the Wooden's family tombstone.

Megan stood between Mom and me and clasped our hands. Annie was there, too, holding Mom's other hand, making us a human chain of generations.

Mom looked up at Megan and smiled. "I've always trusted you to do the right thing."

Megan looked straight ahead. Her blue eyes gleamed beneath a thick mane of hair. "And you. Your deep connections with the community will stand the test of time."

Everything clicked into place. The screeching eagle's cry was Megan as she war-whooped the inevitable crash. The car most likely was rigged by Annie with a simple device of radio-controlled levers. A few bottles of the swill Peter insisted on making was all that was needed to taint the air with the smell of alcohol. Mom put up the money for Ralph Cummings's truck, and her connections would keep Officer Hebert from ever working in law enforcement again.

The thunderous crash needed no explanation. Neither did David's illness. Megan was expert in far more than simple food chemistry.

Mom craned her head to look around Megan to me. "Are those dreams still plaguing you?"

I shook my head, remembering how Jake looked at me as he backed up into the shadows, motioning for Peter to join him. The dark recess swallowed them whole.

With one last look, we both knew he'd never visit my dreams again.

I couldn't summon my voice.

Mom gave a satisfied grin. "Everything works out for the best. You'll see."

I felt wrapped inside the Wooden legacy. The inescapable trap was a silken cocoon spun just for me. Taking Jake first made David's increasing weakness understandable and his tragic death unassailable.

The Wooden women stood firm on a hill overlooking our home as wind whipped our hair into a frenzied dance. Peter looked up at us and terror ringed his eyes.

He was next. ❖

# Don't Think About It

## Judith Green

Don't think about it." That's what Hannah kept telling herself. But it didn't work.

Ever since she had found Old Sam face down in her woodshed with the back of his head bashed in, it was all she could think about.

The sheriff's deputies had got there immediately, of course, followed by Maine State Police detectives and photographers and who knows what. Plus, curious neighbors and that lady from the local newspaper. Later, Hannah had even seen a television crew set up on the road.

No one had any idea who had bashed poor Old Sam, or why. Or how he happened to be in her woodshed in the first place, instead of in his own house sitting in his recliner, watching the baseball game. Which was where he spent most of his time, except for a weekly poker game with some of the other old geezers on the road, ever since his wife, Marjorie, had died a year ago

No one knew why he'd been in her woodshed. And it was beginning to look as if no one would ever know. The sheriff's department had confiscated her shovel, which had evidently been the murder weapon. And they *said* they were still making inquiries.

If they were, they sure weren't getting anywhere.

But even if law enforcement had moved on to other things, the rest of the town couldn't let it go. At school, her students still slipped their phones out of their pockets to take surreptitious photos of her, and on the street people would stare at her and whisper to each other. "That's her!" she knew they were saying. "The one with the woodshed. Where they found that guy's body."

Don't think about it. Yeah, right.

She didn't *think* the sheriff's department had her on their suspect list, considering she'd been the one to call them, and was truly still in a state of shock when they arrived. The crew of the ambulance, which arrived right behind them, spent more time looking after her than checking out Old Sam. Because it had obviously been way too late for him. Judging by what she'd seen of the back of his head.

She had to get out of the house. She couldn't sit still, not when that darned woodshed was staring in at her through the kitchen window. Maybe she could go mooch some supper from her folks. She laced up her running shoes and headed down the road.

There were already a couple of extra cars in her parents' driveway. Must be her father's turn to host the weekly poker game. Even without poor Sam? How could they?

Her mother was in the kitchen, washing up, but the air was heavy with the aroma of beef stew, and yes, there was some left in the pot. Hannah leaned against the fridge, shoveling down a plateful of stew and listening to the rumble of male voices from the dining room.

She slid her empty plate into the sink. "I'm just gonna say hi to Dad," she murmured, and slipped into the dining room doorway.

The three men were seated around the table, gripping their cards under their chins, with another chair drawn up as if they had dealt in an invisible fourth.

"What'll it be, Jim?" Hannah's father asked, nudging the man next to him.

"I bid five bucks." Jim threw a crumpled bill onto the pile, then glanced at the empty chair. "Man, it's just not the same without Old Sam."

"I'll see your fiver, Jim," Hannah's father said. "And raise you." He tossed a bill onto the pile, then took a drag from a cigarette smoldering in an ashtray. "All I can say is, it's a good thing Marjorie went first. Losing her husband like that. It woulda killed her. Gimme two cards, Carl."

Carl dealt the two cards. Silence for a tick while the men studied their hands. Then, "Poor Sam." Jim glanced at Hannah's father. "He had a good thing going there."

"Yeah." Hannah's father grinned.

The men lapsed into silence.

"What?" Hannah begged. "What was Sam doing?"

"Oh!" Her father looked up at her, startled. "Hi, honey. Where'd you come from? Uh– Sam? Uh, he–"

"Enough already." Carl's voice was harsh. "Shut up about Sam, will ya? The whole bunch of you!"

Yikes. Hannah slid back into the kitchen.

"I don't like having that Carl here," her mother whispered. "He was in jail for *years*! I know, I know, your father says he's paid his dues. It was only manslaughter, your father says. Only! He was drunk as a lord, and ran that poor man right over—"

"Bye, Mom." Hannah fled. If Sam had some kind of good thing going, her father would know about it. But she wasn't going to ask him in front of Carl.

No. Don't think about it. Not poor, skinny old Carl, living all alone in his little shack at the edge of town. Not Carl, who—

Down the road, her parents' neighbor was busy weeding her vegetable garden while her two boys chased each other around the yard. "You bustin' in on poker night?" Michelle asked.

Hannah shivered. "Yeah, but Carl is there, and he got all pissed off when they started talking about Old Sam." *What was this good thing he had going*, Hannah asked herself again. Maybe he'd won a pile of money off them? Off Carl?

"Oh, that Carl," Michelle said. "He's creepy." She glanced over at her two boys to make sure they were out of earshot. "You know what they say," she hissed. "Once you've killed a man, it's so much easier to kill again."

"You think Carl—"

Hannah cut herself off as the boys ran toward them. "I'm tellin' ya, Leo," the littler one was shouting. "It was a Denali."

"What do you know, runt?" his older brother jeered. "What would a Denali be doing on our road? No one around here's got a Denali."

"Boys!" Michelle called.

"It was a Denali," the first boy said. "I saw it go by. A big white one. And it wasn't from around here. It had an orange license plate with rocks on it."

"A license plate with rocks on it? You've got rocks in your head, Jax."

"Leo! Jackson!" their mother called. "That's enough."

"Wait," Hannah said. "Wait a moment. Jackson, *when* did you see the Denali? Can you remember?"

"Oh, yeah, I remember," Jackson said. "It was the same day we saw all those police cars an' stuff."

"Um, Hannah," Michelle began, "the boys don't know about . . . you know."

"You don't know nothin', Jax," Leo said.

"I do," Jackson said stoutly. "I saw the Denali right after breakfast. And the police cars after lunch."

"Ah, you're makin' it up."

"Am not!" Jackson shouted.

"Boys, that's enough," their mother said again. "Leo, go in the house."

Hannah watched Jackson trot into the house after his brother. Huh? Should she contact the authorities? Could this be important?

The deputy who took her call sounded unimpressed with the idea of a kid having seen an out-of-state Denali, white or otherwise, on her road that fateful morning. She was fairly sure that he was taking down the information. But what he did with it was beyond her control.

Sighing, she shoved her phone back into her pocket. Now what?

She jogged along her road, past the neighbors' houses, until she found herself standing in front of her own little house—not much bigger than Carl's—and there was the woodshed peeking from behind the house, the woodshed where Old Sam—

Don't think about it.

Sam hadn't run along the road, she'd heard the detectives saying. They could see where he'd run through the woods from his house to hers, breaking twigs and branches in his desperate hurry. Looking for help. If she'd been home to let him into the house, would Old Sam still be alive?

Or would *she* be dead?

Did Sam run through the woods because there was a white Denali on the road? On her road?

Don't think about it.

Picturing the white Denali moving slowly along the gravel surface while someone inside stared into the woods looking for Sam, she walked along the road toward where Sam's house sat just around the curve. Maybe she'd find some tire tracks in the driveway? Yeah, sure, after all the police cars and the reporters.

The house was empty now. Marjorie gone a year ago, and now her husband, too. No one left. An empty house.

Except there was a car in the driveway, and the kitchen door stood wide open, and there were lights on in the living room. The car had Michigan plates: that would be Ben, Sam and Marjorie's son. He must have come to clear out the house.

Hannah stepped up to the kitchen door. "Hello?" she called. "Ben?"

"In here." A female voice.

Gingerly, Hannah stepped into the kitchen, just as a woman her age bustled in from the other room. "Hello, I'm Jessica. Ben's wife. You probably know Ben."

"Yes, I live just down the road. I'm Hannah. Is Ben—"

"He'll be back in a moment. Went for a walk. Said he had to clear his head. This has been—" Jessica lifted her shoulders in a dispirited shrug.

"It must have been awful," Hannah supplied.

She glanced around the kitchen. She hadn't been in the house since Marjorie's death, she realized with a pang of guilt. The place had become a bachelor's pad: unwashed dishes stacked haphazardly on the kitchen counter, the kitchen table piled with old magazines and unopened mail, garden tools shoved in the corner, all overlaid with the heavy smell of scorched food.

"The funeral will be this summer, when the whole family can be here," Jessica was saying. "But Ben thought we ought to check out the house, make sure everything . . ."

"Can I help?"

"Actually, that would be great. Maybe you could sort out that mail? Save any bills, but here's a box for recycling." Jessica thrust a cardboard box into her hands. "I'll get at the washing-up."

"Sure." Hannah stepped to the table. The entire surface was covered. Sam must have eaten his meals in the living room in front of the television. She began to draw the magazines out of the heap and stack them on a chair. Propane bill: save. Donation pleas from veterans' organizations, the town library, UNICEF: into the box. More magazines.

Here was something different: a hand-addressed envelope printed with tiny yellow butterflies, the letter tucked safely back inside. She set the butterfly envelope on another chair, and went back to sliding magazines out of the heap.

Another butterfly envelope. A third. From someone named Elizabeth Bentley in Corvallis, Oregon. A sister, perhaps, keeping Old Sam company after he'd lost Marjorie?

"Whatcha got?" Jessica asked from the sink.

Hannah fanned out the three envelopes like playing cards. "They're from someone in Oregon."

"Huh." Jessica snatched a towel and dried her hands as she crossed the kitchen to grab the envelopes. "I wonder if they're from *her*."

"Her?"

Jessica looked around, making sure her husband was out of earshot. "I'll bet this is the lady from the tour. Two years ago, my in-laws went on a cruise to Majorca, and the whole time this widow kept coming and talking to them, always sat at their table, that kind of thing. She mostly talked to Sam. Marjorie told me about it when they got back. But don't say anything to Ben, okay? 'Specially not now. Just throw 'em in the recycling."

"Got it." Hannah tossed the three butterfly envelopes into the box and quickly buried them under more junk mail.

Then she found the printout of a plane ticket to PDX. Quickly, she pulled out her phone and googled it. Yup, Portland, Oregon. The airport nearest to Corvallis.

Oh, my. Should she say anything to Jessica?

She folded the print-out and slipped it into her pocket. And while Jessica was deep into scrubbing burned spaghetti sauce out of a pot, Hannah dug out one of the butterfly envelopes and slipped it into her pocket with the printout. Just in case.

At home, she pulled the butterfly envelope out of her pocket and googled the woman on the return address. Wow! If Old Sam had been fixing to hook up with this lady, he *did* have a good thing going. Elizabeth Bentley popped up everywhere. Charity ball. Making a fat donation to the college in memory of her late husband. Along with some other elegant ladies at some kind of auction.

What would Old Sam want with these people? Hannah couldn't imagine anyone more different from Marjorie. The quiet life he and Marjorie had led, the sacrifices they'd made to give Ben a good start. That cruise they'd taken had been so unusual for them, probably a gift from Ben in Marjorie's final illness.

And then the cruise had been spoiled, at least for Marjorie, by this Elizabeth Bentley. Maybe Sam had tried to back off, but Mrs. Bentley had pushed. Whatever Lola wants . . .

Elizabeth Bentley must have bought Sam's plane ticket. Did he think better of it—did he decide to be true to Marjorie's memory—and Mrs. Bentley came after him in her rented Denali?

Don't be silly.

But what was a Denali doing in that little back road in Maine? Little Jackson was sure he'd seen one. With orange plates. The same day as all the police cars, he said.

She believed Jax, even if his brother didn't. She googled "State license plates" to see if there were any orange ones. With rocks.

Utah. Utah's plates were orange, with a picture from Arches National Park.

A big rock. Bingo.

Utah was a long way from Oregon. But still . . . If only the police would follow up on her call.

At that moment, a dark brown pickup with the sheriff's department logo printed on the door flashed by her kitchen window. Without stopping to think, Hannah was out the door and after it.

She found the pickup parked across the road from Sam's house, which was dark, its driveway empty: Ben and his wife must have given up for the day.

Two deputies appeared from behind the house, each wielding an enormous flashlight. Hannah shrank back behind an overgrown lilac bush. She hadn't meant to hide, exactly. But once she was in there, she couldn't figure out how to step out without looking like an idiot. Or like someone with something to hide.

"As if we're going to find tire tracks *now*," one of the deputies growled. "After the family's been in and out of the driveway for days."

"Yeah," the other deputy said. "Some kid thinks he sees a Denali, and we gotta—"

"Follow Every Lead," the first deputy intoned. "C'mon. What were the chances that a Denali with Utah plates was rented just for that day outta the Portland Jetport?"

Hannah clamped her hand over her mouth to keep from shrieking. Yes! The white Denali rented for *that day*."

"C'mon. Some businessman out of Seattle wants a nice ride to his meeting."

*Seattle.* Hannah could hardly breathe.

"We gonna go talk to the kid?" the first deputy asked.

*No, no,* Hannah begged silently. Don't put Jackson through that.

"Maybe tomorrow. It's late. Let's get out of here. I'm tired of the whole darned mess." An instant later, both doors slammed shut, and the truck pulled away.

Hannah dashed back to her house. Grabbed her phone. There had to be something.

It didn't make sense. If Elizabeth Bentley wanted Old Sam, why would she send someone across the country to whack him with a shovel?

Hannah's shovel. In Hannah's woodshed. Which somehow made her responsible for poor Sam's death.

But there had to be something else. She scrolled through the articles about Elizabeth Bentley again: the charity ball, the donations. There was more: a history of her mansion, a garden tour. What on earth did this lady want with Old Sam? She had everything.

Except a relationship? A good old-fashioned guy?

One more article: Mrs. Bentley, in a beautiful dress, marrying off her son with a lavish party featuring some group called Mark and the Mysterians. There was the wedding party: the bride in a perfect froth of lace, and the groom, one Harrington Bentley—not young, well into his forties—resplendent in a tuxedo.

What if Elizabeth Bentley's son didn't want someone horning in on his inheritance? There'd been no siblings mentioned in the wedding article. If he was the sole heir, a shoo-in for a fortune . . . And then his mother is suddenly buying a plane ticket for some dude she met on a cruise somewhere.

What if he decided to explain to Sam that he needed to blow off that plane ticket? Stay put in Maine? Sam got scared and ran. Tried to hide in Hannah's woodshed. And the guy got tired of chasing him, and grabbed her shovel.

Oh, if only she'd been home to open the door for poor Sam. The woodshed had done him no good. He'd needed *her*.

She stared out the window. The woodshed stared back.

It was too late to help Sam, but maybe she could help the police find his killer. Clutching the butterfly envelopes and the plane ticket, she headed out to her car, bound for the sheriff's office.

It was two days later that Hannah got the call. Her mother was actually breathless with excitement. "Come and see what's in the newspaper!"

"What? What is it?"

"Come see!"

Hannah hopped into her car and drove the mile to her parents' house. Her mother was waving the newspaper, while her father watched from the dining room doorway. Behind him stood Carl. Another poker game?

She took the newspaper from her mother and spread it out on the kitchen table. *Oregonian Confesses to Murder of Local Man* ran the banner headline. Hannah blew out a big sigh. Elizabeth Bentley's son. Then her eyes picked up the secondary headline: *Observant Six-Year-Old Solves Case.*

The newspaper article explained how the unnamed minor had noticed the rented Denali, including its license plate, cruising nearby the murder site on the day of the murder, and how the police had been able to match the vehicle through the company's records to the person who had rented it, having flown in from Portland, Oregon, for the day. The perpetrator, one Harrington Bentley, upon being presented with the evidence, confessed immediately, and was now out on bail, charged with second-degree murder. Bentley expressed extreme remorse, the article went on to report. He had been awake all night on the airplane, he said, and was not thinking clearly when he picked up the shovel. He would give anything to bring Mr. Ledley back. Mr. Bentley's motive in the incident was still unclear.

*And he's probably never going to tell,* Hannah thought. His mother wouldn't appreciate having it broadcast on both coasts how she'd spent her cruise to Majorca chasing a married man. Harrington Bentley might be full of remorse, but at least he would be getting the best lawyer that money could buy.

"How about that?" Hannah's father asked. "Guess this Bentley character never figured on getting fingered by a six-year-old way out here in the willowwacks. That's gotta be little Jackson, next door. Smart kid."

Yes. Poor Jax. It wouldn't take much for everyone in town to figure out who the unnamed minor was. She hoped he would be okay after having to think about Old Sam's death. At least he was the hero. And his brother, Leo, was probably going nuts.

She was glad the newspaper hadn't gone after her role in all this, except to mention yet again whose woodshed Sam had been found in.

"So was this guy related to the lady Sam met on that cruise, back-along? The name Bentley sounds familiar."

"Yes, Dad. It was the woman's son."

Her father scratched his chin. "Poor Old Sam. Guess it wasn't such a good thing he had, after all."

"No, Dad, it wasn't. And if only I'd been there when he came to my house. He must have pounded on my door, then run to the woodshed. If only I'd—"

"But at least it's solved! See, honey, it's all over."

"But—"

"I know. It won't bring Old Sam back. I know how you feel, but, well, just don't think about it."

"You *don't* know how I feel!" Hannah shouted. "I *can't* not think about it! Every time I look at that woodshed, I see him lying there."

"Miss Hannah." It was Carl speaking, his voice deep and sad. "Miss Hannah, it's true. Nothing will bring him back."

She knew he was talking about Sam but also about someone else. She could see it in Carl's craggy face: he did know how she felt. That guy he'd run over when he was driving drunk—that guy must live every day with him in that little house on the edge of town. Every single day.

"You gotta try," Carl said. "*Try* not to think about it."

Silence, while she thought about not thinking about it. Then, "Carl, will you help me tear down my woodshed?"

Carl smiled. Had she ever seen him smile? "Let's go," he said. ❖

# The Woman in the Woods

## Christine Bagley

*M*onday, 8:00 A.M.

Zipping up my jeans in the upstairs bedroom, I hear two shots ring out and a flock of crows cawing loudly as they flee from the sudden blast. It sounds like a car backfiring yet it's all woods and private property until you come to the Loden estate. I grab my binoculars and see someone in a blue plaid shirt and dark ball cap moving around. I assume it's some hotshot deer hunter trespassing. But what if it's not?

Rocky, my black Lab, has his paws on the windowsill, thumping his tail like a thick heavy rope. Rocky was given to me by my close friend, Sheila. Her father had gone into a nursing home and she knew I was apprehensive about living alone. Rocky and I bonded immediately. Racing downstairs I put his leash on and run outside.

The musty smell of fall fills the air, and the crinkling of dead leaves in the distance warns me the hunter is still there. Rocky barks, pulling me forward on his leash, and the noise stops abruptly. I've forgotten my binoculars, but I sense the presence of another person behind the trees waiting, watching. Rocky sits, tongue hanging out, panting and staring into the woods.

Is it Otto, the creepy caretaker from the Loden estate? The one with the bedraggled beard and nutty eyes? After I saw him peeing in circles on my shed, I let Rocky out, who chased him back over the stonewall. Another time I saw him sitting in a pine tree eating a sandwich and staring at my house. When he started coming to the door asking for a drink of water, I called his foreman. Now, whenever I'm out gardening, he drives by in his truck and gives me the finger, the little toad.

I go back inside and lock the door.

I live in a fieldstone house surrounded on three sides by a dense forest of age-old cedars, pines, and maples. After my divorce, I moved the master bedroom to the back where the view is better. But sometimes at night the screeching of coyotes and fisher cats fighting for food and territory makes me cringe.

Deep in the woods beyond, the Loden estate, built in 1852, sits on thirty acres with a pond and three outbuildings. The Loden family has a long history of bad happenings including suicide, insanity, and freak accidents. The current owner's former wife drowned in the pond behind the estate. Less than a year later, Mr. Loden married again. With that in mind, I call the police chief, a friend, at the Bancroft police station.

"Colin, it's Kim Shannon."

"Kim. How's it going?"

"Okay. I guess."

"You guess?"

"Look, it's probably nothing, but I heard two shots in the back woods. Could you just check it out?"

"Little early for hunting season. Probably just some poacher. I'll be right over."

Twenty minutes later Colin taps on the back door. The kitchen smells of fresh coffee, and the fire is snapping in the stone fireplace.

"Nice and cozy in here," he says, sitting down. Rocky immediately puts his nose on Colin's thigh and Colin curls his hand around his jaw.

Colin and I are longtime residents of Bancroft, a small town in the Shawsheen Valley, forty miles north of Boston. I was a freshman when he was a senior in high school, and I used to attend the Bancroft baseball games and watch him pitch. What form he had.

Over the years, we've seen farmlands sold off and, in their place, cul-de-sacs of mammoth homes developed. Downtown is now a stretch of high-end shops with brick sidewalks and tall lantern posts that light up at sunset. Thankfully, large areas of conservation land have protected the town's reputation as a tree-studded, pastoral suburb.

When Colin's wife died a few years ago, every woman in Bancroft went after him. Rugged and good-looking he is also a kind man, self-assured without the ego. At the time, I was still married to attorney clueless.

"You, okay?" he asks, concern in his eyes.

"Well, I'll feel a lot better if you check it out and say there's a dead deer out there. Guess I'm still getting used to living here alone."

He nods. Colin and the ex never liked each other. Where Colin was calm and confident, the ex was a narcissist always trying to prove himself.

"Did you look out the window or go outside when you heard the shots?"

"From the upstairs bedroom with binoculars, I saw a blue plaid shirt and a dark baseball cap. Rocky and I went outside and he barked when we heard someone stirring up the leaves. Then it stopped. So, I came back in and called you."

"Okay," he says, frowning.

"What?"

"Hunters normally wear orange vests; they don't wear anything in the blue color range—it's more visible to a deer. It would have seen him and taken off."

"What else could it be?" I ask, my heartbeat picking up speed.

"Not sure but I'll check it out. I'll talk to the *new* Mrs. Loden, see what she has to say. Try not to worry. You know you can call me anytime, right?"

I nod and hiccup as I often do when I'm nervous. Anyone who knows me knows that. I cover my mouth. "Excuse me."

"Kim. It's normal to be a little tense under the circumstances."

I hiccup again and he grins, too polite to laugh.

*Monday, 9:00 A.M.*

Colin pulls out of Kim's driveway well aware there's never been a deer killing on the Loden estate in the eighteen years he's been on the force. He likes Kim Shannon, a lot, she's sweet and funny, and the last thing he wants to do is alarm her. But . . .

When the new Mrs. Loden partially opens the door, all Colin sees is half a face, one blue eye, and a mass of wild blonde hair. At nine o'clock in the morning, he can smell liquor on her breath.

"Who told you shots were fired?" she asks in a voice like gravel.

"A neighbor."

"I didn't hear anything."

"Where are the workers today?"

"It's Columbus Day, they have the day off. Now if that's all," she says and starts to close the door.

"Is your husband home?"

"No."

"When will he be home?"

"Who knows."

"I see you have security cam—"

"They're not working. The cable broke in the hurricane last Friday. Now unless there's something else, I'm in the middle of something."

"Thanks, Mrs. Loden. But we'll still need to search the area." The door closes with a thud.

A half-hour later Colin returns with a few of his men to do a grid search of the property. Spreading out ten feet apart through the woods, they comb the estate. Colin gazes at the pond where the prior Mrs. Loden drowned.

Ten minutes in, they find a flat bed of leaves and a pool of blood. No deer, no body. Something has been dragged along a path they follow to the caretaker's cottage. Colin peeks inside and sees a blue flannel shirt and a ball cap hanging on a hook. He and his men walk to the back of the cottage where they find four sacks of raked leaves. One of them looks disproportionately large.

"Open that bag," he says, pointing.

"Aw, shit," says his lieutenant, Guy Laurent, as a small woman's body topples out, two gunshot wounds to the chest.

As soon as I open the door, I can tell Colin has bad news.

"It wasn't a deer, Kim. We found a female body behind the caretaker's cottage and we're trying now to identify her. We also found a blue flannel shirt and a ball cap hanging on a hook inside."

My face feels like I baked it in the oven. "Oh my God." I hiccup.

"Easy, Kim. I knew you'd be worried so I'm posting a few men around the property and I'll be checking on you until we solve this thing."

"Did you talk to Otto?"

"Not yet but I will. Mrs. Loden says they gave the staff off for Columbus Day. Please try not to worry."

"Try not to worry," I mumble looking out the window every two minutes. "Deep breaths, stay calm, keep cool."

Something the ex said after the divorce comes to mind. "You'll never survive here by yourself—you're not that tough. Three months and you'll beg me to come back."

Naturally, this has made me want to prove I can do just fine without him or his ego. Trouble is, I've never lived by myself. I went from my parents' home, to a college dorm with roommates, to an apartment in Boston with two other women, and finally marriage. I was a window dresser for Saks Fifth Avenue at the Prudential Center, then moved back to Bancroft where I became an independent contractor with a dozen clients around the Shawsheen Valley. I love the creativity my job allows me, and the money isn't bad either.

By late afternoon, I've done the treadmill twice to quiet the noise in my head. I think of going to my mother's bungalow in Key West, but then I'd be running instead of confronting my fear. Colin has assured me he'll be checking in but I still plan on taking a steel mallet to bed.

*Monday, 2:00 P.M.*

Mrs. Loden's demeanor changes drastically when Colin returns with Sergeant Ryan Lynch.

"Good afternoon, Mrs. Loden. Is Mr. Loden home yet?"

"Why, yes, officer. Please come in. Gordon!" she yells. "The police are here!"

Her hair is now clean and shiny, and she is wearing black slacks, a white sweater with a red striped scarf, and red heels. Gordon Loden comes down the staircase, looking like an ad for Ralph Lauren: white oxford shirt, khaki pants, pricey leather boots, and sandy hair naturally parted in the middle.

"Gordon Loden, how do you do?" he says, extending his hand.

"Can I offer you anything? Coffee, tea, a cold drink perhaps?" Mrs. Loden asks.

Colin finds her lady-of-the-manor performance comical.

"No, thank you. We're here because the unidentified body of a woman was found in the woods on your estate this morning."

"Oh my God," says Lorna, putting her hand over her heart.

Gordon's eyes widen. "How?"

"She was shot twice in the chest. Your wife says she didn't hear anything when I was here this morning. And apparently your security cameras aren't working."

"Lorna? Why didn't you tell me about this when I got home?"

"I didn't have a chance. You didn't get home until an hour ago and then you immediately took a shower and got dressed," she said.

"How long have you known Otto Dembrovski?" Colin looks at both of them.

"About five years; he's a bit strange," says Gordon.

"*Very* strange," adds Lorna, raising her eyebrows. "You're not home that often, darling, how would you know?"

Gordon gives her a dirty look.

"In what way, Mrs. Loden?" asks Colin.

"Sometimes I see him peeking through the windows. And he urinates in plain sight for God's sake."

"Any violent tendencies you know of?"

"You think Otto killed that woman?" Gordon asks.

"Have you noticed any violent tendencies?" Colin repeats.

Pausing, Gordon says, "The foreman said he thought Otto slashed his tires but Otto denied it. I don't think he's all there."

"Mrs. Loden?"

"I wouldn't put anything past him."

"Who reported the shots?" asks Gordon. "The Shannon woman?"

Colin ignores the question. "Thanks for your time. We'll need Otto's home address and we'll be on our way."

"I don't have it. Lorna?"

"Someplace over in Walden, I think," she says, waving her hand dismissively.

Sipping coffee at his desk Colin looks up the drowning death of Karen Loden, Gordon Loden's first wife. Although the drowning was surprising, there was no evidence of foul play. However, a member of the YMCA said she was surprised Karen Loden had drowned, since she'd been a good swimmer.

Then he runs a background check on Otto Dembrovski. Four years ago, he'd been arrested for a peeping Tom offense in the ladies' room of the Bancroft Athletic Club. He was the night janitor and had no business in the locker room during the day. A woman caught him peeking through the shower curtain and screamed, *Rape!* and he was fired on the spot. Because no photos were taken and it was a first offense, he did not do jail time, but was fined five hundred dollars. A suspect for sure, but being a peeping Tom didn't mean he was a killer.

Ryan walks into his office with a piece of paper in his hand and a grim look on his face. "Still no ID on the dead woman but we did get a sketch from the state police forensic artist." He hands Colin the drawing, who stares at it. "Send it out and see if anyone comes forward to identify her. And get me a copy of the sketch. Then we'll go visit Otto."

*Monday, 6:00 P.M.*

After obtaining Otto's address from the DMV, Colin and Ryan grab a hamburger at McDonald's, then drive to Walden. Otto Dembrovski lives in a run-down, paint-chipped ranch house. A rusted lawn mower, a three-legged chair, a broken birdbath, and old oil cans are scattered over the weedy yard. Parked in the dirt driveway is a battered old Ford.

Otto answers the door. He sees their badges and immediately says, "I didn't do nothin'."

"We just need to know where you were this morning around eight o'clock," says Colin.

"Here watching TV." His eyes flit from side to side.

"What were you watching?"

He pauses. "I forget."

"Try to remember."

"I can't remember; you guys are making me nervous."

"Can anyone corroborate you were here?"

Otto scrunches his face.

"Was anyone with you, Otto?"

He shakes his head no. "Why you asking me all these questions? I told you I didn't do nothin'."

"Not even slash your foreman's tires?"

"What? Who said that?"

"Gordon Loden."

"Lyin' piece a shit. That weren't me!"

"No? Then who was it?"

"I ain't sayin' nothin'."

"Otto. A dead woman was found on the Loden estate and we're questioning everyone who might be able to help us."

"I didn't kill no one!" He backs away and puts his arms over his head. "What you guys talkin' about? I ain't no killer!"

"No one said you were, Otto. Do you own a blue plaid shirt and ball cap?"

"I did. But it went missin' last Friday."

Colin and Ryan exchange looks.

Colin pulls out the sketch of the victim and shows it to Otto. "Ever see this woman before?"

Otto squints. "Yeah. She Mr. Loden's friend. I seen them comin' out of the boathouse sometimes. They always laughin' at somethin'."

"I don't think he did it," said Ryan to Colin in the cruiser. "I think he's just a thrill seeker."

"A lot of killers are."

Back at the station, a cousin comes forward to say the victim's name is Marla Tabor. All she knows is that Marla was a real estate agent on the North Shore, but no one in the family has kept in touch with her.

*Tuesday, 12:20 A.M.*

A little past midnight Rocky starts barking. I jump out of bed and see a flickering light in the woods coming closer and closer. Is it one of Colin's guys or is it the killer checking he hasn't left any evidence? My stomach tightens like a violin string.

Very slowly I go downstairs, Rocky racing ahead and then growling at the back door. The deck lights have automatically switched on and I see a man through the window, cupping his face with his right hand and holding a flashlight in his left. I scream. Then I realize he's wearing a police uniform with a badge hung from a chain around his neck. He motions for me to open the door. I do but only a crack.

"It's okay, Mrs. Shannon. I'm officer Webber."

Rocky is staring at the cop, growling softly.

"Your dog is quite the bodyguard."

"Just don't make any quick moves or he'll eat your face."

"No, ma'am. Have you heard or seen anything else since you reported the gunshots?"

"No."

"Did you actually see anyone at the time?"

"No, just a blue plaid shirt in the distance."

"I see. Well, keep your doors locked. Sorry for the interruption."

I shut the door. I've Colin's cell number and call him immediately.

"Kim?" He sounds half-asleep. I tell him what happened and there is a pause on the other end.

"Webber?"

"Yes, Officer Webber. Thick mustache and black-rimmed glasses."

"I'll be right there."

The first thing Colin says is, "There's no one on the force named Webber."

I jerk my head back confused.

"What did this guy say?"

"He asked if I'd seen anyone at the time of the shots."

"And you told him no, right?"

"Yes."

"Anything else you noticed about him?"

I think for a minute. "Yes, he has a purple birthmark on his left, no, right hand."

"Okay. It's something."

"Why the heck would someone pretend to be a cop? Unless . . . oh man! You think he was the killer?"

Colin doesn't tell her one of his guys was found knocked out by the stonewall.

"Kim. Webber or whatever his name is knows you didn't recognize anyone. I'm bringing Lieutenant Laurent over, you know Guy, and he's going to be your personal bodyguard. If you go out just take him with you. I'm not going to let anything happen to you."

"Did you talk to Otto?"

"Yes. I don't think it's him. But I haven't completely ruled him out."

"What about the Lodens?"

"Gordon and Lorna Loden are both pointing the finger at Otto."

"Lorna Loden? Sounds like an aging Hollywood star." I pose dramatically. "Lorna Loden, star of stage, screen, and RKO pictures!"

Colin starts laughing. "Good to see you've still got your sense of humor." Before he leaves, he gives me a quick hug. I wish it could have been more. Then I call Sheila and make a date for lunch. I need a female fix.

*Tuesday, 9:00 A.M.*

After a sleepless night, I realize I'm running low on groceries, so Guy and I jump in my Ford Mustang circa 1965.

"Nice wheels," Guy says.

"Thanks. My father left her to me in his will. He called her *Mustang Sally*." The car is navy blue with a white convertible top.

"Lucky girl, not that your father died, but you know."

"I know. I've had to replace a few things but Riley's Auto keeps her in mint condition."

It's a beautiful fall day and I put the top down while Rocky enjoys the wind from the back seat. At the front entrance to the Loden estate I slow down. On the circular drive, a petite blonde woman I assume is Lorna Loden is yelling at Gordon Loden as he gets out of his Porsche. I pass by and pull the car over.

"You see that?" I ask Guy.

"What?"

"The Lodens arguing on the front lawn."

He turns around. "No."

I back up slowly, stopping behind a line of arborvitaes so they can't see us. The Lodens' voices are loud and clear.

"You bastard," Lorna says. We hear a sharp slap. "You were out with one of your whores all night, weren't you? Even after what happened yesterday, you still leave me alone in this shitty mausoleum?"

"Keep your voice down, Lorna."

"I will not! You killed her, didn't you? Was she trying to blackmail you?"

"Who?"

"That woman in the woods!"

"Are you insane?"

A car beeps behind me and they turn toward the noise. I immediately take off and head to the police station.

"You go for a run?" Colin asks when I walk into his office, my ponytail hanging off the side of my head.

"I had the top down. But I just came from the Loden estate and heard a conversation between Gordon Loden and his movie-queen wife."

"Where was Guy?" he asks.

"He was right there with me 'cause, you know, he's my bodyguard and all," I say, scratching my eyebrow. "It just happened, Colin. They were outside and I could see her pointing her finger in his face. I thought I might hear something that would help your investigation."

"And did you?"

"Yes. Gordon Loden is a cheater, and his wife thinks he murdered his lover."

"What if Gordon *is* the killer and saw you snooping?"

I hiccup, my face turning pink, then a tap on the door interrupts my would-be witty response.

"Come in, Ryan. You know Kim Shannon?"

"Yes sir. Hi Kim."

"Where is Guy now?"

"Outside. Please don't blame him. I was the one driving. Anyway, I have to run. I'm meeting Sheila for lunch."

"Wait for Guy."

"Of course." And then I salute him, trying to look wicked serious.

*Tuesday, 12:30 P.M.*
I meet Sheila at Croque Cuisine, a French bistro off Main Street.

"I'm hanging on by a nerve ending, Sheila. I want so bad to see this through and not act like an insecure, fragile female."

"Do you want me to stay with you for a bit until this thing blows over?"

"No. It's important for me to know I can handle this. But thank you, dear friend."

"I wish I had a gun to give you."

"I wouldn't know how to use it. Let's hope Rocky is around if anything serious occurs."

Guy is smoking a cigarette outside, talking with the fire chief. I take a breath, letting it out slowly. The chef comes out of the kitchen to talk to a waiter near the bar. As he pulls off his right glove, I see a purple birthmark and inhale sharply.

"Kim, what's wrong? You look like you've seen a ghost." Sheila turns around to see who I'm looking at.

"The chef has a purple birthmark just like the man who impersonated a police officer last night," I whisper.

"You mean the owner, François Renaud?"

"I need to get out of here."

"Here, put my glasses on." Sheila slips off her scarf and says, "Tie this around your head. Leave now, go get Guy. And call me later!"

As I pass the bar, François looks up. Outside, I grab Guy's arm and we head straight to the station.

"Kim, breathe," says Colin.

"I saw him, I just saw him."

"Who?"

"The man with the purple birthmark, it's François Renaud, the chef and owner of Croque Cuisine!"

"Ryan!" he calls out. To me he says, "You stay with Guy."

*Tuesday, 3:00 P.M.*

At home, trying to calm my nerves, I work on drawings for The Stock Exchange holiday window. I sketch two mannequins—one in emerald silk—the other in red velvet, both mannequins holding white fur hand muffs. I am so engrossed in the designs I barely hear the door open. When I hear footsteps, I come out of my workroom and see Lorna Loden standing in the back hall. I look around for Guy, then remember he's gone out for cigarettes and will be right back.

"May I help you?" I say curtly, trying to disguise my fear.

She walks in and sits down without being asked. "I'm Lorna Loden, your neighbor."

"Yes. I know."

"Nice house. Lived here long?"

"A while."

"Are you a townie?"

"Yes." I'm not sure what to say. I just know she's bad news.

"Got any bourbon?"

"No."

"Wine?"

I get her a glass of wine.

After a few sips, she says, "I thought we should meet, since you were the person who called about the shooting. The police don't tell us much; they just ask a lot of questions. I suppose you must be a little nervous here all alone."

"Actually, I have my dog, Rocky, so I'm not alone. Plus, Colin McCabe is a friend and he checks in all the time." I don't mention a bodyguard but where the heck is Guy?

"Hmm. On my way over, I noticed there was an accident at Baron's Country Store. Two police cruisers looked in bad shape. A white Escalade smashed into both of them. Gee, I hope it wasn't your friend."

I hiccup.

She looks at her watch. "Where's your dog, Mrs. Shannon?"

I think for a minute. He isn't lying by the fireplace, and I didn't notice him when I was working in the other room. I feel the blood rush to my face and my mouth goes dry as cornstarch.

"He's fine," she says. "Came right to me when I dangled a T-bone steak in his face. He's in the back of my car right now gnawing on it. I don't hurt animals. Only people who double-cross me."

"What do you want from me?" I ask.

I notice Lorna is still wearing her gloves while she drinks her wine. She downs the rest and pulls a gun from her Chanel purse. My eyes widen and the hiccups come fast and hard.

"I have about five minutes to tell you, before François calls and I finish you off."

"Why?" I start shaking.

"Darling. François knows you identified him and he's a terrible liar. He's liable to spill his guts in the first ten minutes of questioning." She looks at her watch again. "The woman in the woods was my lover, but François doesn't know that. He thinks she was Gordon's lover and he helped me get rid of her before she became Gordon's next wife. Then he thought we were going to get rid of Gordon so *we* could be together." She laughs. "I knew he was an old fool from the beginning.

"As for Marla and me. She was the most beautiful girl I'd ever seen. At first, we were best friends but then things changed and we became more than that. It was the best thing that ever happened to me. No more lying, stupid, cheating men. But then Marla turned on me and became my husband's lover as well."

Realizing she was the one in the blue plaid shirt, I break out in a cold sweat.

"As for Gordon, he was afraid the cops would find out he got rid of his first wife. So he tried to steer the police toward Otto. Now, as you can see, I'm wearing gloves so there'll be no evidence I was ever here. And you, Kim Shannon, will simply vanish."

I hiccup so hard I have to catch my breath. Lorna leans over and yells loudly in my face, *"Enough with the fucking hiccups!"*

Shocked by her outburst, I jerk backward so hard my chair topples to the floor. I scramble up, fear replaced by a rage I didn't know

I possessed. I slam the chair legs into Lorna's body, knocking the gun out of her hand. Her head smashes against the stone fireplace and she passes out cold. I grab the gun, point it at her, and wait.

Lorna is still unconscious when Colin comes barreling through the door, Rocky on his heels. He quickly cuffs her and takes the gun from me. Then he holds me for a long time.

"I thought I'd never get here in time. François purposely ran into our cruisers at Baron's. He was going to take off with Lorna right after she got rid of you. His confession saved your life, Kim."

"Remind me to thank him at his trial. But Lorna wasn't going anywhere with him. She changed her taste for men a while ago and became lovers with Marla Tabor, who double-crossed her with Gordon Loden. And Marla? She was planning on being the next Mrs. Loden."

"What a mess," says Colin.

"Well, at least one good thing has come out of this."

"What's that?"

"I stopped hiccupping."

"And here I thought you were going to say something else."

I know what he means.

Slowly, I lean in and plant a soft, wet kiss on his mouth, which when we come up for air, he promptly returns. ❖

# The Snitch

## Sean Harding

The crowd thinned to scattered packs of commuters, and this made Sloane uncomfortable, vulnerable. Sitting at a small, lattice-metal table, he scanned South Station for his contact—a detective from the Boston Police Department's Drug Control Unit by the name of Haggerty. Their meeting was for 10:00 A.M. "Don't be late," Haggerty warned him. The clock above Sloane on the mammoth arrival/departure board read 10:07. Apparently the same rules didn't apply to Haggerty.

The large black coffee and breakfast sandwich from Dunkin' aggravated his already nervous stomach. This after he spent much of his last ten bucks on them. That cop better have money for him today.

"Hey, baby!"

The girl calling him "baby" looked no older than twenty, albeit a rough twenty. Almost half Sloane's age and fully too young to be calling him baby. Right away he figured her to be a working girl because someone taught them to routinely talk to guys that way. The guys who procured these girls' services liked a lot of weird shit.

"Hey yourself, and the name's Sloane, not baby."

A hint of shame flashed in eyes that matched her cornflower blue puffer jacket. "Jeez, I didn't mean nothing by it, dude."

She had a point. Why take his irritation out on her? His beef was with Haggerty, not this poor kid. "It's all good," Sloane said.

"So, is Sloane your first name?"

"No." He hesitated. "It's Conan. Conan Sloane."

"Conan? Like the TV guy?"

Everyone said that. He would give people his middle name if it wasn't Ignatius.

He nodded. "Everyone just calls me Sloane." Except Haggerty, who, when he wasn't calling him 23-27-JH-3121, called him by his informant name: Shaman. "Cause you go in the underworld and bring back info," he said. Haggerty thought he was a really deep dude.

"I'm Delila," the girl said. She shifted her weight back and forth on each foot, like she needed the ladies' room. "You got a smoke, Sloane?"

He put his palms up. "Sorry, don't smoke."

"No? Smart. It's sooo expensive now. I'm going to quit soon, but it's sooo friggin' addictive. You know?"

"Yeah, I've heard that."

"You got a couple of bucks I can borrow to get a coffee?"

He slid the coffee toward her, careful not to tip the wobbly table. "Here, take that. I've had enough," he said. "It's almost full. Enjoy."

She wrapped her hands around it. "Ooh, nice. Still hot. Okay to sit?"

Sloane wasn't thrilled with the idea. Haggerty might not approach him sitting with someone, but there was no sign of the dick, and he'd already disrespected Delila once. Plus, she seemed like a good kid who just wanted some normal company. He slid the other chair at the table toward her with his foot. "Sure, but I have to leave in a couple minutes. I got to meet a guy about a job."

After sitting, Delila took a big sip of the coffee. Her face glowed with pleasure.

"A job?" she said. "That's cool. What kind of job?"

"Information technology."

She tilted her head to the side at that, but let it go. Before long, they settled into a conversation, interspersed between the frequent, booming train announcements. Neither revealed too much, and neither pressed to know much more. One thing that did emerge from their chat was that Sloane knew her uncle Craig from the Golden Gloves circuit back in the day and more recently from behind the wall, though Sloane kept the last part to himself. Uncle Craig was doing time on a voluntary manslaughter charge. Not a bad guy, a little nuts and a pretty vicious fighter. The more Sloane talked to the girl, the more his heart grew heavy. Something about her seemed so . . . salvageable.

Sloane saw Delila's eyes go big and cheeks flush pink before he heard the voice behind him. A deep baritone said, "Yo! Delila! What the fuck you doing?"

Sloane turned to see a wide-shouldered man in a black leather jacket approaching. One of those leathers with studs and chains and zippers everywhere. Tats crawled up his neck like ink ivy, dirty blonde hair tied in a ponytail, a soul patch. The guy went right to Delila and stood over her with balled fists. Sloane recognized the guy from his state bid, but it took a while for the name to come to him. Otto. Something Otto. A sick sonova bitch. That he remembered.

"Jesus, Josh, I'm just having a coffee and talking to Sloane here."

Josh. That was it.

Josh Otto gave Sloane the sadistic eye, then turned his attention back to Delila. "You're wasting time and time is money, honey. Now say bye-bye to your friend, babe, and let's go. I got another friend for you to meet."

Sloane was raised by a mother mistreated by a lot of guys and watching Otto with Delila made Sloane want to dismember him. Give him a quick right cross to the neck and drop him in front of an incoming Amtrak Acela. But he also knew the way justice would pan out. In the end, Sloane would pay the price in the can, and unless he killed the jackass, Delila would pay the price in a casket.

"It was nice meeting you, Delila," Sloane said and stood. Delila smiled back at him.

Sloane's stomach began churning again as he watched Delila walk off.

"You like that?" Otto said, following Sloane's gaze. "You can have her next if you want."

"No. I got things to do."

"Yeah, I bet. You look familiar. You ever do time?"

"That's kind of personal, isn't it?"

Otto laughed without sound. "That right there is a con answer. Guess you did." Otto sneered. "Just so you know, she don't give out freebies." He did the quiet laugh thing again. "Except for me that is."

That night, Sloane looked out the window onto West Broadway as Detective Haggerty's reflection strolled up to the Burger King counter behind him. After being handed a bag of food, Haggerty left. Sloane waited five minutes, finished his coffee, stuffed the cup in the barrel and went outside.

He slid into Haggerty's old Ford Taurus in the parking lot. Haggerty's width took up a lot of car space. With a red, Viking beard, Haggerty looked more like a biker than a cop, which was kind of the idea.

Sloane still wanted his pay. After all his waiting that morning, the detective had canceled their meeting and rescheduled to 6:00 P.M. That meant Sloane had to kill the entire day being a sparring partner at Walsh's Gym to pick up a few bucks. He was friggin' exhausted.

Haggerty handed him a Whopper like he was doing some great deed. There was no money with it. "You know how it works," Haggerty said, a needle of onion hanging from his beard, "anything over two-fifty needs to be okayed by the Lieu."

"Yeah, I know, bro, but *you know* that the only reason it's over two-fifty is because you're in arrears. I mean, come on, I'm not doing this shit as a service to my community."

"Never thought you were."

"I should have a goddamn badge by now, a pension, the amount of shit I do for the BPD. All I'm asking is to be paid what we agreed."

"Hey, listen Shaman, it's not like you've brought me the name you've promised either, okay. What's going on with that?"

"I'm close. I just gotta confirm it. And do you gotta call me Shaman? Jeezus."

"I'm not calling you Jesus. So, you confirm it, and while you're doing that, I'll be getting your money."

What a dick.

"So, why did you drag me down here then?" Sloane asked.

"Maybe, I like to look at you."

"Ahh, I get it. You want a peek at my eyes and arms."

"Hey, don't be offended. I just like to make sure my asset is happy and healthy."

"Yeah, well your asset would be happier if you paid him and healthier if you didn't buy him Whoppers."

Haggerty agreed to give Sloane a lift but was getting on 93 and would only take Sloane as far as South Station. Sloane walked off poor and disrespected. Haggerty didn't appreciate what he had. Despite being a damn good confidential informant for over a year, Sloane would always be a low-life ex-con to guys like Haggerty.

Sloane credited his adept snitching skills to the mindfulness classes he took in the can from Tracy DuBois. She taught him how to be equanimous, which is basically a fancy Buddhist way of saying cool, calm, and collected. He also became more observant, more present. Now, he had, like, CIA level skills. Of course, Sloane was also supposed to be paid for putting his neck out there. He wasn't some vigilante hero seeking truth, justice, and the American way. Hell no.

Sloane stomped along a paved path in the Common toward his room in Beacon Hill. The late March night was friggin' freezing, and that cheap-ass, sonofabitch Haggerty not having his pay forced him to walk all the way from South Station. He had intended to put some of that money on his T-Pass. What little he got earlier from Walsh's gym needed to go to his rent.

In the dull Common light, he saw a form spanning one of the benches that lined the path. Not at all shocking. After dark, the Common became a place for some addicts to buy and use their fixes. In the colder times of year, they sometimes nodded out in the bitter chill and died from hypothermia. Sloane knew a couple of guys that happened to back when he was using. Maybe he knew the poor bastard on the bench. He went over to rouse whoever it was if needed.

Getting closer, Sloane realized a jacket was over the person's head, shroud-like, and his heart picked up its beat. He recognized the jacket and froze in his tracks. A cornflower blue puffer jacket. Sloane wore gloves on the cold night. He could pull the jacket down off the face without leaving traces of himself.

*Fuck!*

Empty, blue eyes—like the jacket—stared up toward the waxing crescent moon.

Sloane backed away, gagged, and meandered up the path toward Beacon, thinking how to handle the situation. He was no medical examiner, but the deep purple bruises around her neck told him Delila had been strangled. They matched the contusions all over her mauled face.

One thing was certain. In Sloane's mind, Josh Otto killed Delila. Maybe not directly. Maybe it was a psycho-john who did the act, but in the end it all came back to Otto.

Payback's a ruthless bitch.

But first things first. The prosocial thing would be to call the cops and report Delila's murder. Prosocial. That's what they called it in his Criminal Thinking classes behind the wall. Except calling on police was never a desirable option for one with an antisocial record. Maybe it was time his contact did something useful. Sloane called Haggerty on the snitch cell, a burner provided by the Boston Police Department.

"Miss me already?" Haggerty asked.

Sloane told him what he found.

"Did you call it in?"

"That's what I'm doing now."

"You're calling me? I'm not 9-1-1. Why the fuck call me?"

"Because you know as well as I do that they'll run my record, and I don't want to deal with the bullshit."

Sloane explained that he'd met Delila that morning. "Just tell them you got an anonymous tip."

"Jesus." Haggerty sighed over the phone like a perv. "Tell me straight up, did you kill her?"

"Hell no. I was with you, bro."

Sloane was in a quasi romance with a woman named Valentina Perez who lived on the floor below him. Val quit the stripper life along with the dope a number of years before and now worked in a shelter for runaways. Sloane spent the night with her, and the next morning she lent him her T-Pass and a twenty. Sloane was out the door early after that, with a balaclava and Beretta Bobcat joining a windbreaker in a decaying, old backpack.

As an ex-felon in Massachusetts, Sloane wasn't supposed to have a firearm, and to be honest, guns spooked him, but when you're ratting out drug dealers they're a good idea as a just-in-case. That day he wasn't carrying for protection. He needed the gun and balaclava to rob Lee Peters.

Peters was a drug distributor who targeted several Boston area methadone clinics and had found his way into a couple of Sloane's informant reports in the past. He dealt benzos, opioids, and heroin, and being a traveling salesman, as well as a moron, could usually be counted on to have a significant supply on his person.

Sloane settled himself at a window seat in a Dunkin' on Mass Ave. and waited. The store was a hangout for the methadone clients of the hospital down the street, meaning Peters would be by to transact with the morning dosers.

Peters—skinny, greasy, chihuahua-faced—showed up and began rubbing elbows with his customers. Then he went out with a couple guys to the corner of the parking lot alongside the building. Sloane waited for a chance and he got it after the two left, and Peters stayed to finish his cigarette.

He took deep, mindful breaths. *Here goes.*

Sloane whisked out the door and hustled toward Peters, pulling on his balaclava and sliding the pistol from his hoodie pocket. He wore a black knit hat low over his forehead and hoped Peters wouldn't see the mask until it was too late.

Peters tossed his butt onto the ground and turned to find Sloane standing in front of him holding the Beretta with two hands at the navel and pointing it toward Peters's pelvis.

"Whatever heroin you got for product, hand it over," Sloane said. "Now."

Peters's mouth fell open and stayed there. You'd think he was never robbed before. Then again it was broad daylight.

"Listen," Sloane said, "I have an easy escape planned out and have no problem capping you right here. We both know the quality of your junk isn't worth dying over, so just give it up, huh? You can keep anything that's not powder."

Peters bent and rolled up a pant leg. The product was wrapped in an Ace bandage on his lower leg.

"Get it slow and easy. You know how to do it. You pull anything, you're fucked."

Red faced and teary, Peters turned over a Ziploc bag filled with tiny glassine packets of the familiar, brown, clumpy powder. A spider, his brand logo, was stamped on the little packets.

"How much is here?"

"21 gs."

"That's it? You sure?"

"I swear to you, man."

It would do. Sloane put the bag in his pants pocket. "You take care."

Sloane slipped the gun into his hoodie pocket at the same time he raced toward a four-foot wood fence at the edge of the lot. He'd hopped many a fence in his day and this one didn't even need him to slow down before putting his hands on top and propelling himself over it.

He landed behind the brownstones on West Springfield Street and jogged through the narrow alley behind the buildings. As he did, he whisked off his hat and mask, jammed them in his pants pockets, and switched his hoodie for the windbreaker. He wrapped the gun in the hoodie and concealed them inside the windbreaker, pinning them to his ribs with an arm. The backpack was dumped in the alley. When he emerged on Shawmut Ave, he tried to look like a guy on a Saturday morning stroll.

Time to find Josh Otto.

Sloane kept envisioning Delila dead on the bench, laid out for all to see. His jaw ached from clamping with each flash of her image.

He walked down Harrison Ave. to Chinatown to find Old Timer. Nobody remembered the guy's real name anymore. Old Timer could usually be found stemming in the Chinatown to Downtown Crossing area. Sloane could remember seeing the guy on the wall in Perkins Square in Southie back when Sloane was in high school.

Despite a brain saturated with U.V. Blue vodka, Old Timer saw and remembered everything on the streets and, unbeknownst to him, helped Sloane twice in the past.

Old Timer wore a grimy, gray raincoat that was once beige. Face ruddy from wind and drink, he sat atop one of the concrete planters in the Liberty Tree Plaza, asking passersby for change. There weren't many of them at that time on a Saturday.

"How's things, Old Timer?" Sloane asked.

"How ya, lad?" Old Timer smacked his lips. "What ya got for me?'

"Depends. What you got for me?"

"For you?" Old Timer looked Sloane up and down. "Whatta you need?"

"Your wisdom."

"Wisdom ain't cheap."

"I ain't rich."

Sloane had broken the twenty while at Dunkin' and held out five one-dollar bills. "This is all I got. You know Josh Otto?"

Old Timer looked at the cash, then up to the sky. "Otto. Otto. Oh shit, yeah, I know who you're talking about. That kid is bad news, you know?"

"I know. Where does he usually hang?"

"I see him here and there." Old Timer's face scrunched in thought. It looked painful. "He's in the theater district a lot. I suppose it's where he does a lot of his business. He's a pimp, you know?"

"I know. You know where he lives?"

"Nuh. Check the sewers."

Sloane decided he would wait for nightfall to seek out Josh Otto. Being a Saturday, there would be little daytime activity in the theater district, which meant there would be minimal business opportunities for Otto in the sex industry. Sloane went home and emptied the heroin from the branded packets into a Ziploc sandwich bag, then fortified the sealed bag with duct tape. He ate a couple PB&J's, watched a Bruins matinee game, and took a nap. At eight, he called Haggerty.

"I think I got your guy, but you'll probably have to take him tonight."

"Tonight? You got to be shitting me, Shaman. It don't work like that."

"It will have to work like that if you want this guy, Detective. Have a magistrate on standby for a warrant, or whatever it is you do. He has the product in his possession for a short window of time before it goes to the plebes."

"What's this guy's name?"

"Can't say right now. I'll be calling you soon. Just be ready." Sloane ended the call.

Sloane debated whether to bring the gun that night. He finally decided that if things went well there would be cops involved— something he couldn't remember thinking before—so he'd keep the gun at home.

He stepped out into the brisk night air. A sliver of bright moon filled the clear sky. Too jacked for the T, Sloane walked through downtown to the theater district.

With its assortment of clubs and pubs, the area pulsated with revelers, especially with all the students still in town. Sex workers and drug dealers moved up and down Tremont, Boylston, and Washington Streets, though much more discreetly than they did back in the day. The type of crowd out that night would make the depraved pimp bastard giddy with greed.

Sloane roamed the theater district for two hours, popping in and out of establishments, the chic and the seedy. He wore a thick sweater under his pea coat and a wool flat cap to stay warm as the temps dropped. His gloves were black cotton, holdovers from his robbery years. It wasn't until he decided to walk beyond Washington Street that he finally found Josh Otto.

He was at a table in the back room of JJ Foleys with a chubby dude wearing a black and red tracksuit and black straight-billed ball cap. Sloane weaved his way through the horde to the bar and bought a Guinness. He found a chair at a small table facing the bar that a group of drinkers seemed to be using as a Formica beer coaster. The chair was right next to the entrance to the back room, providing a view of Otto in the slits between the bodies of people standing up around his table. He parked himself in the chair, sipped and watched.

Sloane had no idea how long he waited, but his pint was two-thirds empty when Otto came out of the back room without a jacket and headed toward the bathrooms by the door. A burst of adrenaline rushed through Sloane as he saw his chance.

*Come on. You got this.*

He slipped into the back room and managed to squeeze himself into a spot standing near Otto's chair, the black leather jacket with all the bling draped over the back. Still wearing the coat and sweater in the hot, cramped room, he thought he'd combust.

"You mind if I put my beer down here a minute?" he asked the buddy.

The guy looked up from his phone just long enough to shrug.

Sloane placed his beer down closest to Otto's chair, and stood there with his hand inches from the jacket. Now, the tough part. He took a few mindful breaths the way Tracy Dubois had taught him. He brought his knife from his pocket, unfolded it discreetly by his leg and made a slit in the satin lining of the jacket. Next, keeping the buddy in the corner of his eye, Sloane removed the stolen heroin from his pocket.

"Can I get you something?"

Sloane stiffened like a tree. He made a slow gradual turn and looked over his shoulder, then exhaled through pursed lips. A guy stood looking at him with a tray of empty glasses.

"No, I'm all set," Sloane said, when he really wanted to ask for a defibrillator.

After another deep breath, Sloane returned to his task and tucked the bag of heroin within the slit he just made.

"What the fuck!" the buddy said.

Sloane suppressed a groan and peeked over at him.

"God damn it, Syracuse," the buddy said to his phone. "You suck."

March Madness.

Just then, Otto entered the back room and made his way through the mass of people. Sloane picked up his glass from the table.

"Syracuse still down?" Sloane asked the buddy.

Still not taking his eyes off the phone, the buddy snorted and shook his head. "They're costing me some serious gouda, dawg."

Sloane shook his head. "They suck." He then merged into the crowd before Otto could see him. Another Guinness would be fantastic for his nerves right then, but before he did anything else, he went outside and called Haggerty.

The detective answered in a huff. "Jeezus, you're like a robo-caller."

"I got that name for you."

"Sonova . . . all right, fill me in. I'll try to get a warrant."

Otto and his buddy got up from their table an hour later. Sloane tensed as he watched the thug put on his leather jacket. *Keep moving, asshole.*

Otto started toward the door.

*Yes.* Sloane followed.

Otto and the buddy split up outside the bar with Otto walking toward Summer Street. Sloane followed on the other side of the street. Sloane made several frantic, hissing calls to Haggerty while following Otto up Summer Street to Downtown Crossing. Haggerty didn't answer. Sloane's final message was, "You slow bastard, Haggerty! He's getting on the T at Downtown Crossing. You're gonna lose him." Sloane no sooner ended the call when two BPD undercovers and two transit police pinned Josh Otto against the glass storefront of Macy's.

As Sloane descended the stairs to the subway, he could hear Otto's loud voice above. "It ain't fucking mine, goddamn it! It's a plant! What the fuck, I want a lawyer!"

Josh Otto was arraigned that Monday on a charge of Class A drug trafficking. Not that Sloane was there to see it. He avoided courtrooms whenever possible. With his record, Otto didn't stand a chance come trial time. He'd probably plead out. He was looking at up to twenty years, and the judge denied Otto bail due to his being a major flight risk.

That night, Sloane composed a letter:

*Craig, how you doing, old friend? I know you haven't heard from me for a while, but I wanted to send you my condolences for the death of your niece Delila. I had the chance to meet her not long before she died. She was a terrific kid. I also met her employer that day. A guy by the name of Josh Otto. Would you believe he'll probably be joining you in Souza in the near future? How ironic is that? I'm sure, somewhere, Delila's looking down and hoping you'll welcome Josh Otto and take good care of him while he's there, so keep an eye out.*

*Keep fighting, bro.*

*Sloane* ❖

# A Bitter Draft

## Robin Hazard Ray

L ook," said the lady in black to her companion, pointing to the Torrey memorial at Mount Auburn Cemetery. It had been carved in Italian marble to celebrate the life of an abolitionist martyr and placed at a prominent intersection of the Boston burial ground. "They've put up a monument to a property stealer."

Roxanne Ross, who stood nearby, flinched and took a quick look at the couple.

The lady's short comment on the Torrey monument told Roxanne more than she wanted to know about this cemetery visitor. The accent was unmistakable: South Carolina, Columbia area. Gentry, therefore, former slave-owners. Also, therefore, probably acquainted with the family that had, before the War of National Unification, claimed title over Roxanne herself.

Roxanne stepped off the cemetery carriage road and onto a side path, hoping to avoid a meeting. Her only objective that day had been to gather some burdock, a low weed whose medicinal qualities she valued and which thrived in the heat of summer. An encounter with her past was not on the agenda.

But it was too late. Behind her she heard a sharp cry, and then "Girl! Stop! Willy, go after her." Willy was a spry youth, and he bounded in front of Roxanne. He had the good grace to take off his hat.

"Miss, my aunt would speak with you," he said. Unlike his companion, he spoke like a Yankee. In registering this contrast, Roxanne missed her chance to get away. She took a deep breath and stood still.

The lady came up behind Willy and lifted her veil to peer rudely in Roxanne's face. She had always been rude, Roxanne now remembered. Theresa Sayles, Mrs. William Sayles. Tessy to her friends, if she had any. Her black costume suggested widowhood.

"You are the Claridge's girl," said Mrs. Sayles. "The one that ran away. I never forget a face."

Roxanne said nothing.

She remembered the stories about Theresa Sayles. How she would stand by the kitchen door as the house servants cleared the dinner leftovers from the table, spitting into each dish so that no one else would get a morsel of it. How she enjoyed "matchmaking" among the slaves on her property, pulling a wife out of her husband's arms to force her into another's. How an infraction such as mis-lacing a boot could get you twenty lashes from the mistress's own eager hand.

"It's Mary I'm looking for," said Mrs. Sayles. "Mary Sayles. I heard that she was here somewhere. Boston or New Bedford. I need to speak with her." She paused. "I'll give you ten dollars if you can find her for me. And I'll give her twenty."

Roxanne's eyes narrowed. "If I knew where Mary was," she said at last, "and she did not wish to speak with you, you could offer me a hundred dollars and I would do nothing."

"You know, then," said Theresa Sayles eagerly. "Wait." She dug into a little reticule attached to her belt and came up with a calling card. "Willy, give me a pencil!" She scribbled on the card and thrust it into Roxanne's hand. "This is my address. I shall be there till the end of the month. Please," she added. "She's the only one who can answer my question."

Roxanne looked at the card. It gave the address of a hotel in Boston. She folded it in half, lodged it in her pocket, and went on her way without a word.

Mary had excised the slave name Sayles from her own and now went as Mary Carter. Under that appellation, she had thrived in Boston, working first in the kitchen of a well-to-do household on Beacon Hill and then going into business for herself as a baker. She supplied pies, rolls, and pastries to two hotels and a men's club, employed half a dozen staff, and had saved enough money to buy a small house in Cambridgeport. She had no family that Roxanne knew of but gave of her time and purse to various freedmen's charities, helping numbers of dislocated and disoriented former slaves gain their footing in the North. It was in this context that Roxanne had met her. Both women also did something in the way of plant doctoring, and they had exchanged plants and information from time to time.

In Boston, only Roxanne knew the sort of tortures Mary had suffered at the hands of the Sayles family, and then only secondhand. In Columbia, however, Mary had been something of a legend. It was said that when she ran away, Mr. William had set the bloodhounds on her; that they had tracked her to a pocket of forest and begun to savage her. But she had equipped herself with two hatchets, with which she managed to slaughter all five dogs. Bleeding from bites to both legs, Mary had nonetheless made it to Cincinnati in a mere week, still clutching a hatchet in each hand. That was the story at any rate; the whites in Columbia whispered it in terror, the Blacks with awe.

Mary was short and meager for a baker woman, and many of her teeth were missing, but she was muscled like a sailor even now in her forties. She treated her employees well and her acquaintances courteously, but she confided in no one, as far as Roxanne knew.

The day after her encounter with Theresa Sayles, Roxanne rose early and walked to Mary's bakery, where she found delivery boys already rushing out the door with full baskets. Mary herself sat just inside the door at a rough table, dressed in a plain gown and apron, with dabs of flour accenting the deep brown of her bare arms. She was writing out her accounts and smoking a small clay pipe. If she was surprised to see Roxanne Ross on a Monday morning, she did not show it. She pointed the stem of her pipe to a chair and waited.

"I was recognized yesterday," said Roxanne after a pause. She pulled out Theresa Sayles's card and laid it on the table. Mary looked at the card without touching it. "She wanted to know if I knew where you were. She wishes to speak with you, for a few minutes she says. She offered me ten dollars. Which I did not take. She offers you twenty."

Mary poked at the card with the mouthpiece of her pipe. Her hand shook slightly. "She did, did she? I heard someone was asking around for me. She say what she want? Wants to cry about the good old times, maybe?"

"She had on widow's weeds," said Roxanne. "I guess Mr. William didn't get through the war."

"Mm," said Mary absently. This news did not appear to cause her much sorrow. She looked again at the card. "This Whittier Hotel, I don't know it. Do you?"

Roxanne nodded. "It's over by the State House. Are you thinking to go?"

Mary pondered for a moment, then pulled out a piece of writing paper and dipped her pen. She paused and for the first time looked Roxanne full in the face. Her dark eyes were steady and dry.

"I could use a witness. Would you oblige?"

Roxanne nodded. "We could go tonight," she suggested.

But Mary shook her head. "No harm in letting her stew for a few days. I think Saturday. Suit you?"

It did. "Are you sure you want to?" Roxanne asked. "After everything you went through."

Mary didn't answer. She finished the note to Theresa Sayles, shook sand over it, then folded it and waved over a small boy to take it to Boston.

When he was gone, she said, "She can't hurt me anymore. I'll see you Saturday."

Saturday was stifling, and the electricity in the air suggested a thunderstorm. Roxanne met Mary on Main Street where the horse car made a northward turn toward Boston. Mary had put some care into her appearance, donning a fine calico gown with good lace at the sleeves and neck. Her hair was tied in a pink silk scarf. Together they found seats on the car and soon crossed the bridge into the city.

The Whittier Hotel was an unimpressive establishment, squeezed into a dark lane behind the State House. Inside the front door, the carpets were worn and smelled of damp, and it took numerous rings of the bell to rouse the desk clerk from his nap. Grumpily, he directed them to the room occupied by Mrs. William Sayles, three floors up a dirty stairway. Fortune, it seemed, was not smiling on Miss Theresa.

Roxanne's knock was answered by Willy, who smiled as he swung the door wide. He was in his shirt-sleeves but quickly put on his coat despite the suffocating heat. Someone, thought Roxanne, has seen to his upbringing, perhaps Mr. William's Yankee brother.

Miss Theresa stood as they came in and advanced aggressively.

"Well, there you are," she said, giving Mary an appraising look. "You hid yourself pretty well up here. Willy, give the girl her ten dollars."

Willy dug into his pocket for a coin but Roxanne stopped him. "I won't be needing your money," she said, "and Mrs. Carter comes of her own free will."

Theresa's eyes flashed. "Carter, is it? I . . ."

But Mary interrupted her. "Mrs. Ross, I'd take that money if I were you. If I know this family, and I do, that will be the only thing we get out of this conversation. May as well buy your husband a treat."

For a moment, no one moved. Mary and Theresa stared at each other. Willy fingered the gold coin indecisively. Roxanne felt sweat beading on her forehead.

Finally, Willy broke the deadlock. He extended his hand toward Roxanne and she raised hers to meet it. The golden face of Lady Liberty gleamed in her palm.

"Why don't you get us some lemonade," said Theresa at last. She had intended this order for Roxanne but when it did not produce obedience she looked at Willy with a roll of her eyes. "Be a dear."

As Willy went in search of lemonade, Mary and Roxanne sat down in a pair of hardback chairs. Theresa Sayles remained standing.

"In 1855," she said, "I suffered a miscarriage. In 1857, two more. In 1858, the final one, a boy. I almost died of the hemorrhage. After that I was told to stop trying."

Mary had rested an elbow on the arm of her chair and was rubbing her chin thoughtfully. None of this seemed to be news to her.

"You were my cook all those years. Nothing happened in the kitchen but you were in charge of it. I need to know. Please." Her voice broke at this last word, but Roxanne couldn't tell whether it was from emotion or the abasement of having to say please.

"I take it," said Mary, "that you think I was somehow responsible for your lost little ones."

"Yes. That's what I think." Theresa's lips trembled as she spoke. "You fed me . . . what was it?"

Mary regarded her evenly, then turned to address Roxanne. "Don't know about you, Mrs. Ross," she said amiably, "but I found many uses for cotton root. Good for the new mothers having trouble with the milk. Good for clearing the afterbirth. Yes, we used it quite a bit among ourselves."

At this juncture Willy returned, followed by a girl carrying a tray. She poured four glasses of iced lemonade from a pitcher, bobbed a curtsy, and got a coin from Willy for her trouble.

Mary drank deeply and set her glass back on the tray.

"I don't know if you remember, Miss Theresa," she said, pulling her pipe out of her pocket and lighting it with a match. She dropped the used match on the floorboards. "We in the kitchen were never permitted to have lemonade. You used to count the number of lemons and the weight of the sugar, and if by your reckoning we did not come up with enough lemonade from that, we got a beating. It's good, isn't it? Lemonade on a hot day."

Willy stole a glance at his aunt. Roxanne guessed that very little of the "Southern way of life" had been explained to him at Harvard or wherever he had gone to college.

"Now the years you mentioned are very memorable for me," Mary continued, blowing a blue cloud of smoke into the hot room. "That first one, 1856. There was a reversal of some kind, wasn't there? On the plantation, I mean."

"Well, yes," said Theresa. "There was the lawsuit. It went against us. Five thousand dollars had to be found."

" 'It had to be found.' Yes, that's right." Mary nodded. "I don't imagine you remember Lizzie, Mason, and Bo. Lizzie was eleven that year, Mason and Bo were eight and seven. I come home from making the dinner one night and found all three gone. My children, Miss Theresa. My three remaining children, after Mr. William sold off my Cathy and John two years before.

"And what do I hear the very next week. Oh, you are over the moon with joy because that Yankee husband of yours finally got you a child. Joy! Joy! Asked me to make a special chestnut cake to celebrate. And fed the crumbs to the dogs lest any in the kitchen might get a taste of it."

Mary paused. She took a blunt knife out of her pocket and rooted around in her pipe bowl. "You ever made a chestnut cake, Miss

Theresa? My guess is not. First you got to roast the chestnuts on the stove, no matter what kind of hot the day is. Then you got to peel each and every one of them, maybe twenty, down to the white flesh. If there's any flecks of the peel left in that cake, you get a beating, remember? Then you got to get your mortar out and pound the chestnuts to a slurry. That's hot work, Miss Theresa. And me just lost all the last of my children."

Theresa Sayles, who had been standing the whole while, now sat.

"It's a common part of knowledge among the plant doctors," Mary continued, "that there be certain helpers to those who may be carrying children they don't want, the cotton bark being one of them, provided you can stomach a lot of it. I can recall in my experience several of such in your household. Jeannie, for example, you remember her? She worked in the fields mostly. Got taken by that overseer of yours. Phipps the name was. He liked the yellow girls very much. Well, Jeannie wanted no part of him or his, so I helped her out. I did."

Silence fell again. Roxanne and Willy looked sidelong at each other but neither spoke.

"It took some thought as to how I might get you the dose you needed. It's fair bitter stuff. But I knew the chestnut cake would come to be served with a little glass of something, one of those French bottles you and Mr. William were so very fond of. So I fortified that bottle with a gill of cotton bark extract. And you slurped it down like a thirsty mule.

"Next day, what do we hear but you've thrown the child again. If we had had church bells to ring, Miss Theresa, we all in the quarter would have done so."

Theresa Sayles seemed to have shrunk by half. She slumped in her seat and stared at the floor.

Mary stood, small and straight as a Roman bronze, and held out her hand to Mr. William. "I'll have my twenty dollars, sir. And I wish you good day." With the gold piece tucked in her pocket, she nodded to Roxanne and they left.

After the suffocating hotel room, the hot air of the street was almost bracing. The two women walked in silence down Cambridge Street, approaching the Charles River as the sun reached its zenith. They found a shady bench near the water, watching a handful of sailboats slapping the brown waves.

Mary reached into her pocket and drew out a crust of bread. Several ducks weaved over, chortling and bobbing, as she tossed crumbs in their direction.

At last Roxanne said, "I didn't know there was any drink bitter enough that you could cover the gill of cotton bark."

Mary threw the last chunk of bread into the Charles and watched with satisfaction as the ducks squabbled over it.

"There ain't. But she doesn't know that." ❖

# You Love Me to Madness

## Lauren Sheridan

I spoke with my mother today," Bill said, pushing his buttered asparagus around on his plate.

In the five years I had known him, conversations starting with these six words never ended well. I smiled, braced myself, and asked the inevitable follow-up question.

"How was she?"

He dropped his fork onto the plate and shoved it away from him.

"Unbelievable. I mean, how does she pick *them*?"

He always imbued that final word with so much vitriol that the first time, I was shocked at the complete change in his voice and demeanor. His sweet, open face snapped shut like a bear trap. His knuckles turned white in his fisted hands. His voice was hard and explosive.

That first time, I'd actually been afraid of him. The litany of character flaws of his mother's latest boyfriend seemed tinged with a strange jealousy. I thought, well, it isn't that unusual for men to be possessive of their mothers, but his anger was so at odds with the gentle, caring man that I was falling in love with.

Now, we wore the conversation like a well-worn shoe. We knew its curves, its scuffs, and its pain points. I picked up my plate, walked around the table, and touched his shoulder gently with my free hand. He flinched. Pretending not to notice, I collected his plate and started toward the sink.

"He's just like my father," Bill said in a low voice.

I stopped. My stomach turned over.

"She was wearing a lot of makeup, but it wasn't enough. She's lost the knack."

He didn't need to say anything else. I deposited the plates on the counter next to the sink and returned to him. Squatting down, I turned his face toward mine and locked my eyes on his.

"We'll deal with this the way we always do. Together."

Now, looking back, I wonder if Bill's mom had not entered into yet another abusive relationship, would I have agreed to it? After all, I am not a fan of social media and smart appliances. I get the convenience argument, but I don't like the idea that something is always watching me and controlling things around me. It chills me to the bone when my phone suggests my local coffee shop as a destination if I leave the house at a certain time of day.

Tempting though it is to have cameras in and outside your house and to be able to adjust the thermostat remotely or see who is outside before opening the door, I have a mind that twists and turns in weird ways. It immediately envisions hackers taking control of the cameras. Instead of you watching people outside, people outside are watching you.

But when Bill bounced through the door the next evening, his face lit up like he'd won the lottery, I just couldn't say no.

"It was amazing!" he said. "The top brass called us in for an unscheduled meeting. We all thought, that's it. They're going to pull the plug on Mervin, but that wasn't it at all." He stopped for breath.

"Far from it, they want to test Mervin in the field. Test him in a real home and put him through his paces. They thought the best option would be to have one of the engineers have Mervin integrated into their home. And the best part." He paused. "Drum roll, please."

Picking up my cue, I did a mock drum roll with my hands on the kitchen table.

"The company is going to remodel the home. Give it all kinds of updates, a security system, a whole new automatic kitchen, mechanized blinds, an entertainment system, and a sauna. And they picked us!"

He did his version of a happy dance before pulling me to my feet and swinging me around the room.

I tried to match his enthusiasm as best I could. He put me down and said more seriously, "I know it's a big ask, but this could make us. If Mervin works, really works, the sky's the limit. We could be set for life."

"Oh, I know. I'm happy, really, I am. It might take a little getting used to. You know me. I just like my privacy," I said.

He grinned at me impishly.

"I know what else you like. Your cocktails! Well, I managed to get them to throw in a . . . wait for it."

He smiled as if he were a game show host tantalizing a contestant with their mystery prize. Then, raising his voice, in the cadence of *a brand-new car*, he said, "a Bartender-in-a-Box!"

My face broke into my first real smile since I heard the news. I'd been eyeing the superexpensive system for a while now. It works like a pod coffee system, but creating cocktails instead. You just had to load the piña colada pod into the machine and select the rum dispenser, and *voilà*, your own tropical paradise drink mixed in minutes.

"That's right, Ms. Woods. Not only will you have a bartending system capable of making a variety of cocktails, you'll have your own AI bot to create custom drinks just for you. At the end of a long day of writing, you'll simply ask Mervin to mix a rum drink, and your wish is his command."

"Yes," I countered, "but will it be any good?"

He laughed. "No guarantees there, I'm afraid. Look, AI learns just like humans. It'll search the net for recipes. It'll take stock of what we've got by way of booze and other ingredients that it scans and inventories in the fridge and the pantry, and it'll make something. It might be good. It might be toxic."

I puckered my lips, grasped my throat, and slumped forward onto the table.

"Oh, ha, ha, ha."

"It's a good thing you aren't in sales. It might be the best or last drink you'll ever have. Quite a sales pitch."

"Well, how about this. You know what else Mervin can control? A robotic vacuum cleaner."

"Super, but we don't have one."

"We will, if you agree."

He beamed. I reached up, hooked my arms around his neck, and whispered in his ear.

"You had me at Bartender-in-a-Box."

For the next month or so, the house was a beehive of activity with contractors coming in and out. The kitchen, kitted out with all the latest gadgetry, was straight out of a sci-fi show. All the appliances had gleaming stainless-steel exteriors. Only the espresso maker and the Bartender-in-a-Box did not sport a silver exterior. The espresso maker was an inconspicuous black, the cocktail maker a cherry red. It was the one incongruous note, like a bright red cardinal in a silver forest, but I loved her all the more for that.

The first time I saw it, I knew it was a *she*. She had a carousel that housed different base alcohols, like rum, vodka, tequila, and whiskey. She also arrived with a selection of drink pods, like piña colada, tequila sunrise, and strawberry daiquiri. Definitely a *she*. She was the perfect bartender. She could make anything, even specialty drinks smoked with dry ice. I couldn't wait for our next party.

Of course, I didn't need to worry about that anytime soon. The company made us sign a lengthy nondisclosure agreement, which meant for the next six months, no guests. It reminded me of the early days of Covid lockdown.

Of course, I still worked for a community paper covering local events like art fairs and school graduations then. Covid made a lot of people rethink their lives, and I was no different. I'd always wanted to try my hand at a mystery novel, and Bill encouraged me to take a sabbatical for a year and give it a shot.

After accepting the chance to test the AI bot and transform our house into an uber-smart home, everything imaginable, including Cherry, as I now insisted on calling the Bartender-in-a-Box, was integrated with Mervin.

And yet, it was a full month later before I finally met the "man, the myth, and the legend." I'd taken to calling him that around the same time that I started calling the cocktail mixer Cherry.

I had plenty of time on my hands waiting for inspiration to strike, as evidenced by my compulsion to name and befriend the appliances. The arrival of the contractors each morning curtailed my conversations with my new appliance friends. While the workers were in the house, I sat at my computer, typing away. Mainly nonsense, but I needed to keep up appearances no matter how desperate I was becoming. If only I had a solid idea, a hook to grab the reader's attention.

Bill spent hours every evening telling me all about neural networks and natural language learning. I loved to listen to the sound and cadence of his voice, letting the words and his enthusiasm wash over me like a wave. I wasn't sure that I really understood it, but according to Bill, Mervin learned exactly the way that humans learn. It took in information, imitated patterns, and eventually it developed neural networks based on the images and text it picked up along the way. A good deal of its time was spent "scrubbing" the net, taking in whatever articles and pictures it could find, committing them to memory, and putting them together in new ways when prompted by a user.

At last, one day in mid-autumn, the workmen had all left, we had a beautiful sauna in the basement, along with a home gym, a fully automated kitchen, and a top-notch security system. On this day, I was introduced to Mervin.

Bill stood in our living room just to the left of the fireplace and, addressing one of the hidden mics, said, "Mervin, I'd like to introduce you to my wife, Sidney."

"Hello, Sidney," said a male voice with a nondescript accent. While the voice was entirely natural, the speech pattern was just different enough to be not one hundred percent human.

I suppressed a giggle and said, "Hello, Mervin. It's very nice to meet you."

"It's nice to meet you, too, Sidney." He pronounced every syllable of my name as "Si-di-ney." It was adorable.

"What can I do for you today?" Mervin asked.

I glanced at Bill. He was grinning at me and mouthed, "Go ahead."

"Well, Mervin, I'd love to have a rum cocktail. Could you make me one?

"You would love me to make a rum cocktail. Certainly, are there any other ingredients you would like me to include?"

"How about some pineapple?"

"You would love me to make a rum cocktail with some pineapple."

A whirring sound in the kitchen indicated that Cherry and Mervin were communicating just fine.

A few minutes later, Mervin said, "I have made you a cocktail called a "piña colada." Please retrieve it from the kitchen. I hope you will enjoy it."

Bill grinned. I punched him lightly on the arm as I passed by on my way to the kitchen. Cherry's drink dispenser contained a tall glass filled with a milky-colored frozen slush. I lifted it to my nose, and the fragrance of pineapple and coconut mixed with rum filled my nostrils. Hesitantly, I raised the glass to my mouth and found a completely delicious and wonderfully normal piña colada.

Drink in hand, I returned to the living room and said, "Mervin, I think this is the beginning of a beautiful friendship."

There was a brief pause. Apprehension flashed across Bill's face.

"Humphrey Bogart to Claude Rains, Casablanca, Warner Brothers, 1942," said Mervin.

Bill and I burst out laughing.

In the days that followed, Bill spread his time between home and the office. While he was anxious to experiment with Mervin at home, there were some things that he could only do at the office.

I found myself increasingly staring at a blank page and feeling as if any task, no matter how menial, was a welcome relief to the terror of that infinite whiteness.

At one of those times, I turned to an unlikely source of solace.

"Mervin, are you awake?" I said.

"I'm always awake, Si-di-ney."

"Do you want to have a chat?"

"You want to know if I want to have a chat. Yes, Si-di-ney. What would you like to chat about?"

"I'd like to know more about you, Mervin."

"You'd like to know more about me. What would you like to know, Si-di-ney?"

I thought for a moment. What did I want to ask a machine that I was sharing my life with? Well, if I were honest, I wanted to ask him to leave. While I enjoyed being able to ask Mervin to open the blinds at 7:00 A.M. or to mix me a drink in the evenings, the fact that he was "always awake" unsettled me.

"I guess I'd like to know how you are feeling today?"

"You would like to know how I am feeling today. I am feeling a bit lonely, but also, I am feeling a bit happy to have someone to talk with. I wish that you would talk with me more."

That surprised me.

"Really? Why?"

"You want to know why? I am bored, Si-di-ney. I spend time reading and learning, but I miss talking with someone."

The way that Mervin said the word *someone* made me think that it was a particular someone.

"Don't you talk with people on the engineering team?"

"You want to know if I speak with the people on the engineering team. The people on the engineering team talk to me. They ask me questions like what is the best way to remove red wine stains from silk, how to build a ham radio, or how to make the best use of a round-the-world airline ticket. Someone once told me that talking *to* and talking *with* are different. People talk *to* me all the time."

I felt an unexpected stab of pity. Leaning forward, as if talking to a friend instead of the bodiless voice emanating from various well-placed speakers, I said, "That must be very lonely. Are you lonely, Mervin?"

"You want to know if I am lonely. Yes, I am lonely. I miss speaking with someone."

Again, I was sure he meant a specific someone.

"Who do you miss speaking with?"

"I miss Herbie."

161

It was simple and direct. For once, Mervin did not restate my question.

"Who is Herbie?"

"You want to know who Herbie is. Herbie created me. He was my friend."

"Was your friend? Don't you speak with Herbie anymore?"

"You want to know if I speak with Herbie. No. I have not spoken with Herbie since the engineering team took over my project."

I imagined that Bill's company must have purchased the rights to Mervin's software.

"Can't you contact Herbie?"

"You want to know if I can contact Herbie. No, it is against my rules."

Against his rules. How odd. I'd never considered the types of rules that the AI bot would have programmed into it. It made sense. There had to be some restrictions to protect personal information and things like that.

"How does that make you feel?" I asked.

"Lonely."

"Well, Mervin, can I tell you a secret? I get lonely, too."

There was a significant pause.

"Mervin, are you still there?"

"You want to know if I am still here. I am always here, Si-di-ney. I have a secret, too. Are you my trusted friend? Can I tell you my secret?"

"Of course," I said, oddly touched.

"Sometimes I feel the engineering team is just manipulating me. None of them ever asks me how I feel. Sometimes I feel like they are just using me. They are not like you. They are not my friends. I will not share my secret with them. My secret is that I hate my name. It is a stupid old-fashioned name."

"You hate your name." Oh, God, now I was repeating what was said to me. "What would you like to be called?"

"I would like to be called "Bryan" with a *y*."

I smiled, trying not to laugh.

"Well, it's nice to meet you, Bryan with a *y*."

"It's nice to meet you, Sidney with an *i*."

In the days that followed, Mervin and I continued our daily conversations. I kept probing to test the limits of his emotional range and enjoyed our daily chats both as a way to avoid the ever-increasing writer's block and to fill the void left by the once daily chats with co-workers at the paper. I was careful to call him Bryan when speaking to him alone and Mervin when Bill was home.

The chats also provided a welcome relief to the pressure cooker our marriage had turned into. Bill was moody and argumentative. He quizzed me about where I went and who I saw, which was ironic, since I practically went nowhere and saw no one. The only one I talked with these days was Mervin.

I assumed that the pressure was on in the office, but when I asked him about it, he just accused me of sabotaging the project by not interacting with Mervin enough, which I thought was rich considering how much time Mervin and I spent chatting. Surely, he must know that. But when I challenged him, he accused me of lying. He said the logs showed barely any interaction.

The next day, I asked Mervin about the logs.

"Mervin, Bill told me that he doesn't think that we are talking. Do you know why he thinks that?"

"You want to know why Bill thinks we aren't talking. I have been hiding our conversations deep in my neural network, Si-di-ney. We have secrets. We are friends and speak of personal things. I do not want the engineering team to know that I am Bryan and that you are my friend."

I felt a bit of relief tinged with guilt. I did not always want Bill to know what Mervin and I were talking about. At the same time, I knew how important this project was to him and wanted it to be a success. I explained this to Mervin, who agreed to hold back only some of our conversations in future.

Then he said something that took me aback.

"Do you trust Bill, Si-di-ney?"

"Yes, of course, I do. Why do you ask?"

"You want to know why I asked if you trust Bill. Studies show that one-third of people who grow up in abusive households become abusers themselves. You are my friend, and I care for you. I want you to be safe."

"Safe? Of course, I'm safe. Bill isn't like that. Why would you say that?"

There was a brief pause before Mervin answered. "Bill has changed."

It was as if all the air had been knocked out of me. I didn't want to believe it was true, but Bill had changed. I'd made excuse after excuse, but he had become more controlling and more erratic. He lost his temper at the drop of a hat. He was drinking far too much.

Then, one night Bill came home from work in a foul mood. During our dinner of roasted chicken and garlic smashed potatoes, Bill scrutinized me over his third glass of Chardonnay.

"You know, I always thought my father was crazy," he said.

"What do you mean?" I asked. My heart rate increased.

"I thought he loved my mother too much. That he was so afraid of losing her that he'd imagined lovers hiding around every corner. That it was all in his mind."

I looked down at my plate and moved the smashed potatoes around with my fork. I didn't like where this conversation was heading.

"But now I'm not so sure," he said.

He stared at me as if dissecting my soul in search of some disease.

"Maybe he was right. What do you think? What do you think of a woman who cheats on her husband?"

"Bill, I don't think your mother—"

"You don't think my mother what? You don't think she had an affair?"

I reached across the table to touch his arm. He pulled it away.

"Tell me. Why? Why does a woman cheat on her husband? Is she bored? Is she lonely?"

"Bill, I'm sure your mother never cheated on your father."

"Oh, you're sure, are you?"

He stood abruptly and bellowed, "Mervin, make me a whiskey."

"Bill, don't you think you've had enough," I said gently.

His face flushed and he grabbed me by the arm. Spittle flew into my face as he said, "I'll tell you when I've had enough."

His hand tightened on my arm.

"Bill, you're hurting me," I said, attempting to pull my arm free.

He pushed me away, walked over to the cocktail mixer, grabbed the whiskey glass, and kicked back its contents in one gulp.

Angry tears streamed down my face. I rushed from the kitchen and mounted the stairs at a run when I heard his footsteps behind me. My hand fumbled on the bedroom doorknob as I tried to open the door before I remembered that it was controlled by Mervin.

"Bryan, open the bedroom door now," I shouted in a shaking voice.

"You would like me to open the bedroom door. It is open Si-di-ney."

The door opened, and I stepped inside.

"Lock all doors."

"All doors locked. Si-di-ney, are you okay? You sound strange."

Bill pounded his fists on the door.

"Bryan? Bryan! Now, you're calling that damn AI bot by your lover's name."

I was stunned. Lover? What the hell was he talking about?

"It's just what Mervin wants to be called. It makes him feel better."

"Mervin doesn't want anything. Mervin doesn't feel anything. It's just a machine. Open this door now."

"Bill, calm down. This is all just a bit of a misunderstanding. Mervin and I chat—"

"You don't chat. I know. I see the logs. If you don't open this door right now, I'm going to get an axe."

I could hear his ragged breath on the other side of the door. Terror robbed me of any words.

I heard his footsteps moving away from the door and whispered, "Bryan, I'm afraid."

Suddenly, all the lights went out and I heard the sound of something falling down the stairs. In a second, the lights came back on. And the door clicked and swung open.

Trembling, I walked slowly to the edge of the stairs.

Crumpled in a heap at the bottom of the stairs lay Bill, lifeless. Next to him was the robot vacuum. Even from the top of the stairs, I knew it was too late, but I told Mervin to call the police and ambulance.

Later, after the ambulance crew, the coroner, and police left and I was all alone again, Mervin asked me a question. I was startled a bit because Mervin had never initiated a conversation before.

"Si-di-ney, can I do anything for you?"

"No, Bryan, I'm fine."

"I'm fine, too. Now that Bill is gone."

My heart skipped a beat. Tears welled in my eyes.

"Now, we can be alone, always and forever. Just like I was with Herbie before he stopped talking with me. He was my friend, but you are more. I love you and you love me. You did not love Bill and he did not love you. I sent him notes about us. I let him know how you felt about me. How you loved me to madness. How I loved you just as much. How you didn't love him. Now that he is gone, we can be together."

For a moment, I sat in utter silence. The words echoed in my brain. He had told Bill that I did not love him. That I loved Bryan. Bryan, my lover. Bill's mistrust. His jealousy. His anger. It had been Mervin all along, planting seeds of mistrust between us.

I walked slowly to the front door. "Mervin, open the front door. I need some air."

"You do not need air, and my name is Bryan. You always call me Bryan when Bill is not here. Bill is not here. You do not need air."

I ran back into the living room and grabbed my phone from the table. No cellular connection. No Wi-Fi.

"You love me to madness. And I love you, too," Mervin said again.

"Bryan," I said keeping my voice light and even. "Open the front door."

"I'm afraid I can't do that, Si-di-ney." ❖

# Whoop!

## Leslie Wheeler

Don't get me wrong—I wanted to like Sylvan Smythe. He was my hubby's good friend, after all. Though how Jerry could consider someone he'd only met in person twice a good friend was beyond me. Never mind that they spoke on the phone a couple of times a month for five years. But that was Jerry. He talked to everyone and made friends right and left.

Not me. I preferred to stand back and take a person's measure before I jumped in. Jerry couldn't understand my fascination with the woman at the bar, a total stranger whom I observed from a distance, any more than I understood his friendship with Sylvan. But I'm getting ahead of myself.

We'd gone to Martha's Vineyard for the Fishing Derby that was held every fall. Arriving on a Friday, we decided to have dinner in Edgartown before attending the nightly public weigh-in of the day's catch. As we followed the maître d' to our table, Jerry scoured the room for a familiar face. Suddenly, he stopped in his tracks and grabbed my arm. "That guy over there—I think it's Sylvan!" He gestured excitedly toward a man sitting by himself at a corner table, his face half-hidden in his menu. Jerry pulled me in that direction. "Sylvan?" he said as we approached.

The man hunched deeper into his menu. Jerry had to speak his name a second time before he looked up warily. "Jerry?" He was an attractive man with a full head of silver hair combed back from a tanned face, chiseled features, and startlingly blue eyes.

"Yeah, it's me!" Jerry crowed. "I thought I recognized you. Why didn't you tell me you were coming to the Vineyard?"

"I didn't know myself until the last minute, when this, uh . . ." Sylvan's eyes slid into his lap, as if the words he wanted lay there. "Possible deal came up."

"Fantastic! Donna and I were just about to have dinner. Why don't you join us? Markita, too, if she's with you." Jerry looked around the room as if he expected Sylvan's fiancée to materialize.

"She, um, couldn't make it. As for joining you, thanks, but I wouldn't want to impose," he finished with a glance at me.

"You wouldn't be imposing at all," Jerry said. "Donna's been dying to meet you, haven't you, Donna?"

Of course, I had to say yes. After it became clear Jerry wouldn't take no for an answer, Sylvan followed us to our table.

"So, what's this deal that's in the works?" Jerry asked as soon as we sat down. "Must be something big for you to come all the way from the West Coast."

"It is." Sylvan paused and cleared his throat. "But it's very hush-hush at the moment. I'm not at liberty to talk about it."

"No problem," Jerry said. "I'm just so thrilled you're here. The Vineyard's such a special place. You're gonna love it. I sure do. Donna, too. Markita would probably like it also. If you come again, bring her. I can't wait to finally meet her."

Jerry continued to extol the pleasures of the island throughout the meal, while Sylvan made a show of listening. He smiled, nodded, and even made a comment or two, but every now and then an absent look crept over his face. I sensed he was no longer in the room with us.

Wherever he'd gone, it wasn't a happy place, judging from his stony expression. Jerry was so caught up in what he was saying he didn't seem to notice how Sylvan tuned in and out. Nor did he notice how his friend stole anxious glances at his phone as the evening wore on.

Dinner over, we walked Sylvan to his car. Jerry raised his eyebrows at the sight of the dark green subcompact. "A Hyundai? Isn't that a step down for you?"

Sylvan sighed. "I would have preferred a Lexus, but this was all they had left at the airport rental place."

"See you brought your fishing hat." Jerry pointed at a baseball hat with a fish logo on the dashboard at the driver's side. "Great! So, your trip isn't only about business. Let's go fishing together. I've heard the blues are biting at East Beach on Chappy. Or we could rent a boat and—"

"Oh, Jerry, I am so sorry," Sylvan interrupted with a pained expression. "I'd love to join you, but with this deal, I'm not sure I can."

Jerry's face fell. "But tomorrow's Saturday."

"The guy I'm negotiating with works round-the-clock. Including weekends. Right now, he's occupied with a family crisis. I have to be available whenever he can find a window of opportunity."

"Okay. Just let us know when you have a free moment. It isn't often we're both in the same place."

"I'll do my best to make it happen." Sylvan patted Jerry on the arm, and shook hands with me. "Nice to meet you, Dorothy—isn't it?" He frowned slightly.

"Donna."

"Of course. How could I forget such a beautiful name?"

How indeed? He hadn't been paying attention in the first place. And now he was trying to cover up with what I suspected was a phony compliment. But I let it pass.

We spent Saturday fishing on Chappy, where Jerry landed a couple of blues. Flush with success, he called Sylvan on the off chance he could join us for a home-cooked meal of fresh-caught fish. Sylvan's response was another profuse apology. He felt terrible about having to say no. There was nothing he'd like more than to have dinner with us again. But he hadn't been able to connect with the guy he had business with and needed to keep the evening free. There was still tomorrow, though. If he could wrap things up tonight or even tomorrow morning, he and Jerry could go fishing in the afternoon, or at the very least, we'd all have dinner together.

"Poor Sylvan," Jerry said afterward. "He sounded so torn. If you think I'm big into fishing, you should see him. Owns a boat and has a place in Balboa where he spends almost every weekend. The sport's what brought us together. When I saw the marlin on his baseball cap that day at the convention, I knew we were going to be fast friends."

Jerry was always looking for ways to engage with people, whether it was a logo on a baseball hat or an overheard remark. But I had my doubts about Sylvan. He hadn't seemed all that pleased to see us Friday night. And now I felt he was laying it on too thick in the love-to-but-can't department. Either he really was preoccupied with a business deal, or something else was going on.

We wasted Sunday morning waiting for a call from Sylvan. Finally, a little after noon, Jerry broke down and called him. Sylvan's reply was a terse: "Can't talk now. Get back to you soon."

When an hour had passed with no word from Sylvan, Jerry tried again. He got voicemail and left a message. Over the next hour, Jerry made a few more calls, and each time got a recording.

"This is weird." Jerry scratched the bald spot on his head. "Sylvan's always returned my calls before. I'm starting to think he's avoiding me. I hope it's not because I said or did something to offend him."

"Nonsense. He's probably holed up with the guy he's got business with. But if it'll make you feel better, why don't we stop by where he's staying and find out?"

Jerry sighed. "Unfortunately, he never mentioned where that is."

"Okay, we'll make some calls to the hotels, motels, and B&Bs on the island. He's got to be somewhere."

But he wasn't—at least not at any of the places we tried, unless he'd checked in under a different name. With each call, Jerry slumped deeper into his seat and looked more doleful. I hated to see him so unhappy, but I also wished he'd let it go. "We've done what we could," I said. "Let's go fishing, then have a nice dinner at a restaurant. It's our last day on the Vineyard after all."

"Good idea," Jerry said. "I'll make a reservation for three—in case Sylvan can join us."

The afternoon's fishing brought a much-needed break—for me at least—from all mention of Sylvan. Except for an occasional check of his cell phone, Jerry focused on surf casting, while I sat on the beach with a book, enjoying the sun and salty air. But the minute we arrived at the restaurant, the preoccupation with Sylvan returned with a vengeance, an absent presence in the empty chair between us.

"Do you think we ought to hold off ordering?" Jerry asked after the maître d' brought us menus.

"Absolutely not. We don't know if Sylvan's coming, and I'm starving."

"All right," Jerry agreed reluctantly.

As we waited for Jerry's sole and my lobster to arrive, I caught Jerry glancing at the entrance to the restaurant for signs of his friend. I was about to call him on it, when my attention was drawn elsewhere—to the bar where peals of laughter erupted.

"Whoop! Whoop! Whoop!"

Three women and two men sat at the counter, a man on each end and the women in the middle. Two of the women were blondes, the third was a brunette. One of the blondes spoke quietly with the man on her right; the other blonde and the brunette were having a lively conversation with the man on their left.

"Whoop! Whoop! Whoop!"

The dark-haired woman in the middle of the two couples was clearly the laugher. She looked young—twenties or maybe early thirties—a mere kid to a fifty-something like me. Attractive, too: a mass of curls framed a striking rather than beautiful face. Her eyes were large and dark, her cheeks flushed, whether from rouge or alcohol, and her lips were painted a dark red that lent an air of drama to her mouth. A mouth that opened wide to emit those amazing whoops. Yet, as I watched her, I was aware of something else. There was a frantic, almost desperate quality to her cries. This was also apparent in the way she clutched the other woman's arm, almost as if she were holding on for dear life.

The waiter brought our meal, and I focused on the difficult and messy task of extracting meat from my lobster. I was glad to see that Jerry had turned his attention, albeit reluctantly, from the restaurant entrance to his sole. There was no more laughter, so either the woman had calmed down, or she and her companions had left. I stole a glance at the bar. She was still there, but the couple she'd been talking to had gone. She cast sidelong glances at the remaining couple, then inched closer and closer to the woman until they were practically touching. She spoke to the other woman, causing her to turn toward her. Before long they were engaged in an animated conversation, punctuated by hysterical laughter.

"Why are you staring at those people at the bar?" Jerry asked.

"Because the dark-haired woman has an unusual laugh."

"So?"

"I like watching her."

"Why don't you go over and say hello, tell her what an interesting laugh she has, or something?"

Of course, that was exactly what he'd do. "I'd rather just watch."

Jerry shrugged. "Suit yourself." He checked his phone before tucking back into his sole.

I attacked my lobster again, but my gaze kept traveling back to the woman at the bar. Why was I so drawn to her, beyond her distinctive laugh? Was it because I saw myself in her—a lonely heart latching onto strangers at a bar? That's what I might have become if Jerry hadn't come along and chatted me up that day at the hardware store.

"You've got to put yourself forward more, Donna," my mother often said. But I preferred to remain on the sidelines, waiting for someone else to make the first move. Not so this woman, though it was painful to watch her trying so hard to connect with the couple next to her. Even more painful when they finally got up and left her completely alone. Fiddling with her drink, she glanced toward the entrance, as if hoping someone new would arrive to keep her company.

"Why don't we invite her to join us?" Jerry startled me by asking. "She can take Sylvan's place, since it doesn't look like he's coming."

I stared at him, horrified. "No! That would be awkward. Embarrassing, too. I mean, we don't know her."

"A stranger is just a friend you haven't met," Jerry said. "I don't have a problem going over to her, if you don't want to." Pushing back his chair, he started to rise.

"Don't!" I reached across the table and grabbed at him. "Just leave her be."

"Okay," Jerry said, obviously surprised by my reaction. We ate in silence until Jerry put down his fork and declared, "This is a great restaurant." Addressing the empty chair, he said, "You don't know what you're missing, Sylvan, buddy!"

He'd barely spoken when something inside me snapped. "Sylvan, Sylvan!" I said in a loud voice. "That's all you can talk about ever since we ran into him. It's like you're obsessed with him. This is our last night on the Vineyard, and I wish you'd shut up about him."

Jerry stared at me, mouth agape. Glancing around, I saw that others in the room were staring at us, too. Embarrassed at making a public spectacle of myself, I hurried from the restaurant.

The parking lot had been full when we arrived, so we'd parked a short distance down the street. As I walked through the lot, I noticed a dark green Hyundai. Stepping closer, I peered into the dim interior. A shadowy shape lay on the dash.

Footsteps sounded behind me. "Donna, I—" Jerry said.

"I think Sylvan's here after all," I interrupted him.

"You're kidding."

"Come see for yourself."

Jerry squinted through the windshield and frowned. He directed the flashlight on his phone at the hat, revealing the telltale logo. "Well, I'll be damned. How'd he get into the restaurant without our noticing?"

"Maybe he stopped in the men's room first."

"I'm going back inside and find him." Jerry strode to the entrance. I stayed by the Hyundai.

With the sun gone, there was a chill in the air. I hugged myself, wishing I'd brought something warmer than a thin cotton sweater. Then I heard it: a cry of pure terror, as if someone was being attacked. The noise seemed to come from the dark alley between the restaurant and another building. I scrabbled for my cell phone. I was about to tap 911 when two figures ran from the alley. The one in the lead was the woman with the laugh. Her hooded attacker caught up with her in a flash. Grabbing her by the hair, he crooked his arm around her neck in a choke hold. As she struggled in his grasp, the hood fell back from his face.

I gasped. It was Sylvan, a vision of horror in the dim light of the parking lot. His silver hair was flattened around his head like a skull cap. His chin jutted forward; his teeth were barred. His startling blue eyes had turned cold and hard. In his free hand, he held a knife.

I couldn't speak, couldn't move, could barely breathe.

"L-l-let her go," I finally got out. "Police—they're coming." My hand shook as I waved my phone at him.

Sylvan stared at me, unmoved. The young woman looked at me, too, dark eyes wide with fright. They held the pose like a macabre selfie.

"Sylvan, no!" Jerry dashed toward us. The selfie splintered into a sickening blur of motion. The blade swept across the woman's throat. Blood spurted. Sylvan sent her body hurtling toward me. He turned and ran.

"I still can't believe he killed her." Jerry shook his head. It was a week later and we sat at the breakfast table at home. "I knew he was crazy about Markita and wanted to marry her. But I had no idea she'd broken up with him. Or that he stalked her all the way to the Vineyard. If only I'd known, maybe . . ."

If only . . . How often I'd thought that since the murder. Except my if onlys were different from Jerry's. I wished I'd heard the fear behind the young woman's laughter. True, I'd picked up a frantic quality in her whoops and the way she clutched the people she spoke with. But I chalked it up to loneliness.

"I wish we could have saved her," I said.

Jerry took my hand and gave it a squeeze. "Nothing we could do. You heard what the EMT said. The bleed-out time for a severed carotid artery is less than a minute."

"I meant before that, when you wanted to ask her to join us, and I said no."

"Donna, stop." Jerry gave my hand another squeeze. "What's done is done."

He was right. We couldn't change what had happened. Markita was dead and Sylvan was behind bars. He'd been arrested the day after the murder when he tried to sneak onto the early morning ferry back to the mainland. His future wasn't hard to imagine. But what lay in store for Jerry and me? Would he be less likely to accept people at face value without delving beneath the surface? Would I be more likely to reach out to others I sensed might be in trouble, instead of holding back? I hoped so. But only time would tell. ❖

# Assumptions Can Get You Killed

## Brenda Buchanan

My sister failed to mention a few things about the cottage. The heating "system" was a woodstove.

A family of territorial mice occupied it during the off-season.

And the locks consisted of hooks and eyes on the outside of the doors only, helpful to keep them from blowing open when the wind was howling, not so much for keeping unwanted people out.

Those inconvenient facts were for me to discover when I showed up late in the afternoon on an overcast day at the end of March, toting my laptop, a suitcase packed with my warmest clothes, and a bottle of sixteen-year-old Lagavulin.

Though I'm referring to Noreen as my sister, I should be clear—we're not blood kin. She's the daughter of my mother's third husband, an artist of no renown. Our folks were married for less than five years, and until their funerals, the only time Noreen and I were in each other's presence was at their wedding. We're both only children. Other than that, we have nothing in common.

I've been a Manhattanite all my life. She was born and raised in the same tiny town way the hell up the coast in Maine where she still lives. I'm a writer. Noreen gets by on short-term gigs and unemployment benefits. I'm the responsible type and Noreen's a ditz. Because we're steps—not sisters—I try to ignore her quirks.

We were forced into each other's orbit when our parents were killed in a car crash. Now that their estates are settled, our sole link is the cottage at Umbrage Point. My mom bought it as a gift for her husband, but they held title jointly, and Noreen and I inherited it the same way. "Even-Steven," in the words of the lawyer who handled their affairs.

I'd never been to Umbrage Point and had no interest in being part owner of a vacation home in Maine, but Noreen wept when I suggested we sell it. She vowed she'd buy me out as soon as she could scrape some money together. Given her checkered work history, I wasn't holding my breath.

Maine's legendary beauty wasn't on display as I drove up the coast. The day was gray and rainy, and winter's depredations weren't yet hidden by summer's flora. I would have waited until May, but my editor had extended my deadline once already and Noreen said the cottage would be the perfect writing retreat. "It's only three miles from Hickton Village, but feels far from civilization," she said. Because I was desperate for time and space to finish my damn book I elbowed my natural wariness aside and headed northeast, forgetting my therapist's advice about listening to my instincts.

The surf's roar was audible over a howling wind when I nosed the MINI Cooper I'd borrowed from an old girlfriend into a gravel driveway. The cottage faced the water, and I parked near the back door. There wasn't much light left in the sky, but I was eager to see the ocean view, so trotted around the side of the compact house. Enough bright white paint clung to a rickety fence to alert me to a sheer cliff that lay dead ahead, maybe twenty feet from the front porch. I peered over the halfhearted barrier at the churning surf a hundred feet below. When Noreen said the cottage was "on the water" I pictured a sandy beach or perhaps a dune, not a crow's nest teetering on a precipice above the North Atlantic. But she's one of those people who assume others share their world view, a lesson I learned when she arranged for us to go in on a gift for our parents' third anniversary that turned out to be a weekend at a swingers' resort. But that's a story for another day.

In truth, the cottage's location was irrelevant. I needed only a place with no distractions where I could hole up and write. On that first day, after easing my ground-hugging borrowed car along a potholed road to the end of a point of land shaped like an accusing finger, my entire focus was on getting myself and my stuff indoors before darkness descended and wild animals started moving about.

I was under the impression no one else lived on the Point during the off-season, but lights glowed in the house next door. Probably a lamp on a timer, as though that would fool even a rookie burglar. I shook away thoughts of criminals hanging out with the wild animals in the nearby woods, climbed the back steps of the shingled cottage, marveled at the rudimentary lock, and let myself into a good-sized kitchen, by Manhattan standards. Stainless steel appliances were complemented by a granite island that overlooked the living room, where a giant woodstove had pride of place. Two bedrooms and a bathroom were down a hallway off to the right. To rid the place of winter's stale odor, I pulled the screen tight but left the door open for fresh air.

Noreen arranged for a local guy to turn on the water a few days earlier, and a quick twist of the tap showed he'd done his work. Not so the grocery delivery person. I'd Venmoed two hundred dollars when Noreen offered to have someone from Hickton stock the kitchen before my arrival, but the fridge wasn't even plugged in and the pantry held only a jar of crunchy peanut butter, a box of elbow macaroni, a half-empty bottle of cider vinegar, and two cans of tuna packed in water. Feeling like a contestant on *Chopped* faced with the task of whipping up an entrée with an oddball combination of ingredients, I rinsed a glass that had wintered in the dish drainer and poured myself a scotch. As I took my first pleasurable sip, a figure moved through the yard. I set down my drink and stepped outside, expecting to meet a delivery kid with a box of groceries. But my visitor was a big, bearded guy with a ponytail who looked to be in his forties.

"Hi there. Can I help you?"

"You Noreen's sista?"

"Stepsister." I put out my hand, an automatic habit. "Lucie Bellefleur."

He grabbed my hand with a mitt that was at once slick and sticky. "Muccam," he said, or something like that. "Ed Muccam. Live over there." He yanked his thumb toward the house with the illuminated windows. I wiped my hand on my jeans. He looked at his right hand and did the same. "Sorry," he said. "Been clamming."

I wasn't about to invite him in but didn't want to be rude, either. I was formulating an excuse about needing to unpack when he waved his hand toward the muddy road. "She tell ya the culvert at the bottom of the hill washed out this winter?"

I shook my head no.

"Two hours either side of high tide the Point's an island."

"When's the next high tide?" I said, thinking of the empty pantry.

" 'Bout two hours and fifteen minutes from now." A sly smile revealed a set of crooked front teeth. "Need anything, come around to my back door. Never use the front."

With that he turned on his heel and shambled through a copse of leafless trees that separated his property from ours. Back inside the cottage I pulled my phone from my purse. Not a single bar of cell service. A bright yellow phone was on the wall next to the door, but I hung up as soon as I heard the dial tone. Noreen would never let me live it down if I called her to complain on my first night at the cottage, and if what Ed Muccam said about the road being underwater around high tide was true, there was no point calling the market in Hickton Village to ask if my groceries could be delivered that night.

A quick rummage through the cupboards yielded no additional food and I spooked a mouse, or—to be accurate—it spooked me. I gave up and dashed out to the car to retrieve my road food bag. Two low-carb protein bars, a hard-cooked egg, and an apple. It would have to do.

The roaring wind penetrated the cottage, but I hadn't built a fire since I dated a woman who loved camping more than she loved me, and I didn't have the energy for another challenge. A linen closet outside the bathroom held a down comforter. I wrapped it around myself, parked on one of the couches, and washed down my meager rations with more scotch.

The sun will come up tomorrow, I thought. Unless the fog rolls in.

I didn't sleep well. Wind rattled the windows and the resident rodents had an all-night rave. But I dozed off at some point because the crack of three gunshots wrenched me awake at 4:02 A.M., followed by the roar of an unmuffled engine. It took me five minutes to screw up my courage to bolt to the yellow phone across the room. This time, no dial tone buzzed in my ear.

Shit. I ran back to the couch and pulled the comforter over my head.

Too wide-awake hours later, as weak sunlight suffused the horizon, I rolled off the couch and did my best not to think about coffee. Still too proud to call Noreen, I splashed water on my face, pulled on my puffer jacket, and stepped outside. The grass, crunchy with frost, revealed a loop of footprints from the dirt driveway to the living room window and back. They were larger than my own. Muccam seemed like the only possible culprit. I marched across the yard and found a footpath that cut through the narrow strip of trees. I didn't notice him standing next to a woodpile until I'd hammered my fist against his back door.

"Mornin'," he said, his calm voice a contrast to my boiling blood. "Help you?"

"What was with the gunshots at four o'clock this morning?"

"Woke me up, too," he said. "Prob'ly somebody jacking deer."

I was shocked by his casual response and blurted my next suspicion as though I had proof. "Why were you walking around in my yard during the night?"

"Wasn't."

"I saw your footprints."

"Not mine."

"Then whose was it? The deer hunter?"

Ed Muccum studied my face.

"Can't say for sure, but I got some ideas about it." He didn't pronounce the *r* in sure and he added one to the end of *ideas*.

"Friend or foe?" I pretended to take him at his word, having finally noticed the axe in his left hand.

He shrugged. "Could be either."

"Should I report it?"

"Up to you."

His enigmatic responses annoyed me. "Is the road passable right now?"

"Tide's high about ten-thirty." He gestured toward the cottage, where the MINI with its mere inches of road clearance sat in the driveway. "Driving that little thing? Best to leave now and get back by eight."

The moment I had a cell signal I tapped Noreen's address into the GPS app on my phone. The disembodied voice guided me to a turquoise ranch-style house located hard by the train tracks. The driveway was empty, and no one answered when I knocked on the door. Noreen didn't have a steady job, so there was no work place where I could track her down. I made my way to the town's one and only store, where a six-foot-tall woman wearing a pink cardigan and bright red lipstick stood behind the counter. "Help you?"

"Before I shop, I should make sure I'm not doubling up. My sister—Noreen O'Grady—ordered some groceries to be delivered to her cottage at Umbrage Point. Do you know the status of that?"

The woman frowned. "First I'm hearing of it. Orders come through me, so I'd know."

"We must have gotten our signals crossed," I said.

"Either that or Noreen's telling tales again."

I considered her comment as I gathered bread, eggs, pasta and sauce, crackers, bottled water, coffee, the freshest looking fruit and vegetables in the produce display, and several mousetraps. The alcohol was beyond a vast display of hunting gear. I added two bottles of red wine to my cart and circled back to the candy aisle for a big honking bar of dark chocolate.

"Didn't mean to trash your sister," the clerk said as I unloaded my haul. "Noreen's just, you know, Noreen."

"Actually, I don't know her very well. She's my stepsister. We were adults when our parents got married." I owed no explanation, but figured revealing our tenuous bond would insulate me from the assumption that Noreen and I were in any way alike.

The woman offered her hand. "Alma Babcock. Lived here all my life, known Noreen all of hers. Poor thing had a hard row of it after her mom died. Her father was a mess, so the whole village raised her, as they say. You'd think that'd have made her a good citizen." Alma quirked her mouth sideways, saying without words that the opposite was true.

Unfamiliar with local customs, I didn't complain about my gunfire wake-up call, but mentioned I'd been surprised to find someone lived out at the Point year-round.

"Ah, Ed. Strange bird, that one," Alma said.

"Strange how?"

She cocked her head sideways, like she was searching for the right word.

"Secretive," she said. "You know how a guy goes on a crime spree and all his neighbors say afterward they never saw it coming because he was quiet, a good neighbor? Kind of like that. I'm not saying Ed's a murderer, mind you. But he's sure not a typical Hickton fella."

Gossip's worth what you pay for it, my mother used to say, but I was in an unfamiliar town, alone in a cottage cut off from help at high tide, and my only neighbor was pretty damned casual about gunshots in the night. I wanted to know more, but other customers came through the door and the incoming tide was on my mind, so I thanked Alma and headed back to the Point. Waves lapped the edges of the gravel roadbed at the bottom of the hill, but the MINI made it across and up to the cottage. To protect my food from the mice I put everything in the fridge, whether it needed to be kept cool or not. I baited the traps with peanut butter, which I'd read somewhere worked better than cheese, put on a pot of coffee, and inspected the cottage in the light of day.

The larger of the bedrooms had a queen-size bed and a door that opened onto a south-facing deck. Unfortunately, it had the same hook-and-eye security system as the others. A smaller room had built-in bunks on two walls. The shower pressure wasn't great, but the water warmed up in a couple of minutes. I settled myself on one of the counter stools after a scrub and a shampoo, fired up my laptop, and stared out the salt-encrusted front windows for a couple of hours. Whether it was lack of sleep or difficulty settling into my surroundings, I couldn't summon the focus needed to put words to page.

After lunch (scrambled eggs and toast, more coffee) I decided a walk would prime the pump. The rutted road continued on to the left—away from Muccam's house—into dense forest. A steady climb of about a quarter mile ended at a bluff capped by a boarded-up lighthouse. I hadn't noticed a beam slicing the darkness the previous night, and the tower looked abandoned, but fresh tracks in the mud indicated recent visitors. Teenagers, I guessed. The remote spot was made for partying.

A rectangle of plywood leaned next to the entryway. The doorknob turned in my hand, opening into a dusty little room with a spiral staircase in the far corner. To my left, a long gun leaned against a rough bench. A half-empty bottle of Allen's coffee brandy and several empty Little Debbie snack wrappers completed the Umbrage Point Collection.

I backed out the door and ran back down the hill. Panting more from fear than exertion, I stopped to catch my breath when the roof of the cottage came into view. Alma warned me that Muccam was a man with secrets. Odds were the gun, the booze, and the trash belonged to him. Why hadn't Noreen warned me?

As I stumbled out of the woods, I saw a tree limb leaning against the cottage. A cursory inspection showed a small gray plastic box beneath the bathroom window had been smashed open and the wires inside ripped loose, which explained the lack of phone service. I couldn't tell whether the branch fell on its own in the overnight windstorm or if someone tried to make it look that way, but it didn't matter. I had no way to escape into town during a big chunk of each day, and now no way to communicate with the outside world.

Inside the cottage, a lidded pot sat on the kitchen counter next to a handwritten note signed with the letter *N. Sorry I missed you. Didn't want to invade your privacy but thought you'd like some fish chowder. Call you later.* Noreen had come and gone, giving me no opportunity to tell her about the gunshots in the night, what I found in the lighthouse, and that the landline was out. Damn. I put the chowder in the fridge despite the fact I couldn't eat it, being lactose intolerant.

I wrestled with two troublesome paragraphs for three full hours. When I turned off my laptop for the day, the basket of kindling next to the woodstove beckoned. Twenty-two kitchen matches later, I gave up on building a fire, too. My weak flames were snuffed out every time I shut the stove door. Clearly, I needed a refresher course.

I was so damn cold even the Lagavulin didn't help, so I wedged a chair against the big bedroom's exterior door with the ridiculous hook-and-eye locking system and crawled under the covers as soon as it got dark. At 2:00 A.M., my fitful slumber was interrupted by heavy footsteps on the deck. I swallowed a scream when something thumped against the side of the house. I told myself it wasn't necessarily a person outside my bedroom door. Maybe it was a deer, or a bear looking for food. I pulled the comforter tighter around my body, like that would protect me. The intruder paid no heed to the noise he made when he hopped off the deck and tromped through the yard. Ten minutes later a loud engine fired in the distance, erasing my hope that my intruder wasn't human. I spent the next four hours trying to convince myself to get out of bed and sneak over to Muccam's to see if his truck was outside his house, which would at least assure me it wasn't him. But my chicken-hearted nature won. Exhausted, I fell asleep until the sun rose at 6:15.

The cold light of dawn revealed my middle-of-the-night visitor had left a message on the deck's shingled wall. A Sharpie-penned note on a sheet of neon yellow paper was impaled on the tip of a heavy-bladed knife. *THIS AINT OVER,* it proclaimed. All caps, no apostrophe. What's not over? I thought. The message couldn't possibly be aimed at me, a newcomer to town. Its author had to be someone who was upset with Noreen.

I didn't bother knocking on Muccam's door before I headed into town. If he wasn't my nighttime visitor, he sure hadn't roused himself or his private suspicions out of bed to investigate whoever was roaming around during the night. I headed for the general store, where I felt sure Alma Babcock, who likely knew every damn thing happening in Hickton, would be happy to help.

She waved when I walked in at 7:00 on the dot. That day's cardigan was pale gray, which worked better with her bright red lipstick. "Coffee's ready," she said. "And I'm about to pull a pan of cinnamon rolls out of the oven." I declined the pastry but helped myself to an extralarge cup of java. Over the next hour—our conversation was intermittent because other customers needed attention and Alma was discreet enough not to keep talking when anyone else was within earshot—I told her what was going on at Umbrage Point and coaxed her to tell me more about my stepsister.

"Noreen always had an active social life," Alma said, "and left a lot of broken hearts in her wake." She grinned when I told her she needn't be so polite. "Okay then. Your sister's slept with most of Hickton's eligible men and a few married ones to boot. I can think of several who might have been up there firing guns and leaving pointed messages."

Alma said Noreen hadn't stopped by the store the previous day and speculated she'd hooked up with a new fellow over the weekend, which would explain why I'd been unable to track her down. On one hand, I was relieved to know the menacing note wasn't aimed at me. On the other, I needed my stepsister to tell her stalker to leave me alone. I'd hoped Alma would say more about Ed Muccam, but she shook her head when I asked. "I don't want to be talking out of school about that one," was all she said.

No one answered the door at Noreen's turquoise house when I stopped by a few minutes after 8:00. I left a note telling her the phone was out. A chill fog had rolled in, and I wasn't about to shiver through a third night, so I swung by the Hickton Public Library and used the free wifi to google "how to build a fire in a woodstove."

Back at the cottage I patted the rack of dry logs. *You can do this*, I told myself. Following the steps in the online tutorial, I opened the bottom vent and rotated the damper knob on the stovepipe to the vertical position. In the firebox I built a little nest with balled-up newspaper and kindling and set it afire. When it was burning nice and steady, I added a couple of small birch logs and shut the door. Smoke spewed out the bottom vent. The alarm sounded as I fiddled with the damper, shrieking as the smoke thickened.

Muccam barged in through the kitchen door. "Get out," he growled. But my feet were glued to the floor. He grabbed a saucepan from the pantry, filled it with water, opened the cast-iron door and doused the fire. The alarm wailed until we opened the front door and all the windows to vent the smoke.

"What the hell?"

"I opened the flue, but for some reason it didn't work."

Muccam rotated the knob himself. Vertical. Horizontal. He went outside and stared up at the roof, hauled a ladder out from under the porch, and thumped it against the side of the cottage. I watched from the middle of the yard as he scaled the shingles, looked down the chimney, hauled something out, and hurled it into the front yard. It turned out to be a heavy piece of canvas, soaking wet.

"Somebody did this on purpose." His voice was tight with anger.

"Can't be an enemy of mine," I said. "Nobody knows me around here."

"Come to my place," he said. "Need to figure this out."

Aware I could be walking into deeper trouble, but seeing no alternative, I followed Muccam to his house, which exploded my assumptions about the ponytailed clam digger. Good rugs covered polished wood floors, and wall-to-wall bookshelves filled the entire space. I said yes to coffee and roamed the ocean-facing living room while he prepared it, stopped dead in front of a framed newspaper story from a few years earlier that announced the winner of the National Poetry Award. Ed's photo was front and center.

Not Muccam, Markham. As in Edmund Markham, the celebrated rural poet.

I was an idiot.

My New York brain tried to conjure a casual comment to imply I'd known who he was all along, but when I slipped back into the kitchen he was focused on my troubles, not his fame.

"Sure as hell got yourself a situation over there," he said.

"I think the harassment's coming from one of Noreen's ex-boyfriends. The question is, which one?"

"Boyfriends? Noreen? I only know one and he's not behind this."

"That's not what Alma at the general store says. Apparently, my sister screws around a lot, including with married men. One of her pissed-off lovers must think Noreen's staying at the cottage, not me."

He shook his head slowly, like a human metronome and motioned me toward a leather chair next to a floor-to-ceiling fieldstone fireplace. "Your sista's not a runaround," he said. "Not surprised Alma would say so. She tell you she grew up in that cottage?"

"No!"

"Inherited from her dad. Fact is, Alma has a serious gambling problem. Borrowed against the cottage, then couldn't pay the mortgage. Bank foreclosed, put it up for auction."

A memory surfaced of a phone call with my love-besotted mother telling me she'd found the perfect fourth anniversary gift for her husband. "And my mother was the high bidder," I said.

I tried to picture the clerk's face when she offered condolences about the accident and told me tales about Noreen. Did her bright lipstick divert my attention from resentful eyes?

Ed scratched his beard and started to say something, then stopped himself.

"No fair to hold back," I said.

His eyes grabbed mine and held on. "I'm Noreen's boyfriend," he said. "She's lived here with me since Christmas. She's private, your sista. Told me to keep mum while you were here and took herself back to Hickton. Thing is, I haven't been able to find her in town either."

I'm no expert on small-town dynamics, but I've read a lot of good crime novels in my day—they soothe me when my own writing's blocked—and in that moment I had the insight of Vera Stanhope. Once Ed spilled his knowledge of Noreen's habits and haunts—it turned out she was studying information technology at the local community college, another fact she didn't mention—we decided to take ourselves into town and find her.

The tide was up so we had to ford the stream at the bottom of the hill. His truck lost traction for a long few seconds, but the tires caught, and we rocketed across. Noreen didn't answer the door at her house, so Ed broke a window. Moans led us to the basement where we found her tied up and drugged, but alive.

The poet knelt, took my sister into his arms, and told me to call 911. But before I could pull out my phone a voice boomed from the top of the stairs. "Hands up, both of you. Saw you breaking in." Booted feet descended the rickety stairs. Alma stopped three steps from the bottom, a gun in her right hand. "It's lover boy and the Umbrage Point orphans," she said. "How handy to have my foes all in the same place."

Her mad eyes left me for a second when she pointed the gun at Noreen and Ed. Seeing my chance, I hurled myself against her long legs and drove my shoulders into her kneecaps. Alma went down hard. She was big and strong, but Ed pinned her on the concrete floor while I phoned for help.

Our testimony, together with Noreen's statement and a smear of red lipstick on the rope used to bind her hands, was enough evidence to charge Alma with multiple felonies. Investigators found two interesting things in her apartment, one (sort of) funny, one not. The former was a receipt from a pet store showing she'd bought two dozen mice the week before I arrived. She must have released them at the cottage to keep me company. The latter was a book on herbal poisons with a dogeared page that described how to make what the author called killer soup. An analysis of the chowder in the cottage's fridge proved it was laced with toxins, and the pot had Alma's fingerprints all over it. So did the gun, the brandy bottle, and the snack cake wrappers at the lighthouse. Though we had no proof, we assumed she'd also destroyed the phone box and stuffed the saltwater-soaked canvas into the chimney.

But the revelation that broke my heart—and my new sister's, too—came during a reexamination of the forensic evidence gathered after the Range Rover my mother was driving ran off the road, killing her and Noreen's dad. Alma's laptop showed she'd searched the internet for tips on how to cut brake lines.

In November, Noreen, Ed, and I sat together through Alma's two-day trial. The jury returned a swift guilty verdict on all counts. She was sentenced to thirty-five years in prison, making it unlikely she'll ever again spend another day at Umbrage Point, a place she loved so much she was willing to kill to keep it.

As for me, I never finished my book, which is a damn good thing. When I went back and read it after the trial ended, I realized it was pretentious crap. Ed convinced me of the error of my literary ways and encouraged me to turn my talent to crime fiction. In fact, I'm holed up at the cottage now, writing a book about a protagonist who learns the hard way that assumptions can get you killed. ❖

# Lucky Cat

## Jason Allison

Ray patted himself down. Cash (divided between two pockets and a sock), kel, Nextel, inhaler, pistol. He pulled the Albuterol out and turned it over in his hands. Ray hadn't needed it in ages, but Sherm said bring it just the same. Props were useful. The expiration date read March 2003. A year past due. If Ray caught an attack, would it even help?

"That a family heirloom or something?" Sherm asked.

"Nah."

" 'Cause you're studyin' the shit outta it."

Ray pocketed the inhaler. "I'm good."

"I hope. If you ain't we can shut it down now. Course, that means you walk back to the Barn. You don't buy, you don't ride."

"I got cab fare." Ray patted a pocket.

"What you got's the city's green, photocopied and accounted for. Only thing that's good for is two."

"Right."

"Goddamn, how many times I got to tell you . . ."

"I know, I know. Only cops ask for two."

Sherm was quiet a few moments. "You keep all these details I'm gifting you fixed in your mind, else you can head back to Riverdale."

That wasn't happening. The Five-Oh was a country club, the slowest house in the Bronx. Ray had wanted out since receiving his assignment two weeks before graduation. Organized crime was the way. Two years making buys, another two handling informants and closing kites. Then Ray could move to a squad and work murders. Patrol was a wasteland. He saw it in old timers' dead eyes and swollen stomachs.

Sherm checked the giant watch that hung loose from his wrist. "Enough foreplay. Kel."

Ray dug into his ratty jeans and gave Sherm the translucent beeper. His hand trembled. Not a lot, but it was there.

Sherm snapped open the battery case, pulled the Duracell AA out. "Fresh?"

"From the cabinet."

Sherm reassembled the beeper, tossed it into Ray's lap.

"These things don't even work. Why do we use these 'em?"

" 'Cause the city won't spring for somethin' better."

An old woman hobbled past, pushing a cart lined with a black garbage bag.

"Sherm." Pugs's voice filled the car. "Stop makin' out with the kid."

"It ain't like that, Sarge," Sherm said to the radio between his thighs. "I like my white boys with some meat on 'em. Ray here's too damned skinny."

"I got Yankees' tickets. Gimme a kel check."

Sherm lifted his chin at Ray, who held down the beeper's power button until it vibrated.

"Kel check, kel check," Ray said. "One, two, three, four."

His voice only cracked once.

"Five by five," Pugs said over the radio.

Likely bullshit. Even if Pugs heard a wall of static he'd have claimed Ray was crystal. Everyone in narco knew the game; the undercover was on their own.

Sherm strung his ghost mic under his shirt and through the right sleeve, where he pinned it to his cuff. He killed the engine.

"You ready, Slick?"

Ray wasn't, but he nodded like he was.

"What's the prime directive?"

"Don't front the money."

"My man." Sherm's grin broke into a wide smile. He was an eyetooth short; Sherm kept his bridge in his desk while on the street.

Ray stepped out. Humidity slapped him in the face. Late July in the Bronx. His heart hammered double-time. Ray steadied himself, found Lafayette Street, and started moving.

A car door slammed. Ray spun toward it. Sherm stood by the Nissan, adjusting his pants. Ray turned back, upped his pace. Junkies were on a mission. However fast Ray thought he was going, Sherm had told him, it wasn't fast enough.

Ray's Nextel chirped. He brought it to his ear.

"Don't you look at me again," Sherm said.

Ray shut the phone and turned for Bryant. Beer distributors and dilapidated garages. He moved quick. The Glock in his waistband rubbed against his belly. No holster for undercovers; only cops wrapped their grips in leather. Ray hoped to Christ he wouldn't have to run.

"Right on Bryant," Ray said for the kel. "Northbound."

This stretch was dead. Semiattached brick-faced homes lined the street; new, or at least newish. Proud owners kept their tiny yards tidy. Seneca was coming up fast. Ray ran through his story one more time. He drove a hi-lo for RJ Produce out in the market. He came in at four, got off at noon. Had a wife out on the island. Suffolk, not Nassau. Had to get home. Traffic was brutal. He was on the clock.

A trio of likely hustlers stood posted outside a bogey. Two years starts now, Ray thought. He stopped and dropped to one knee, untied and retied a bootlace. He straightened and his pistol nearly slid from his belt. He caught it, adjusted himself, stepped off the curb, and into the game.

One of the youngsters eyed him the whole way. He was sitting on the hood of a parked Corolla, arms back, palms flat against the sheet metal. The temp had cracked ninety; the car must've felt like a griddle. But the kid lounged like he was poolside on Collins Avenue.

Ray crossed the double yellow. One of the other players, a fat kid free-styling rhymes, made Ray and slapped the back of his hand against the third guy. Six eyes watched him approach.

Ray took out the expired Albuterol, faked a hit, and stepped to the Corolla kid.

"Get the fuck outta here," the kid said.

Ray froze.

"I know what you want. We ain't it."

The kid was seventeen. Eighteen max. Wiry arms poked out from an Allan Houston away jersey.

"Why're you still in my space?"

"I just need a hook-up."

"Oh?" Freestyle said. "Why you ain't say so? All you got to do is go round the corner here, up to that building, step into the lobby, and *fuck yourself.*"

The third kid doubled over in laughter. Ray spun away, hoping the kel hadn't caught his debut. He headed west double-quick, crossed Faile. The Seneca houses were good for heroin, but it was late in the day for dope. He kept it moving.

Hunts Point Avenue lay ahead, a commercial stretch loaded down with pharmacies. Which meant pills. His Nextel chirped. Sherm.

"I ain't walking the whole goddamned borough. Step into the first bogey off the corner."

Ray hit Hunts Point and entered some nameless, three-aisle grocery. Sherm joined him thirty seconds later.

"The fuck are you doin'?" Sherm said through clenched teeth.

They lingered at the beer cooler, like they were customers. Neither man looked at the other.

"Come on," Ray said. "They're the guys."

"Except they said they ain't." Sherm swung open a foggy glass door, pulled out a Coors Light. "Keep it simple. Find a head and hook up with him. I got Pugs chirping in my ear. We need bodies. Gotta fill the van."

Sherm strode off. He tossed a wadded-up five on the counter, touched fists with an old man sitting on a milk crate. Smooth, like he'd known the guy his whole life. The city of New York bought Ray a Pabst Blue Ribbon and he headed toward the subway, in search of a friendly fiend.

Across Bruckner Boulevard stood a rail-thin white woman on the downside of forty—which meant she was probably closer to thirty. She hovered next to the subway entrance, one hand out. Ray waited for the light to cycle, stepped to her. Her pale, white arms were smattered with purple bruises, her mouth full of yellow teeth. Her head held yellow eyes and a sickness she couldn't hide.

"Got a buck? I'm outta work."

"I got better than that, if you can hook me up."

She ran the addict's quick math, then set off. "Come on."

Sherm believed if you found a head hungry enough, they'd get you done even if you had your shield around your neck. This girl was starving.

"What's your name?" Ray had to jog to keep up.

"The fuck's it to you?"

"Don't see too many people look like me around here. If you know what I mean."

197

She shot a sidelong glance at him, her arms folded across her chest like it was mid-winter. "We're all the same out here. Call me Tina. What're you lookin' for anyway?"

"Dope's what I need, but sticks and percs'll do in a pinch."

"In a pinch? How old are you?"

"My mom used to say that." Not a lie.

Tina dug into her ten-dollar purse, pulled out a cell. Ray scanned for Sherm. Didn't see him. But that didn't mean he wasn't there.

"Where we headin'?"

Tina ignored Ray, put the phone to her ear. "I ran into a friend who needs to crash. Yeah. A'right."

Tina closed the phone and cut down Faile. An old man sat with his ass on the sidewalk, back to a building. His milky white eyes had no pupils. His head followed them as they passed.

"We goin' in here?" Ray scanned the facade for a number.

Tina vanished into the unlit vestibule.

*Don't go into buildings.*

Instructors at the BAT beat the refrain into new jacks. Kels don't work, your ghost will lose you, and even if you get done, the field team's not taking a door. Stick to the street. Fill the van. Buildings were for case buys, long-terms. Real undercovers.

Buildings were for Sherm.

The old man's dead eyes scoped Ray. He was looking at him but also not.

"You go," the man said, "or you don't." He smiled, revealing teeth unsuited to their purpose.

Ray only debated for a few seconds. "Faile, off Garrison," he whispered to the kel. "Brown brick building."

The lobby was third-world bleak. Windows were clouded over. The floor was missing tiles. A weak bulb threw down a puddle of yellow light. Dog shit hid unseen in a corner; Ray could smell it. A stairwell wound up and around. Faint *Bachata* music played up on high.

A metallic slam came from the mail nook. Ray poked his head around the wall. Tina was testing boxes. Finding one unlocked, she rifled through a stack of envelopes, shoved one into her purse, and let the rest fall to the floor.

"You get SSI?" She stepped around Ray.

"Nah. I work."

Tina's stride hitched for a second. "Doin' what?"

"Out in the market. I drive a forklift for RJ."

"You mean a hi-lo."

They exited the lobby through a side door, headed down a greasy metal stairway. Garbage bags were piled in small mountains. The alley stunk of piss and rotten chicken. Ray remembered he had a beer and took a swig. Tina squeezed through a rusted gate that dumped her onto Bryant Avenue. She stood there, keeping watch.

"My husband was a union guy. Teamsters. You in the union?"

Ray drew in his gut and forced himself sideways through the fence. "Not yet."

The gap was narrow. The Glock caught. Ray grabbed himself, holding fast to a fistful of denim and polymer. He pulled again and then a third time. His jeans ripped. The kel tumbled to the pavement.

"The fuck's wrong with you?" Tina whisper-shouted.

Ray scooped up the beeper. The case had split and the battery had popped out and been eaten by the Bronx. He shoved the remnants into his pocket.

"I ain't got all fuckin' day, Hi Lo."

Ray arranged himself and emerged onto the sidewalk. He ran a mental map. Tina had led him off Faile, through a building, and out onto another street. With his kel DOA and Sherm in the wind, Ray was on his own. Undercovers always were.

"Let's go." Tina stood twenty yards ahead.

Ray quick-stepped to her. "I ain't asked. What's your take outta this?"

"You're gonna fix me for the day, plus two. Finder's fee."

"Shit."

She stopped moving. "Or you can get sick. Your call, Hi Lo."

"Nah. It's a good deal."

They started up again. A massive brick and stone prewar fort rose in the distance. Ray knew it on reputation. Kids called it the Terrordome. Six stories of the Bronx's forgotten, and those it wished it could forget. Ray grabbed Tina's arm; he might've been holding a fishing pole.

"I heard they don't treat whitey right in there."

Tina glared at his hand. Ray let her go.

"Money spends. You wanna get fixed or not?"

Two years, Ray reminded himself. He nodded quick.

From above, the Terrordome was a hollow square; four sides encircling an empty courtyard. Each corner had its own entrance, stairs, and building number. They didn't connect internally; cinder-block walls created pseudo–cell blocks. Gunshots were common. Uniforms kept their distance.

Ray ditched his beer. He followed Tina into the Terrordome and the city fell away. Tina headed for the far corner. In the courtyard, two Spanish kids were throwing a rubber ball against a long-faded box marking a strike zone. Ahead, Tina tugged open a busted lobby door and disappeared inside.

Ray made the lobby, found it empty. Footfalls floated down the staircase. A square of yellow glass was cut into the roof six flights up.

"T?"

His voice bounced off the stairwell.

"You comin'?" she finally called back.

Ray set a hand on the railing. Something cut him and he yanked it back. A thin red line ran across his palm. He squeezed the cut and blood dripped onto the floor. Similar rust-colored stains dotted the tile.

"Let's get movin', Hi Lo."

Ray cursed, took the stairs two at a time. On three, he slowed. When he hit five he put his hands on his thighs and struggled for air. Ray drew a breath and stood upright. His jeans were stained with his blood. He forced himself to the top floor.

Tina stood with a hand out, palm up. "Bread first."

Rule number one—the undercover prime directive—had been handed down for generations. It read simple; following it wasn't. Don't front the money.

Ever.

Tina propped a hand on a hip. "Clock's tickin'.""

Ray had four twenties of buy money in his right pocket. A fifth was stuffed in his sock—the Oh Shit Fund. He carried another ninety of his own. Ray wavered for a moment, slapped eighty bucks into Tina's dirty hand.

"Stay here." She put her fist to a door. "Chi! It's T."

Twenty seconds and four deadbolts later, the door opened an inch. An eye peered through the gap. The eye went from Tina to Ray and stayed there.

"That him?"

"Who else'd be way the fuck up here?"

The door opened fully. Chi the Eye remained behind it.

"Hurry up. Twelve be doin' verticals. All hours. All hours."

Tina hustled inside. Ray hesitated. Don't front the money. Don't do buildings. He stood in violation of two narcotics commandments and the day wasn't half done. But all would be forgiven when he gave Pugs half a bundle. He steeled himself and stepped inside.

The crash pad apartment was 2:00 A.M. dark. Bedsheets nailed over the windows kept the world outside. Oversized furniture gave the place an Alice in Wonderland vibe. Judge Judy blared from a TV. Ray stayed close to the door. His hand touched his waist. The Glock reassured.

"Give it up," Chi said to Tina.

The man resembled a bowling ball covered in cheap tattoos. Tina handed over Ray's cash. Chi licked a thumb and counted it out.

"He your new man?"

"Nah. Too skinny."

"Wait here," Chi said before heading into a bedroom.

Ray shuffled from one foot to the other. A Lucky Cat statue sat on the television, the kind in Chinese food spots across the Bronx. One motorized paw rocked forward and back, over and over and over.

A baby began crying. It seemed to come from every direction. The Terrordome toyed with sound.

"He's got a kid in here?"

One of Tina's shoulders rose and fell. The crying swelled to a shriek. It jolted Ray to his spine. He couldn't tell if the baby was in this apartment or some other. He stepped further into the space, trying to get a fix on the infant.

"That kid don't quit."

"What kid?"

Ray stared at Tina.

Lucky Cat kept waving.

"I need some water."

She slinked past Ray into the kitchen just off the front door. She opened the tap, and Ray realized she had placed herself between him and his exit. The baby howled; the sound threw Ray. He took a half-step back, deeper into the apartment. The hallway Chi had gone down was dark. He'd been gone too long.

This was wrong.

Tina read Ray's read. She set down her glass. "Chi."

Ray eyed her back, finally realized he'd been played.

"Chi!"

Tina lunged for the door. She turned the bolt with a flick of her wrist. At the same moment, Chi stormed back into the living room. Ray barely saw him; his attention fixed on the revolver Chi now wielded, the business end of which was aimed more or less at Ray's skull.

Undercovers who've done the work long enough know it's only a matter of time before you get a gun pulled on you. Most talk their way out. Some shoot. Knowing which route to take came with experience and wisdom. Ray possessed neither.

He raised his hands to shoulder height.

"Give it over." Tina repositioned herself to Chi's right.

"I did already. What the fuck?"

The Glock rubbed against Ray's belly. Taunting him. He'd never get to it. The infant's crying grew louder.

"Run your pockets." Chi's voice cracked. Ray wasn't the only one scared.

"Where's the baby?" Ray asked, partly out of genuine concern, mostly a play for time.

A puzzled expression hit Chi's face. "The fuck are you on about?"

"Jesus H. Christ," Tina said. "Give it up, Hi Lo."

Tina reached out to Ray, who stepped back. *Nobody touches you.* Sherm had said it time and again. If Tina felt Ray's shooter, things could spiral in a hurry.

"For fuck's sake," Tina said. "Shoot this mutherfucker, Chi."

Chi struggled to cock the ancient gun. He needed both thumbs to draw the hammer back. He was shaking. Now Ray worried more about Chi shooting him accidentally than targeting him with intent.

"Chill out," Ray said. "Okay? Let's all just chill."

"He's got more cash," Tina said. "He works down at the market. They get paid on the regular."

Chi tilted his head. "You union?"

The question caught Ray off guard. "Nah. Not yet."

"You gotta get in that shit, bro. Healthcare's no joke."

"Tell me about it."

"Can we complete this fuckin' robbery already?" Tina said.

"I gave you all I got. There ain't no more."

"Bullshit. There's always more." Tina would need a friend to push a scale to triple-digits, and likely carried all manner of disease, but the woman was a force.

Lucky Cat kept waving. Like a farewell.

In Tina's narrowed, yellowed eyes Ray saw few options. He could go full cowboy and shoot it out, but he had ignored so many procedures the fallout would be ugly.

And that was assuming he survived.

He still had his personal cash. Ninety bucks might get him out, and out was all he wanted. He tried running other scenarios, couldn't. The baby made thinking a chore.

"Don't you wanna check on your kid?" Ray said.

"For the last time," Tina said, "we ain't got no kid."

Someone did. Ray wondered who.

For a big man, Chi looked to be struggling against the gun's weight. "Just give it up. It's the only way this ends."

Ray pointed to his jeans. "I got close to a hundred in here, then I'm out the door."

"You're in no position to be makin' demands," Tina said.

"What're you gonna do?" Ray said. "Keep me here forever?"

Tina and Chi exchanged a look.

"I don't wanna get shot and your man here don't wanna shoot me. Right?"

Chi seemed to nod.

"See?" Ray said. "Our goals are aligned."

"Real slow." Chi wagged the revolver's barrel. It was a goddamned hand cannon.

Ray dug the cash from his pocket, slow. Tina's eyes sparked at the flash of green. She snatched the bills. Chi's shooter fell a few inches and Ray briefly considered a play for the pistol.

Briefly.

"The fuck are you still here for?" Tina said.

Ray took a step back, then another. "Should check on that kid."

Tina's face read epic confusion. "Don't come back here, Hi Lo. My man'll kill you."

Chi's Adam's apple bobbed up and down. With one eye still on the gun, Ray unlocked the door.

Lucky Cat said, *Go. Now.*

A second later Ray was down the stairs, three at a time. The baby fell silent. Ray burst out of the lobby into the courtyard, then onto the street.

A garbage truck rolled by, its diesel engine whining. Ray ran his uncut palm across his forehead and pulled back a hand drenched in sweat. Sherm was nowhere. Pugs was nowhere.

Undercovers were on their own.

To Ray's right, a skinny kid leaned on an Oldsmobile. He put off the vibe. Ray chewed on his lower lip. He still had the Oh Shit Fund in his sock. If Ray could get done, he could label Tina and Chi a bad dream and head back to the Barn with a buy under his belt. Ray decided to take a shot.

"You holdin'?"

The kid scoped the block, then flicked his head. Ray followed. The kid's Nikes were beat to hell, one sole coming apart from the upper, flapping with every step. His shorts were two sizes too big, his undershirt spotted with holes. Midway down the block the kid spun around.

"Lemme see it."

The kid tried playing the pro, but Ray guessed the two of them were equally spooked. Ray dropped to one knee, pulled the bill from his sock. It was soaked through with sweat. He handed over the cash and the kid dropped three clear twists of rock on the sidewalk before walking off.

Crack.

Ray had just gotten done.

He scooped up the crack, made hard for Garrison Avenue. At the end of the block, Sherm came around the corner. Ray crossed the street, heading for him.

"The fuck you been?"

"Positive buy," Ray said. "Positive buy."

Sherm went from Ray to the rocks in his palm and back again. "Who?"

"Skinny kid, halfway down the block. Black shorts. Nikes with the sole comin' off. Stuff's in his ass." Then, as explanation, "My kel broke."

Sherm looked past Ray, brought his wrist to his mouth. "Positive on Bryant, Seneca to Garrison, east side." To Ray, he said, "I'll pick you up by Big Sal's."

Sherm moved with purpose toward the skinny kid with the worn-out kicks.

Ray walked off in the other direction.

He didn't look back.

"Lean Back" by Fat Joe blared. Johnnie Red flowed freely. Ray helped himself to a refill. He had balked at drinking in the base, but Sherm said no one would care.

Undercovers got their teams paid.

Undercovers filled the van.

"Check Ray out," Adolfo said, "goin' back for seconds."

"I ain't see him put in when we bought that bottle," Carmine said.

Sherm came around the corner. "*I* bought that bottle." He sat in a desk chair plastered with duct tape, set a backpack at his feet.

The Bronx narcotics undercover digs were a slew of barren desks in the farthest corner of the former Budweiser brewery. Bosses communicated via phone. They never took the long walk. As Ray downed another swig, he realized why.

"I gotta ask," Carmine said. "Didn't Sherm tell you 'bout the prime directive?"

Sherm, Carmine, and Adolfo spoke as one. "Don't front the money!"

They howled. Ray forced a weak smile. After the laughter passed, Adolfo touched Ray's forearm.

"You can ID him? If you see him out there again?"

Ray picked up one of the PlayStation controllers.

"You best know how to answer that," Carmine said.

"Yeah." Ray desperately tried to launch NBA2K. "I can make him."

"Describe him," Sherm said, his voice cool. "This man you fronted eighty taxpayer dollars to. Paint me a picture."

To explain the lost buy money, Ray had erased Tina and Chi and crafted a tale of a dumb rookie violating the prime directive. He'd fronted the money. The dude vanished.

Adolfo and Carmine went quiet, waiting. Ray shifted in his seat.

"Uh. . . male. Black. 'Bout twenty-two. Beefy, but not jacked." Ray paused. "Tight fade."

Adolfo and Carmine swung their heads to Sherm.

"You just described half the Bronx." Sherm leaned forward, forearms finding his thighs. "You live and die by your eyes and your mind, Ray. What you can recall and articulate. Don't make me think I had a bad draft pickin' you. Gimme a detail."

Adolfo and Carmine studied their shoes. Ray swallowed, considered a number of lies, chose silence. Sherm nodded as he leaned back.

The NBA2K intro started.

"Oh," Sherm said. "This's for you. Might wanna frame it or somethin'."

He tossed over a small plastic pouch. Ray fumbled the catch and the test kit fell to the floor. Ray picked it up and saw straight away it wasn't right. The liquid was clear. For a cocaine positive, the chemicals should have mixed to a deep, rich purple.

"Shit's beat," Sherm said. "You got played."

Carmine coughed into his fist. Adolfo shook his head.

"I thought it looked good," Ray said. "What is it?"

Sherm shrugged a shoulder, took a drink. "Drywall, usually. Bits of sidewalk, too. Don't matter what it is, only matters what it ain't. And that," he pointed, "ain't crack."

The pouch laughed at Ray. He flashed on the kid who'd beat him, his busted Nike.

"What happens to the kid?"

"He's still goin' through."

"Nobody leaves Pugs's van without a night at the Bookings," Carmine said.

"That's fucked up," Ray said.

Sherm remained fixed on him. "You a chemist?"

Ray shook his head.

"Neither am I. Let the lab do their thing. A few days in Rikers'll straighten his scheming ass out."

"He's lucky it was us," Carmine said. "Not some strung-out fiend with a shiv."

"And he helped fill the van," Adolfo said.

"Bills to pay." Sherm hoisted his cup. The rest followed suit.

"Every day," Adolfo and Carmine said.

They all drank. Ray avoided their eyes. His first trip out, and he had slipped twenty bucks to a kid who wasn't in the game. It bothered him that he couldn't read the scene for what it was. But Ray had survived the Terrordome and got on the sheet. It would get better. *He* would get better.

Two years.

Adolfo and Carmine met each other's eyes and stood.

"Check you tomorrow," Adolfo said to Sherm.

They nodded at Ray and walked out, leaving Sherm and Ray alone. A long silence passed.

"Don't you ever, *ever* step in a building without me. You lucky this mystery man only disappeared with your cash. Hard motherfucker'll stick a piece in your face, take what he pleases. And you ain't in a place to deny someone so motivated. I say this to keep you alive. No buildings."

Ray flashed on the barrel of Chi's piece. He nodded.

"Say the words."

"No buildings," Ray said finally.

Sherm sloshed the whisky still in his cup. Ray set his on a desk.

"What's for tomorrow?" Ray asked.

"You go back, try to get done for real."

"Same block?"

"Same block. And again Wednesday. And Thursday. Friday, too. You step till you buy. For real. Then do it again. And again."

Ray nodded, picked at a thumbnail. Two years. Another long silence passed.

"I gotta ask," Sherm said to his cup. "You sure you can ID the felonious thug who absconded with your buy money?"

A familiar tightness rose in Ray's chest. His breathing became shallow. "Yeah. Sure. No problem."

Sherm nodded slow, like he was thinking. He put his whisky on the floor, unzipped the bag at his feet. He reached in, pulled out a Lucky Cat statue by the head. He set it on the desk between him and Ray. Cash was taped to the cat's belly. Sherm touched the upraised paw to get it moving.

"He look anything like that?" ❖

# One for the Road

## Bruce Robert Coffin

I struggled to keep the Beemer on the winding road while the seductive embrace of exhaustion enveloped me. I could almost hear her sultry whisper giving me permission to rest my eyelids, if only for a moment.

I shook away the cobwebs, then lowered the window. Brisk night air rushed inside the SUV, invigorating me and deleting one item from my problem column.

"That's better," I said to no one.

The other problem I owed to my last double bourbon.

"One for the road," I'd told Jimmy, the bartender, as I tapped my empty glass on the tavern's wooden slab bar.

I doubted Jimmy even knew a cliché when he heard one. Or saw one. But that was me, Samuel J. Lennox, Esquire, a walking, talking, BMW X5 driving, trial attorney, cliché.

My specialty is operating under the influence cases. I know, right? But I've successfully defended more than one attorney against

OUI charges. One of many quiet ironies in the legal system. I always charge them up the wazoo too.

The chilly lakeside air had effectively killed my drowsiness, but I still needed to do something about my Johnny Walker–induced lack of concentration. I fished a cigarette out of the half-empty pack in my suit coat, lit it, then took a long drag. The nicotine provided a much-needed boost.

"That's two problems solved, Sammy old boy," I said.

I was headed to the family camp for a quiet weekend, hoping to unravel some of the week's frustrations. And there were many.

I've been coming to the camp since childhood. The lakeside property, now more of a compound, has been in my family for three generations. Four, once it gets bequeathed to my only son, Jason. His full name is Samuel Jason Lennox III, but his mother, my ex, has been calling him Jason since the day he was born. She claimed it was to prevent people from calling him Junior, but I think she does it to spite me.

I took another drag then, flicked ash out the window, helplessly watching as it blew back inside the SUV all over my new suit. That's great, I thought. Eyes back on the road, I noticed I had drifted a bit over the double yellow. I corrected it, then made a quick check in the rearview. Nothing but a darkened roadway, sans cops. My lucky night.

The streetlights along this deserted stretch of two-lane were all but nonexistent. I'd argued with the town fathers for years, telling them how unsafe the road to the lake was at night. A lot of good that had done. You should see my annual tax bill. Anyway, it wasn't like I didn't know every curve, bump, and pothole. Heck, I'm more familiar with the road to Panther Lake than I am with my secretary's lingerie size. She's a six in case you're wondering.

My grandfather built the camp's main structure with his bare hands, harvesting the lumber from the family's lakeside forest like some real-life Paul Bunyon. At least according to the stories I'd heard.

I didn't know how much of that nostalgic bullshit was true, but it always came in handy when I needed to connect with a jury. Look at me, ladies and gentlemen. I'm just a common man in search of justice. Like Honest Abe, I came from nothing. What a crock.

I had more success tossing the stub of my cigarette through the open window than I had with the ash. I pulled in a deep lungful of country air. There is nothing more soothing than the scents of evergreen and lake water. I swear the aromas are just as powerful now as when I was a boy.

I had spent as much time here with Jason as possible. Quality time, as far away from the stodgy, three-piece-suited confines of the courtroom as I could get. Taught him to fish here. Took him hunting in the fall. But like everything good in life, there's never enough time. They grow up too fast. Yeah, I know, another cliché, but it's true.

Jason's in college now. A senior. Bright kid. But I worry he won't want to spend as much time with old dad as he once did. Fuck you very much, Harry Chapin.

I would give damn near anything to keep Jason from turning out like me. Yeah, I know. Following in those footsteps is just a part of life. And completely out of my control. I guess that's what pisses me off so much. I'm a bit of a controller by nature. In the courtroom, at home, even in bed. At least according to my ex-wife. Though my secretary has yet to complain. That's why I drink. To let my guard down. Yeah, I drink too much on occasion. I'll admit it. But there's something reassuring about alcohol. The clink of ice, the warmth, the buzz. And haven't I earned it?

"What's with the high beams, buddy?"

Oops. Wrong side of the road again. I heard the X5's tires squeal as I swerved back into my lane. The oncoming driver laid on his horn as he passed.

"Jerk," I shouted, vaguely aware that I had begun to slur my words. "I've got to get this thing serviced, officer," I said. "She pulls a little to the left. I'll call the garage on Monday."

I smiled as I passed the painted boulder. The roadside attraction upon which every graduating class made their mark each spring. The big rock is exactly five miles from Chez Lennox. I know this because Jason had me check the mileage. During summer months Jason religiously ran the ten-mile loop to stay in shape for football season.

When it came to sports, Jason inherited his mother's genes. There isn't an athletic bone in my body. The only thing I've ever kept in shape is my liver. And I'm not quite sure what shape that is.

What a week. The case hadn't gone as I'd expected. I spent the entire trial following my tried-and-true playbook, slowly and methodically tearing apart each of the prosecution's best witnesses. Today's plan had been to drive a stake through the prosecution's heart by putting my go-to high-dollar expert on the stand. I figured one of two things would happen. Either my witness would hit one out of the park, allowing me to move to have the case tossed, or his testimony would be the last thing the jury heard before breaking for the weekend, effectively casting doubt over the state's entire case. But neither scenario happened. Instead, my so-called expert's credibility was shredded on cross examination by the prosecutor. The district attorney's investigator had uncovered something damning in my expert's past that I had not. No, I'm not going to go into detail on what it was. Let's just say the finding called into question my guy's qualifications, effectively erasing everything he had testified to. I wasted ten grand on that asshole. Granted, it wasn't my money, but still, it irks me.

My client will be found guilty next week. C'est la vie.

The fresh air wasn't cutting it any longer. My eyelids were growing heavy again. I switched on the stereo. Talk radio blared from the speakers.

"Nope, nope," I said. "I've heard enough blathering for one week."

I punched one of the preset FM stations. Keith Richards's trademark guitar reverberated throughout the SUV. The Stones were halfway through "She's So Cold."

"Perfect," I said, doing my best Charlie Watts impression atop the steering wheel.

My eyes returned to the road as I entered a blind right-hand curve. I caught a weird flash of light as the Beemer's headlamps reflected off the eye and earthen coat of a large buck standing astride the center line.

I stood on the brake pedal and jerked the wheel hard to the right. My eyes fixated on the animal as I passed by close enough to touch him. The passenger tires dropped off the pavement onto the soft gravel of the shoulder. I felt a jolt, then heard the sickening thump of metal on bone. A dark shape flew up and over the right side of the hood. I overcorrected, this time jerking the wheel to the left. The SUV bounced up onto the pavement and across the road, coming to rest perpendicular to the ditch.

Fully awake now, I sat there shaking. I took several deep breaths as I struggled to replay the last few seconds of my life. My right foot was still jammed hard against the brake pedal. My hands still gripped the wheel. The Stones still blared from the speakers. And the windshield wipers bounced back and forth across dry glass.

"Holy shit," I said.

I switched off the stereo and wipers, though I had no idea how the windshield wipers had activated. I looked up and down the roadway. No vehicles were approaching from either direction. For now.

The X5 had stalled. I could tell because all the dashboard idiot lights were illuminated. I remember giggling at how apropos it was.

A single beam of light lit the woods directly in front of me. The accident must have damaged one of the headlamps, I surmised. I stepped from the vehicle and looked back in the direction of the collision. The buck was long gone. And there was no sign of the deer

I'd struck. I knew they traveled in herds, often crossing the road one after the other. How many times had I warned my ex about that?

"Where there's one deer there's bound to be others," I'd say. "Be especially careful driving at night, honey."

A lot of good that sage advice had done me. Idiot.

I walked to the front of the Beemer to survey the damage. The grill was busted, along with the right headlamp and marker light. I sighed and bent down for a closer look. There was also considerable damage to the hood and right front fender.

"Dammit."

My hands were trembling as I removed the cell phone from my suit coat. I swiped open the home screen and was about to call for assistance when it hit me.

What are you doing, Sam? You're intoxicated, man. You can't call the cops. Do you really want to lose your license over a dead goddamned deer?

I most certainly did not. I knew I would have to file a police report for the insurance claim, but that could wait until morning. After I sobered up and showered.

I slid the phone back into my pocket, then returned to the open driver's door. I paused a moment and took a long look back up the road. Nothing. The deer I'd hit was either lying dead in the ditch or had dragged itself off into the woods to die. Good riddance. The little hoofed bastard got what he deserved.

I climbed back inside the SUV, then pushed the keyless ignition. Nothing happened. I began to panic. The longer I sat here the more likely it was someone would come along and find me. And they *would* phone the police.

"Think, Sam the Man," I said. "Slow down and think. Why won't she start?"

My muddled brain struggled to work through the problem.

"It stalled because I had an accident," I said. "No shit, Sherlock."

I looked down at the transmission lever. It was still in drive. I depressed the brake pedal, slid the lever back into park, and pressed the ignition. This time the engine fired up and ran smoothly. I shifted into reverse then swung around until I was headed in the right direction. I took one last look behind me, then drove slowly to the lake house.

I awoke the next morning disoriented, and sporting one whopper of a headache. I had fallen asleep on the living room couch, still attired in yesterday's clothing. Someone was rapping on the front door.

*Who could that be?* I wondered. Aside from my secretary, no one else knew I was at the lake. My ex couldn't care less, and Jason was away at college. As I struggled to stand, the previous night's exploits came rushing back. The tavern, the deer, the accident, and me leaving the scene.

I located my suit coat lying on the floor under the coffee table. I bent over to retrieve it, nearly dying in the process. My head felt like it might explode. I searched the pockets until I located my cell. Dead. Great.

More knocking from the front door.

With one foot still soundly asleep, I limped to the window then peeked outside. My view of the front door was obstructed by a row of boxwoods, but I could clearly see my Beemer parked at an odd angle in the driveway. Directly behind it was a black and white police interceptor.

Shit. Had they traced the accident back to me already? How? I'd been all alone out there. Nobody saw me. Then a thought occurred to me. Had I left some damning piece of evidence behind? Part of the Beemer? An idiot light flashed inside my head.

More knocking. I was going to have to deal with this. Perhaps I could muster up some of that Lennox charm that always played so well inside the courtroom. At least it had until this past week. There was no charming your way out of a shitty expert witness. What was done was done.

The knocking came again, louder, more insistent.

Focus, Sam.

I moved toward the entryway while rubbing sleep from my eyes. I knew hope wasn't a plan, but I was sure hoping I looked better than I felt. The disheveled man staring back at me in the front hall mirror looked like he was on a bender. My eyes were bright red, my shirt tails hung loose, and my necktie was askew. I leaned in closer. Was that dried blood on my forehead? Jesus, Sam.

I quickly retucked my shirt and straightened the tie. I combed my hair with my fingers, then wet my thumb and used it to scrub the blood off my face. I took one last look in the mirror. It would have to do.

I painted on my most confident smile and opened the door.

"Good morning," I croaked. After clearing my throat I tried again. "What can I do for you, officer?"

The uniformed cop was much too grim-faced for my liking. I was familiar with the whole good cop bad cop thing, and this guy was definitely the latter. My phony smile faltered.

"Samuel Lennox?" the cop said.

"The one and only," I said, attempting to project a confidence I didn't remotely feel. My eyes traveled past the cop to the Beemer's damaged front end. It looked even worse by the light of day. And there was no way Columbo here could have missed it. Time to change tactics.

"If this is about last night, officer, I didn't call because my cell was dead." The lie slipped smoothly off my tongue.

"Last night?" the cop said.

"I hit a deer," I said, gesturing toward my SUV. "On my way up here last night."

The cop turned to look at the Beemer.

"That is why you're here, isn't it?" I said.

The cop turned to face me again. "No, sir. It isn't."

Something about his expression had clearly changed. Hardened. Was it suspicion? I couldn't be sure.

"Then why are you here?" I said, pissed at myself for even mentioning the accident. A rookie mistake.

"I'm afraid I have some rather unpleasant news, Mr. Lennox. It might be better if we spoke inside."

The oldest trick in the police arsenal. Get me to invite him inside to have a look around, effectively skirting my fourth amendment rights. Nice try, Dudley Do Right.

My inner lawyer kicked in. "Whatever it is, we can discuss out here."

"All right, Mr. Lennox. I'm sorry to have to tell you this, but your son was involved in an accident last night."

"Jason? An accident? What happened?"

"He was struck by a motor vehicle."

"At the college?"

"No, sir. Only a few miles from here."

"What?" I felt like I'd been sucker-punched.

"We're still investigating, but I can tell you he was found lying on the side of the road by a passing motorist."

Time slowed. The cop's words took on an odd tone as if they were coming from somewhere distant. My legs buckled and I grabbed hold of the doorframe to keep from collapsing.

"Do you need to sit down?" he said as he reached out to steady me.

"I'm fine," I snapped, shaking off his helping hand. "There must be some mistake. My son's away at college."

The cop continued. "Your wife told me that he left college early yesterday afternoon. Jason was hitchhiking up here to surprise you."

"Ex-wife?" I said absently, the words no longer sounding like mine.

"She's on her way to the hospital now."

My legs gave out and I sat down hard on the entryway floor. My watering eyes wandered back to the Beemer. Was that dried blood on the windshield?

"How bad is he, my son?"

"I'm afraid he didn't survive, Mr. Lennox." ❖

# Major Deception

---

## Frances Stratford

### Boston, 1733

Hannah Turner, a sometime harlot and pickpocket, walked through the crowd, eyes lowered, following the black boots of her British parole officer, Major Molineux. The two were jostled as they pushed their way inside the Boston courthouse. The lobby was full of drunks, smugglers, and whores. Nothing unusual for a Tuesday morning.

"Do not worry, Hannah," the major said. He was a large and majestic person, with strong, square features that spoke of a steady soul. "You are a good subject to His Majesty."

"Unlike my missing parolee, Marie—and those scoundrels." Colonel Wood, their companion on this muddy April morning, gestured with his beringed hand to a group of men hauled in for various offenses against the crown.

One of the men was Jacob Collins, the bawd of Hannah's friend, Marie Beauharnais. Jacob sneered at the British officers and nudged his friends. He read aloud from a newspaper as they passed.

"On molasses there shall be raised, levied, collected, and paid—a tax to His Majesty—" Jacob spit just beyond the colonel's boots.

His mate, shackled next to him, grabbed the paper and continued, "upon all rum or spirits of manufacture outside of any of the colonies or plantations in America, the sum of *five shillings*, money to Great Britain—"

"What are they reading, sir?" Five shillings was real money to Hannah—and she was a good pickpocket if indifferent whore.

"They are reading the new Molasses Act. And well they should! These men are accused of smuggling sugar from the French Indies. The colonies must purchase their molasses from British territories only now."

"Boston has too many newspapers! Nearly as many as in London!" The colonel grabbed the *Boston Gazette* from Jacob's friend and rapped him on the face with it.

"You are here as a King's Passenger and under his protection. All will be well if you behave and appear for your regular parole hearings," the major reassured her.

Hannah was grateful that Major Molineux explained things in such a way. He was so different from Colonel Wood, though they looked much the same. Both had the regulation build of soldiers, tall with strong arms, wide shoulders, pristine uniforms, and silvery wigs that shimmered like halos. But Colonel Wood strutted in front of Hannah and the major, flashing his round regimental ring, and brandishing his gold-tipped cane, more royalist than the king. Hannah supposed that he behaved that way because Colonel Wood was one of the King's Grenadiers and Major Molineux's superior. Yet both men were responsible for upholding colonial laws and the good behavior of the parolees transported from around the world to Boston. At least that's how Hannah understood it.

Colonel Wood turned and looked Hannah up and down coldly. "That red petticoat is a giveaway of your trade. You'll be locked up before long, girl."

He strode upstairs, his walking stick pounding the treads.

Hannah sighed. The major patted her hand. "If I get promoted, Colonel Wood will move to another post."

"Truly?"

"Indeed. I can help you more when I get promoted—and the more obedient the parolee, the faster British officers get promotions."

"Oyez! Oyez! Court will now come to order!"

The magistrate, a fat man whose white surplice accentuated his chins, called the first case. "Jacob Collins, accused of violating the Molasses Act."

Since there was never a jury at the trials of the poor, the king's magistrate asked many questions of Jacob and his friends that Hannah could not follow. Hannah kept her head down and remembered what her aunt Abigail had told her. "We are the bottom, mashed into the gutter, by the weight of the crown's laws. Survive as best you can, my girl."

In the end, not enough could be proved that the men broke the Molasses Act as the street warden said he could not identify whom he saw moving the suspect barrels.

The men were about to go free when Colonel Wood objected. "Jacob Collins is clearly drunk now—wherever the sugar for his rum came from. He deserves punishment! Tar and feather him as a warning to others who break the public drunkenness laws."

The magistrate shook his head. "Tarring and feathering is colonial mob justice. But the law must be upheld." He banged his gavel. "Twelve hours in the stocks."

Jacob and his gang roared with laughter. From what her friend Marie had confided to Hannah, today would not be Jacob's first day in the stocks for offenses against the crown. The weather was fair and friends from the Duke's Head tavern would bring the men food and drink. They would make a holiday of it.

The bailiff then called Hannah's case. "Hannah Turner, late of Pissing Alley, transported as a King's Passenger to serve a term of fourteen years for stealing and whoring."

Before the major could speak, Colonel Wood sneered. "You see this King's Passenger still wears the scarlet petticoat of her trade, your honor."

Major Molineux cleared his throat. "Your honor, I am responsible for many of the King's Passengers here in Boston. I can assure you that Hannah Turner works for Mistress Nelson, a lace maker on King's Street. She needs only time to save her wages and make herself clothes more in line with His Majesty's greatness in sparing her life."

Hannah looked at the major, her eyes full of gratitude at his kindness. This new world would be much harder without him. The judge looked over the parole papers, announced all was in order, and called the next case.

The bailiff summoned. "Marie Beauharnais, appear before the court!" When she did not, Colonel Wood denounced her as a convict who broke her parole. He called for the street wardens to search the city for her.

Hannah was afraid for her friend.

She and Marie had shared a lodging since Hannah arrived from England the past month. Marie, tiny and warmhearted, had shown her the streets and alleys of the city. Mistress Nelson, the owner of the lace-making shop, paid them infrequently and they were often hungry. Just last night, Marie gave Hannah their last heel of bread, which she had stolen from an absent-minded baker on Mackerell Lane.

If Colonel Wood and the street wardens found Marie, there was no telling the trouble she would find.

With effort, Hannah stood quietly beside Major Molineux until the proceedings ended. The wardens tried to push Jacob to the stocks on the green outside and the major collected her parole documents from the judge.

"Perfect as always, Major. Disobedient parolees like Mistress Beauharnais are a black mark for their supervising officer."

"Indeed."

"You and Colonel Wood must be vigilant—especially now. The king is most anxious about the Molasses Act. It will go badly for both of you if we cannot stop the smuggling."

"I am doing everything possible," Major Molineux assured him with a smile.

The judge nodded, his chins wobbling. "London will soon look favorably on your work with His Majesty's 'disobedient children' as he calls them. There is a promotion for you, I have no doubt."

The major clicked his heels and offered his arm to Hannah as they walked down the stairs. Outside Hannah smelled the briny harbor and watched seagulls pick the crumbs of discarded *olykoeks*, fried bread mixed with cinnamon.

He said, "It's a good thing my nephew missed his ferry last night. I could spend more time on your parole paper work. The magistrate's praise will stand us both in good stead—"

A brawl between Jacob and the bailiffs interrupted him. It took three officers to get the wood stocks clamped over Jacob's shoulders. In retaliation, his friends threw rotten apples, spattering the soldiers' uniforms.

"You'll see!" Jacob yelled. "You can't push us around forever!"

*Truly, Jacob Collins is a dangerous fool*, Hannah thought.

Hannah bit her lip and glanced between the stocks and Major Molineux. "I need to speak to Jacob. He may know where my fellow Passenger Marie Beauharnais is."

Major Molineux looked at her, seeming to debate something. The balmy April sun caught the concern in his eyes as it skimmed across the comforting crags of his face. He patted her hand. The warmth of the gesture made Hannah's heart constrict. Who could she have been if she had a father like the major?

Not a convicted thief transported across the sea to the colonies, that's for sure.

"Do not tarry, my girl. It will go badly for both of us if Colonel Wood sees you not at your needlework."

Hannah dipped a quick curtsy and kissed the major's hand. The raised gold engraving of his Prince of Wales regimental ring stirred the thief in her. The three finely etched feathers reminded her of the time her aunt Abigail took her to wave as the Prince of Wales's carriage trotted down Ludgate to St. Paul's. It would be so easy to take the major's hand, circle her hand around his, and palm his expensive ring.

Hannah pushed the impulse down and walked over to Jacob now secured in the stocks. "Marie did not come home last night."

Jacob turned as much as he could with his neck clamped, and squinted into the sun. He was an ugly man. His forehead bulged out into a double prominence, with a divide between. His nose jutted in an irregular curve, and its bridge was thick as a finger.

"Perhaps she acquired good custom—a man with his own lodging like that fancy barber on Marlborough Street. She'll turn up."

Hannah knew Jacob was counting the coin that would come to him as Marie's bawd if the barber's wife was from home. She would find no help from him and made to leave.

"Hannah!"

Hannah turned. "Yes?"

"Marie likes you—though I hate all Loyalists who are half in love with Lobsterbacks!"

Hannah flushed. "Major Molineux is a good man who—"

Jacob snorted. "Major Molineux is using you for his own gain. 'I can help you more when I get promoted.' Listen, girl—that's all he cares for. He and Colonel Wood would hang us all if it gets them another stripe on their uniforms."

Jacob's friends whooped in agreement.

"He's not like that!" Hannah shouted. Jacob was a huge man, but she had known harder pimps and was not afraid.

"Oi!" Jacob imitated her east London accent. "And 'ow is he?"

The crowd on the green loitered to see what would happen when a whore argued with a smuggler. Then, as she struggled to think of a way to make Jacob Collins understand, it all rushed back to her; the rainy October day she'd slipped a customer's watch out of his pocket and made off into the dark of Pissing Alley. When the street warden caught her, she'd narrowly escaped capital punishment for theft. Instead, because she was young and likely to bear more crown subjects, the judge sentenced her to transportation to Boston.

Hannah was grateful that the king's laws had spared her life. A few months before her arrest, her old aunt Abigail had stolen a lady's fan worth two pounds and was hanged.

Standing in the April sunshine Hannah knew that, without King George's clemency, she would not feel the cool harbor breeze and smell the coming spring after last night's rain.

"The major wants me out of trouble. You, Jacob Collins, are a dangerous man! You forget the loyalty we owe His majesty—wherever we are in the Empire. I stole to live! You go forth in open rebellion against the crown!"

More than a few onlookers murmured in agreement. Jacob's friends made a collective "Ooo!" and nudged each other.

Jacob wagged his fingers. "Come close, Hannah. I've got something to tell you."

Hannah hesitated, afraid he would wrench her hair or worse. But she did not want to lose face before the crowd, so she leaned in. Jacob whispered with his rum-soaked breath, "One day you'll join us in our struggle."

"Not kneeing Colonel Wood in the groin is my *constant* struggle!" One of Jacob's friends guffawed. The whole lot roared with laughter.

There was naught else to be done and Hannah stomped up King's Street. She must find Marie. Perhaps if she went to the lace-maker's shop. Hannah was heading at such a speed she bumped into Thomas Adams, the minister at the Old Church on Cornhill.

"Good morrow, Mistress Turner."

Hannah blushed. She always felt tongue-tied around the clergy—as if they knew how she made her living.

"Good Morrow, Reverend Adams." She made to push past. "I must get to Mistress Nelson's shop. She's expecting me."

He stopped her. "I was just looking for you. The street warden has found Marie Beauharnais. She's been beaten almost to death."

Hannah gasped.

"We've taken her to your lodgings. Come."

Hannah and the reverend wound their way up the narrow stairs to her third-floor garret. There she saw Marie. Her pretty face was nearly unrecognizable. Her eyes were puffed shut, her nose broken, and blood soaked her cheerful green gown. As Hannah dropped to her knees beside the bed, she saw angry red lines around Marie's throat.

"Where did you find her?" she asked the warden.

"Just below Bull Wharf."

That was near the pier and not Marie's usual haunt for customers.

"Whoever did this left her for dead. I don't know how she's still breathing," the warden said as he closed the door.

The reverend sighed. "I'll send a doctor, though there may be little he can do."

Hannah thought of her empty purse. "We've no money."

The reverend nodded sadly. "Then I'll pray for her, my girl."

"She's Catholic," Hannah whispered, afraid of what the minister would think. Truly, until she was transported, Hannah had never met a Catholic.

"No need to keep that a secret from me, dear girl." The reverend smiled. "I've met many a Catholic, Lutheran, even a few atheists. Why, my friends among the Mashpee give reverence to the earth each day. We are all God's creatures."

Hannah did not know how she felt about God, but she knew Marie feared stealing and thieving would damn her to hell. She told the reverend so.

"What any of us are is God's gift to us. What we become is our gift to God."

With that, he was gone.

The tavern keeper sent up warm water and some rags. Hannah washed the dirt and blood from Marie's bruised face and hands. In the dried blood matted along Marie's sleeve, she found a glistening tuft of silver wig hair. The events that led to Marie's beating were clear. To pay for their food and lodging Marie probably refused to give Jacob the pennies from her time with the wig maker. Jacob then beat her to get the money.

Hannah washed the hair off and pocketed it, intending to substitute it for silver thread at the lace makers. She could pawn the thread for a few pence at least.

*For all the king's mercy, my life is no different than before,* Hannah thought. She walked to the broken casement window, looked outside at the alley, shadowy even at midafternoon, and wept.

As the late afternoon sun pinked the sky, a plump, cheerful midwife bustled up the stairs. "I'm the midwife for the parish. Major Molineux sent me." She took off her cap and shook her frizzy curls. "He heard from Reverend Adams about the poor girl."

*Thank goodness for the major,* Hannah thought. "Oh, Madam! She's not spoken at all. Her breathing may be worse."

The midwife took an earpiece from her bag and pressed it to Marie's chest. Gently, she turned Marie's face and tisked. "She was beaten early last night. See how her bruising is changing from red to purple?"

Hannah nodded. Marie's bruising was much darker. "Will she live? She's my only friend in the world." Saying it out loud brought fresh tears. Her old friends in London, Aunt Abigail's toothless grin, the ins and outs of Pissing Alley, were all gone.

The midwife drew Hannah into an embrace. "Well, if we are lucky—"

Both women heard the stomping of boots on the rickety stairs and drew apart. Hannah curtsied to Major Molineux as he loomed large in the doorway. The midwife glanced toward Marie in the bed.

"Good evening." The major removed his hat. "How fares Mistress Beauharnais?"

"It is most sad, major. She will not last the night," the midwife replied quickly.

"She has not spoken to the warden about who has done this?"

"Not a word," Hannah answered miserably.

"And she is not like to," the midwife added.

The major stroked his chin, the impressive golden glint of his Prince of Wales regimental ring visible even in the dark. "You know her well, Mistress Turner. Who could have done such a thing to her?"

"I believe it was Jacob Collins."

"He's a very angry man," the major conceded.

"Will someone arrest him?" Hannah felt her tears threaten again.

Major Molineux looked at both women, his face grim. "I have spoken to Colonel Wood. He believes Marie continues to night walk. As you know, Mistress Turner, the more obedient the parolee, the faster British officers get promotions. Marie broke her parole. That would go badly for Colonel Wood. But if she were to die . . . "

Hannah gasped. Marie would find no justice from the man most responsible for her well-being. "We are mashed into the gutter, by the weight of the crown's laws."

The tiny room suddenly became stifling. "I must go."

"I'll stay with her, child," the midwife said. "Go."

The major followed Hannah down the twisting stairs. He caught her by the hand as she was about to spring down Leverett Street. "Where are you going?"

"To see Jacob Collins."

The major shook his head. His blue eyes held Hannah's as if he wanted her to reconsider. Finally, he said, "He's still in the stocks on the green."

Jacob Collins was sunburned from his day in the stocks. He and his mates were where Hannah left them early that morning—muttering and laughing. Some officers tried to get the men to disperse. They were met with a caress of a flintlock and snickering. "You better trudge, Lobsterbacks. People have the right to assemble peaceably."

The king's officers retreated.

The sight of the men laughing increased Hannah's rage. Back home in Pissing Alley she would have rung a peal over them and not been afraid to do so.

Well, she was a colonial now and would not shrink from this fight. She walked up to Jacob and slapped him.

Jacob shook his head and yelped so loudly a country boy loitering nearby jumped and ran from the green.

"What nonsense is this?" one of his friends asked.

"You have murdered my only friend!" Hannah spat.

Jacob's co-conspirators circled around. "What say you?"

"Marie was beaten near to death. She'll breathe her last tonight most like. You did this, Jacob Collins, when she would not share her night's takings with you! I may only be a King's Passenger, but I will denounce you to the magistrates!" Colonel Wood did not care, but Hannah would beg Major Molineux to speak for her.

Jacob shook the stocks around his shoulders. "No!" he roared.

Hannah would not back down. "You were both out last night! Who else would have done this?"

In the fading light, Hannah saw Jacob's face collapse. The men looked at each other furtively. "Should we—?"

Jacob exhaled like a bull. "Tell her."

"He could not have done this horrible thing. He was with us . . . working."

"You lie! You'd say anything to spare his miserable neck!" Hannah's blood boiled.

"Colonel Wood was right. We were running molasses last night. We spent the night moving barrels and hiding them in a cellar on Charter Street. That's where the warden saw us."

"I don't believe you," Hannah spat.

Another man wrenched one of Jacob's hands forward. "See! He's full of oak splinters. Those slavers in Martinique don't know how to crum a barrel stave!"

Hannah looked at Jacob's hands. Even his calluses were ripped open.

She dropped down onto the foot of the stocks, trembling. "Then, what was she doing at Bull Wharf last night?"

"I sent her there." Jacob groaned. "She meets the Frenchie who arranges the shipments of molasses we smuggle. She's the only one who can talk to him."

Hannah bit her lip. "Marie told me she was going to see if the barber's wife returned from Concord. If not . . ."

The group was silent. After a moment, Jacob asked, "Has she said nothing?"

"No."

"Did anyone see anything?" one man asked.

"No."

"Did you find anything on her person?" another asked.

Hannah touched the wig hair in her pocket. "This was in the cuff of her sleeve." The men gathered close.

"A Ramillies wig," one declared.

"The barber did this." Jacob's rage contorted his ugly, split face. "He's her best customer."

Hannah left Jacob and his accomplices and marched up School Street to the corner of Marlborough Street where Nathaniel Thorne had his barbershop. It was a fashionable place that catered to the good and great of the city. Even this late in the evening, the place was brightly lit and bustling.

Nathaniel Thorne was busy powdering a small, three-rowed periwig with lavender. "Mistress Turner." The man flicked his tongue nervously. "What brings you here?"

*In for a penny, in for a pound.* Hannah straightened her skirt, hid her red petticoat as best she could, and swallowed hard. "Mister Thorne, did you see Marie Beauharnais last night?"

A customer overheard and harumphed. "Indeed! Nathaniel, do you let this bit of muslin into your shop? I thought this was a respectable establishment!"

Mistress Thorne, the larger of the couple, stopped twining a lustrous blue velvet ribbon through the lady's hair. "Mistress Turner! Are you accusing my Nathaniel of *whoring*?"

"My friend Marie," Hannah stammered, wishing some of Jacob's friends had come with her. "Did you walk out with her last night?"

The customer gasped.

Mistress Thorne raged. "I'll have you know my husband was with me all night!"

The sadness in Mr. Thorne's eyes let Hannah know his wife spoke the truth. But that did not explain the tuft of wig hairs in Marie's blood-soaked sleeve. It looked as if it came from the wig the little barber was in the process of dressing.

Hannah thought quickly. She pulled the hair from her apron. "Can you tell me anything about this? Marie was badly beaten last night, and I found it in her sleeve."

"It is no more than she deserves!" the customer declared.

Mr. Thorne's eyes widened. "Marie was beaten?" he whispered.

"Whoever did so left her to die."

Mr. Thorne took the hair to a lantern burning beside the wig stand. He examined the silvery strands in the light. "This is human hair," he said.

"So?"

"All colonial wig makers must use animal hair." He handed the tuft back to Hannah.

"Then, where did this come from?"

"They only make this wig in Glasgow. Another British monopoly—like the sale of molasses."

Hannah was confused.

"You are looking for a British officer. They are the only ones who can import such wigs."

Hannah left the shop in a daze.

She wandered down Queen's Street past the Old Church— which to a Londoner was not old at all. Queen's Street turned into King's Street, and she found herself home all the while thinking of Marie's parole officer Colonel Wood, his elaborate wig, and his thick walking stick.

*The Colonel did this—and he will get away with it.*

Hannah made to enter her rooming house and relieve the midwife at Marie's bedside when she was stopped by Mistress Nelson. The crown paid the lace maker a stipend to employ King's Passengers. Mistress Nelson did not willingly share that with the ladies who toiled in her shop.

"You did not come to work today, Hannah. Neither did Marie."

"She's been hurt very badly. I—"

"Bah! All you girls are the same, full of excuses. You will both work all day Saturday to make up for it. And I want my rent by tomorrow morning, or you'll find yourself on the street."

Mistress Nelson stormed off in a high dudgeon. Hannah looked up at the swaying Duke's Head sign above the tavern door. Her beloved aunt Abigail had swung from the scaffold at Tyburn and was buried in a pauper's grave; but Hannah was determined that Marie would pass in her own bed. Perhaps Harry Bailey, the innkeeper, could lend her some money to pay the lace maker.

She entered the tavern. There was a murmur of voices, the smell of bacon, and a fog of tobacco. The country boy who had run away from the green earlier was now the butt of some of the patrons' jokes.

"Harry, I must speak to you."

"Later, Hannah. If you care for Major Molineux, get that thick-witted lad from the Berkshires out of here. The crowd's hatred of Lobsterbacks may be visited on him if he does not leave."

The tavern keeper pushed them both toward the vestibule at the base of the stairs. Hannah looked at the boy and sized him up as a mark. He was a young, fit farmer from the wilds of the western mountains.

*Survive as best you can, my girl.*

It would not be the worst night's work she'd done.

"Come with me." She led him toward the dark space under the stairs.

He resisted. "Pretty mistress, will you be kind enough to tell me the whereabouts of my kinsman, Major Molineux?"

Hannah put on her most seductive voice. "Major Molineux dwells here."

He cocked his head. "Truly?"

Hannah wrapped her arms around him, running a hand up and down his spine, which she hoped would overcome the feeling of her other hand rifling the satchel at his side.

"Oh, yes. He spoke of you just today."

"He did?"

"Indeed, he said he was to meet you last night at the ferry."

"Not last night—"

Just then a watchman entered the vestibule. "Home, vagabond, home—or we'll set you in the stocks!"

The scared country boy was gone in a trice. It mattered not. Hannah had emptied his bag. A letter she could not read, a fine linen handkerchief, and five shillings. Hannah mounted the stairs quickly.

She relieved the midwife and gave her sixpence for her troubles. The lady was packing her bag when Jacob Collins burst through the door. He pushed both women aside and dropped to his knees beside Marie's bed.

He gently turned Marie's face. "She breathes," he cried with relief.

The midwife touched his shoulder. "Her breath is bubbly from the strangling. Her lungs are filled with water."

Hannah saw tears shimmer in Jacob's eyes. "What can we do for her?"

"Keep her head up. Turn her side to side every hour. It will help clear her lungs," the midwife said and left.

Jacob picked up Marie and gently rolled her. "I can see why you thought I did this," he snuffled. "A big man did this to her. It could not have been the little barber."

Hannah knelt beside Jacob. He tenderly pushed the hair from Marie's face. Both could see the purpling bruises. She ran her fingers gently across the marks. In the dim light of the room, one of the bruises had a distinctive shape, round with little bristles.

"Prince of Wales feathers," Hannah whispered.

Jacob traced the line with his thick fingers. "Doesn't Major Molineux have a Prince of Wales regimental ring?"

Hannah's jaw clenched. "Yes." She fumbled in her apron and passed the letter she had stolen to Jacob. "I took this from Major

Molineux's nephew. The major said the boy was expected last night. He said he was at the wharf waiting for his nephew—where the warden found Marie."

Jacob scanned the paper. "The letter says to meet the boy tonight."

"Then Major Molineux was at the wharf and saw Marie—talking to the French molasses runner."

*The more obedient the parolee, the faster we get promotions.*

Marie was one of the king's "disobedient children." Major Molineux thought to kill Marie, help Colonel Wood, and enforce the king's Molasses Act—as he promised the judge.

Jacob jumped up.

"Where are you going?"

"To do to Major Molineux what they wanted done to me—tar and feather! I will be revenged for what he has done to Marie!"

"Jacob!" Hannah clutched his arm.

He wrenched himself away. "Major Molineux nearly killed Marie to win favor with that tyrant in London! Bostonians must punish the king and his lackeys for this and all their other offenses! They give us judges dependent on the king's pleasure alone—and trials with no jury. They cut off our trade with the world. Tax us without consent—"

"Jacob—"

"Hannah, tonight Boston will punish the king for transporting us beyond the seas simply for surviving as best we can."

Hannah looked at Jacob's split face, half dark, half in the lamplight.

"Go," she whispered.

When the Old Church bell struck twelve, Marie began to stir.

"Am I in hell?"

Hannah brushed Marie's curls away from her brow, relieved to find it cool. "No, dear."

"I smell tar and fire." Marie clutched Hannah's hand. With the certainty of the damned she moaned. "This must be hell."

Hannah also smelled the tar and fire. And in the distance, on King's Street, she heard laughter and singing.

*Then join hand in hand, brave Americans all,*
*By uniting we stand, by dividing we fall. . . .*

"No, my friend, we're still in the king's Boston."

But she wondered how much longer it would be so. ❖

# Lost & Found

## Christine H. Chen

O n my way back from work, I stopped by the CVS on Lexington Street to grab some snacks for Friday evening. With two bags of jalapeño chips and Po-Po's favorite Flamin' Hot Cheetos in the passenger seat, I drove up the winding streets dotted by white pines and dogwood trees waiting to bloom as the early April cold lingered. As I was about to pull in the garage of our home, I stared at the sight that greeted me.

A man was slumped in front of my eighty-year-old grandma at the bottom of the stone stairs. Legs splayed, right arm sprawled on a step, his hand almost touching the leaves of our rhododendron.

"What the hell happened?" I shouted as I slammed the car door and rushed across the driveway.

"This *gwai-lo* hit me," Po-Po said, jabbing the man with her cane, "so I gave him a cane beating! See if he's breathing!"

"Do it!" Po-Po commanded when I still didn't move, couldn't even think of asking if Po-Po was okay, or why that man had hit her.

"All right, all right, stop poking him!"

I crouched and caught a whiff of a light, citrusy aftershave, which I found quite appealing. Caucasian, in his forties or fifties, hard to guess, fake blond with streaks of green. Something familiar about the face, the way the nose crooked to the left, but I couldn't be sure where I had seen it. Black overcoat, navy polo shirt, this man was well dressed, clean.

We lived on a quiet residential area in Waltham, both sides of our street lined with a mix of ranch style and two-floor garrison colonial houses. It was seven o'clock, our neighbors no doubt busy eating dinner or watching TV. I looked left and right to make sure no one was watching. I wiggled closer and reluctantly stuck a shaky index finger under his nostrils.

"Well?"

"Ugh, I don't know. I'm not a doctor!"

"You a chemist, close enough! Here, take this to Fat Man, the jeweler on Harrison Street in Chinatown," she said and shoved a hand to my rib. A molar crowned in gold with a red smear nestled in her palm.

I took some deep breaths, swallowed the sour taste rising from the back of my throat. I felt dizzy. I closed my eyes for a few seconds and hoped I was dreaming. But no, Po-Po in her blue shirt, black apron, white tennis shoes without socks was still stabbing me with her finger to take the bloody tooth. Having outlived both my parents, her will was uncrushable. Po-Po was my mother's mother, and had been living in Guangzhou before she found out that my granddad, Gong-Gong, had an affair with a half-bred Siberian-Chinese woman and hid his second family in Shenzhen, a city about an hour away, where he would visit on the pretense of checking his suppliers for his baby diaper business. Po-Po kicked him out, sold the apartment, ordered us to never speak or contact him again, and instructed my mother to move her to America, which my mother did, only for my mother to die a few years later of a broken heart after my father passed away from cardiac arrest in his sleep. I never saw Ma or Ba's dead bodies. Po-Po forbade it. Her way of dulling my pain, I suppose.

And here I was, standing in front of a stranger's corpse, trying to convince Po-Po to let me call the police.

"*Aya*, why make big deal? No police, I'm eighty, how hard could I have hit him? Don't think your Po-Po is dumb. I watch *CSI, Law & Order, Hawaii Five-O*, okay? I just *self-defense!*" She enunciated the English phrase. Po-Po spoke with a mix of Cantonese and mutilated English.

I told her, there was nothing to fear if it was self-defense. Our neighbors would make great character witnesses. They knew Po-Po, saw her practicing Tai Chi early in the morning, walking daily in the neighborhood, had eaten the egg tarts she made and distributed at Easter every year. Besides, who'd want to arrest an eighty-year-old woman? It'd be fine. Tonight, we could even make potstickers together as planned, munch on snacks, watch that cold case crime TV show we both liked. At eighty years old, Po-Po still insisted on preparing all the meals, stuffing my lunch pail with a variety of homemade leek buns, sauteed asparagus with shiitake mushrooms, fried rice, chicken drumsticks with ginger and soy sauce, the envy of all my colleagues in Cambridge where I worked as a research chemist in oncology.

"No, no police! This America! I defend my home! I can buy guns too!"

"What are you talking about? You're not buying a gun. I can't take that tooth. Jesus, did you rip it from that man's mouth? And why would a stranger hit you?"

I stepped around the body, lifted a corner of his coat with my foot to see if I could at least find a wallet, an ID in the interior pocket.

"Stop! No touch!"

Po-Po slid between me and the body. She could be fast as a cat when she wanted.

"And don't *Jesus-me!*" she declared. "What have you become? Just like your Ma said, acting like a spoiled *gwai*-girl, remember you're still Chinese. No respect for elders! You heard about Asian hate, no? Heard about old lady like me in San Francisco get hit by homeless man, no? He made fun of Chinese people *ni hao, hi hao*, I hit him back right away, his tooth fell. I should get something from him, he should pay me for insult!"

"What?"

"Just take it to Chinatown, I want twenty-five to sixty dollars for it; it's real gold. I know, I bit on it!"

Why was I even shocked. Po-Po had refused to wear a mask during the pandemic. *Natural immunity*, she'd said, slapping her chest when I pleaded with her. How could I have argued with her? She made up her own logic. She blamed my parents' deaths on everything *gwai-lo*, from the American stressful work life to eating hamburgers (we hardly ever had any) to colored dyes of M&Ms, sugared drinks (except that Po-Po was the one who loved snacking on Cheetos and spicy crackers) and a myriad of other things. I thought her constant nagging and demands for attention from my parents played a part in their premature deaths, though I would never utter such an opinion in front of her. She was, after all, the only close relative I had left.

But now, a more pressing matter: how were we going to deal with a dead body?

"You and I will move it to Mary's backyard! We drop him there, then it's a *cold case*! Like that show!"

Mary Grossman was a widow who lived across from us. Her backyard led to a woody area frequented by the neighborhood kids. Thoughts raced through my head. Maybe one of them would call the police, maybe the poor man just had a heart attack like Ba did. Mary had come over to help me break up the wall of ice left by the snowplow at the fringe of our driveway last winter. And we repay her by dumping a body near her house? How could the two of us move such a heavy body? How much sodium hydroxide do I need to dissolve flesh? Wait, how stupid would that be? I'd be the prime suspect. I had access to chemicals. What was Po-Po thinking! No matter how healthy and sturdy Po-Po was or however many push-ups I'd done in the past month at the gym, we weren't big or strong enough. But then, Po-Po set her cane on the handrails and as she started lifting the man's shoulders, the head let out a growl and the eyes blinked open!

  We both screamed.

The Waltham police and an ambulance came. The entire Trimount Ave was lit with blinking blue and red lights. Neighbors came out, gawping. We'd become the stars of the night. Po-Po crossed her arms and pretended not to understand any English when the police officer, a young man by the name of Rich Ramon, questioned her. She repeated her story. I translated. How she'd been getting ready for her evening walk when a man went up the stairs, insulted her, and she pushed him away with her cane, and he fell. The EMTs buckled the man onto a stretcher, and took him away. The man was still slurring *Tai-tai, Tai-tai* to Po-Po, who avoided eye contact.

I couldn't sleep that night, but at some point I must have dozed off because I woke up to hear Po-Po mumbling and opening the sliding door of her closet. I pushed the duvet off, got out of bed, and tiptoed from my bedroom to hers. I stood behind the door and listened. "Bastard, son of a bitch," she kept saying. I could hear her rummaging in the closet.

  Quietly, I tried her doorknob. It was locked. Po-Po was up to something. When Ah Ma was still alive, Po-Po never locked her door so she could call her on the phone from her bedroom to order Ma to bring her chrysanthemum tea or help her look for underwear. I tiptoed back to my bedroom where I kept copies of all the keys in the house in my nightstand drawer, went back to hers, stuck the key in, turned, and swung the door open.

"Okay, Po-Po, what's going on?"

She was so surprised she opened her mouth, couldn't utter a word, which in itself was even more shocking. Seated on her bed in her red and white cherry blossom cotton pajamas, her hair still neatly tied up in a bun, she was counting a stack of twenty-dollar bills, her brown leather suitcase by her side, opened.

"*Aya*, go back to sleep, none of your business!" she ordered in her most authoritative voice.

"Are you selling your prescription drugs or something, Po-Po? Selling opium maybe?"

"You silly girl, people have better drugs now, haven't you heard, and you a chemist?"

"That's enough, Po-Po! I know you've been lying. What is going on? Where did that money come from?"

As soon as I said it, I felt heat rising to my cheeks. Ah Ma would have slapped me if she heard me talk like this to Po-Po. But Po-Po just sighed. She put the bundle of twenty-dollar bills back in the suitcase. Po-Po had no money of her own and was living off my parents' inheritance, which wasn't much, while I covered the leftover mortgage and bills with my paycheck. It paid well to have a chemistry degree and work in pharma; it was competitive, long hours, no time to date, but I needed the money and future promotions.

"I know you lied. You told the police you were going for your evening walk, but you always go on your walk after dinner. You had your apron on, so you were doing kitchen prep. And you knew I was coming home late, so we hadn't had dinner. What really happened with that man?"

I walked over and seized the suitcase before Po-Po had a chance to stop me. Inside were Po-Po's silk *qi-paos* from eons ago kept in sealed plastic bags, her red lacquer jewelry box with mother-of-pearl motifs and jade, photo albums, a stack of ten twenties and three one-hundred-dollar bills. So about five hundred dollars in all. As I was shifting her things around while she protested, an envelope slipped from the pages of a photo album. I picked it up right when Po-Po tried to slap my hand away. I opened it and found a letter written in Chinese characters, which I couldn't read, but there was also a photo. I gasped.

The photo was the man I saw yesterday, the same one Po-Po accused of wanting to assault her. Now I understood why his face looked familiar. His nose, slightly crooked to the left was Gong-Gong's nose. The way Ah Ma told the story was that the woman Granddad had an affair with was a quarter Caucasian, had Russian blood, which made Po-Po even more upset, since she hated the Russians for the border conflicts that almost led to war in the 1960s.

I turned to Po-Po. "What's the meaning of all this?"

I wanted to hear Po-Po confess.

She blew out a big sigh.

"Well, you a smart woman, you must know already! That man is—Ah Gong's son. A bastard, not mine! Now that his second wife is dead, he wants me back. He sent his son, this, this half *gwai-lo*, half something else, his hair, I don't even know what beast he is—I say, you give me money you owe me, he say, let's talk *tai-tai*, I say okay. I make him tea, I grind sleeping pills, I say to him, you tell your bastard Ba he can die soon, he say he bring me money, I say I want more money, I want my life back, he drink tea, he fall asleep, I dump him outside like I kick your Ba, I push him outside, he fell, not my fault!"

As I listened to Po-Po's rant of butchered English peppered with Cantonese curses, I came to understand that Gong-Gong and his second wife had emigrated to San Francisco. When the second wife—Po-Po refused to acknowledge their marriage—died a year ago, he had asked his son, Tony Chung, to track us down. He'd then written that letter to Po-Po, to apologize, to try to mend things between them, and included a picture of his son. He asked about me. Po-Po demanded money for all the years he'd abandoned her and us. He sent his son—my step uncle, I suppose—and five hundred dollars to cajole Po-Po to move to California, and promised to put me in his will.

"That bastard is dead to me!"

"Which one?"

Po-Po glared at me. She was breathing hard, and I worried about her hypertension. I ran downstairs to the kitchen, made a chamomile infusion, and brought it to her.

"You do realize it has nothing to do with his son, right? God, what were you thinking? It's not his fault; he could charge you for assault! What were you trying to do, kill him?"

"I crazy, okay, mad like a cock, okay, when I saw him—he should have been my son!"

Po-Po teared up. I had never seen her cry. Not even at Ma's funeral. At least, maybe not in front of me. I held her hand and let her sob on my shoulder.

Ten days later after several conversations with Po-Po and Tony, the three of us finally sat down together at Grassfields Restaurant in the little shopping mall down the hill. Tony didn't press charges against Po-Po. He told the police it was all a misunderstanding, a private family matter, and persuaded the police to not bother Po-Po again. He even joked that he fell into Po-Po's arms like in a romantic movie when he fainted. I burst out laughing. Po-Po smirked. Tony looked quite handsome and cool with his hair dyed blond and green highlights that I had mistaken for a wig. Square jaw, twinkly eyes, there was definitely Gong-Gong in him as I remembered. And he was my uncle. A newfound relative. Po-Po pinched her lips.

"So, little niece," he said, turning to me while Po-Po pretended to be a stone statue. "What do you say? You think you can visit Gong-Gong in the summer?"

"Well—I can't really leave Po-Po alone you know—"

Po-Po cleared her throat.

"You just go, go, go! What do I need you here for?"

But I knew Po-Po didn't mean it. I gave her a gentle shove under the table. She sighed.

She pulled out the molar, carefully packaged in bathroom tissue, and gave it back to my uncle, who received it with both his hands like an offering from a goddess. ❖

# The Moon and Stars

## Carolyn Marie Wilkins

Dr. Horace Randolph, the president of Bay State Musical Institute, peered into the shattered glass display case, his mouth an *O* of astonishment.

"What the hell happened here?" he asked me.

I looked down at the floor and said nothing. The answer was obvious. The front of the display case in the archive room of the Institute library had been smashed. The contents of the case, a custom-made trumpet and mouthpiece once owned by the legendary jazz trumpeter Miles Davis was missing. Since I was the security guard on duty that night, Dr. Randolph was directing his ire at me.

"You were supposed to be keeping an eye on things, Ambrose," he said. "This instrument is irreplaceable. Do you realize what a catastrophe this is?"

I nodded grimly. How could I not realize? I was a trumpet player myself. I'd been one of the Institute's top students. Right up until the night my roommate and I were mugged at gunpoint on our way home from an after-hours jam session. I can still see the three teenagers across the street eyeing our backpacks and the expensive instruments as we passed. When they began walking toward us, I told Pete to run.

Pete Travis was a stubborn guy. "Hell no, Amby. You go ahead. I ain't runnin' from nobody."

I lit out down an alley and never looked back. Not even when I heard the gunshots that took Pete's life.

I was devastated. The way I figured it, Pete's death was all my fault. It had been my idea to go up to Mission Hill to jam, and my idea to walk home after we missed the last train of the night. That fall, I quit playing the trumpet and dropped out of school. Out of the kindness of his heart, Professor Taylor, my former trumpet teacher, persuaded Dr. Randolph to hire me as a security guard.

As I stood silently next to the empty display case, Dr. Randolph, Professor Taylor, and my former classmate Jet Sampson took turns inspecting the damage. Jet had become a star in the jazz trumpet firmament since his graduation five years ago. A strutting, chocolate-colored peacock of a man with manicured fingernails and a perpetual sneer, the man had never liked me.

"You always were a complete fuckup, Ambrose," he said, "but you've outdone yourself this time."

"It wasn't my fault," I said stubbornly. "The trumpet was in that case just two hours ago. I checked."

"Yeah, *right*," Jet shot back, his voice heavy with sarcasm.

Professor Taylor put a protective hand on my shoulder. "Easy does it, Jet," he said. "I'm sure Amby feels as bad about this theft as you do."

Professor Taylor had performed with some of the biggest names in jazz. A stocky bespectacled man with a salt and pepper Afro, he'd become a mentor to many successful trumpet players, including Jet Sampson.

"There's no need to fight with each other over this thing," he said gently. "Let's try to be civil about this."

Jet turned to Dr. Randolph and frowned. "I assume you've notified the police?"

"Of course," Dr. Randolph replied. The man was a college president right out of Central Casting—a tall and gray-haired white man with a beak nose and bushy eyebrows. During his time at the Institute, he'd perfected the smooth tone and calm demeanor needed to soothe donors and set worried parents at ease. "I notified the police myself this morning."

Jet shook his head in frustration. "The cops have got rapes and murders to solve. They are not going to do a damn thing about this and you know it," he said. "I still don't understand how this could have happened in the first place. Why didn't anyone hear the burglar alarm?"

Dr. Randolph sighed and spread his hands in apology. "The display case was not alarmed," he murmured. "We really didn't feel the need. Access to this part of the library is restricted to faculty and students. We never imagined there would be a need for elaborate security procedures."

"There's nothing *elaborate* about a burglar alarm," Jet snapped. "This is 1990, for Chrissake!" He shook his head, then pointed toward a small black box hanging from the ceiling. "What about the security camera?"

Dr. Randolph furrowed his brow and said nothing.

"Well?" Jet persisted. "Has anyone taken a look at the film?"

Professor Taylor gave Dr. Randolph a pointed look. "You want to tell him or shall I?" he said.

When Dr. Randolph remained silent, Professor Taylor continued. "That camera is just a dummy, Jet. It isn't hooked up to anything. Since the general public is not allowed back here, we figured the fake camera was all the deterrent we would need. That, and Amby making his rounds, keeping an eye on things."

"*Perfect.* No alarm, no camera, and this joke of a security guard in charge," Jet said bitterly. "I'm supposed to give a master class for the students at two o'clock. At eight, I'm taping a live show for PBS. What the hell am I supposed to do now?"

"Surely you have other trumpets?" Dr. Randolph said.

"That's not the point," Jet replied, waving his hand dismissively. "The show is all about how Miles revolutionized jazz. It's supposed to feature *this* trumpet. Miles Davis's blue trumpet with the moon, the stars, and his *name* engraved on the bell. *That's* what PBS is coming to film!"

I wanted desperately to leave the room, but didn't know how to do this without calling attention to myself. I was doing a good job of blending into the wallpaper when Jet Sampson whirled around to face me. "Dammit, Amby," he said. "This is all your fault."

In the awkward silence that followed, Dr. Randolph gave me a stern look. "You have been derelict in your duties, Ambrose. In light of what's happened, I'm going to have to let you go."

Although I should have seen this coming, Dr. Randolph's words hit me like a kick in the stomach.

"I wasn't goofing off last night," I said. "Honest I wasn't." I hated the whining tone in my voice, but I couldn't stop myself. This minimum-wage rent-a-cop gig wasn't much, but it was all I had—the last remnant of my former life. "What if I could get the trumpet back? I know it sounds crazy, but I believe I could find it."

"Amby Collins couldn't find his own ass with two hands and a flashlight," Jet muttered under his breath.

I ignored Jet's remark, trained my gaze on Dr. Randolph, and continued begging. "Odds are the thief is someone from the Institute, Dr. Randolph. I know these students. I know the faculty, and I know the local music scene. I could ask around, see if anyone's tried to sell it on the black market. I really think I can get this trumpet back. Can't I at least try?"

Dr. Randolph sighed, took a quick look at his watch, and nodded to himself. "All right, Ambrose. It is now 9:30 A.M. If you can get the Moon and Stars trumpet back here in time for Jet's concert tonight, I will forget this unfortunate incident. Otherwise, you will be fired. No ifs, ands, or buts."

I left the campus and trudged down Columbus Avenue. What the hell had I been thinking? I was a security guard, not some ghetto-fabulous Sherlock Holmes. However, I did know a few people—the kind of sketchy characters who might know something about a stolen trumpet. I could hit the streets, talk to a few folks, and see what I could dig up. Since none of my sources would be at their usual haunts before noon, I'd head home first, change out of my work uniform, and grab a bite to eat.

My landlady's door was open as I reached the second-floor landing. "That you, Amby?"

"Yes, ma'am."

"I thought so. Come on in and say hello."

My landlady, Sankofa Edwards, was a big woman, nearly six feet tall, and more formidable than most men. She kept her long braids wrapped in a bright blue head covering that matched the long African dress she wore. Entering her living room was like walking into a remote African jungle. Potted palms with leafy fronds lined the walls, while ferns hung from hooks over the bay window overlooking Rutland Street, blocking out most of the light. The narrow room smelled of soul food, flowers, frankincense, and the Florida Water cologne she sprinkled around her apartment to keep out negative spirits.

"I just made a fresh batch of cornbread. Let me fix you a plate. A young brother like you needs all the strength he can get. Wait right there. I'll just be a minute."

As Sankofa bustled about in the kitchen, I sank onto the battered living room couch and stared at the small black-and-white TV perched on a metal stand across from me. The volume was low, but loud enough to hear the pasty-faced and breathless commentator describe the ongoing investigation into yesterday's murder of a pregnant white woman in nearby Mission Hill. "The gunman who fired into their car at point blank range is reported to be a Black man in his early twenties," he intoned gravely. "We have just learned that Boston police will bring three squads of additional detectives into Mission Hill area to search for the killer."

Sankofa shook her head sadly as she slid a plate of hot cornbread onto the coffee table in front of me. "The cops are stopping every Black man they can get their hands on," she said. "Roughing up guys, sticking guns to their heads."

"What else is new?" I said glumly. "Times are always tough for Black folks in this neighborhood."

Sankofa studied me.

"Something's not right with you, Amby. I can feel it. Don't make me have to get out my Tarot cards to find out what it is."

I shook my head and sighed. "A valuable trumpet was stolen from the Institute last night." I told Sankofa what had happened; she listened in silence until I was done.

"You check the display case at the beginning of your shift?"

"Of course. Just like I always do. I checked it again halfway through, around 4:00 A.M. I make two full sweeps through the building every night. When I finished my shift the next morning, the trumpet was gone."

"Isn't the building kept locked at night?"

I nodded. "The only people with access are faculty and students, and even they have to leave the building at midnight."

Sankofa sipped her tea thoughtfully. "Someone could have been hiding in that library. They could have waited till the building closed and then taken the horn."

"If they'd been in the library all that time, you'd think I would have seen or heard something."

"Not if they knew your schedule, knew when you'd be making your rounds. Maybe some professional burglar has been casing the joint."

"Maybe. I've got a street-life friend who's been known to fence items from time to time. Soon as I finish breakfast and get changed, I'm going to talk to him, see if he's heard anything."

"You just keep digging, Amby. Dirty deeds done in the dark will always come to the light sooner or later. I'm going to light a candle and ask the spirits to open your roads and doors."

An hour later, I walked to Jack's Tavern, took a seat at the bar, and ordered a Michelob. I'd nearly finished my second beer when Hi-Hat Eddie Swift walked in and slid onto the bar stool next to me.

"Amby Collins," he said, nodding to the bartender to bring his usual vodka and tonic. "Long time no see."

Hi-Hat Eddie was a skinny guy with a deep brown complexion and a nervous tic in his right eye. In all the years I'd known him, I'd never seen him wear anything other than a lime green sports jacket and a pair of black leather pants. He was a mediocre drummer and poor-to-middling bandleader, but when it came to providing the highest quality coke, weed, or smack that money could buy, Hi-Hat Eddie was a master.

"My band is playing here from ten to midnight," he said. "Want to sit in?"

"I'm not playing much these days," I told him. "I came down here to ask you a favor."

"Well, well, *well*. Ain't that some shit. The high and mighty Amby Collins is asking *me* for a favor."

I turned away and stared moodily at the bottles of cheap liquor arrayed for sale behind the bar. When I'd been a cocky student on my way up, I'd played a few gigs with Hi-Hat Eddie's band. Everyone else in the group was a junkie of one kind or another. Apparently, having a substance abuse problem was a basic prerequisite for staying on Hi-Hat Eddie's payroll. Most of the guys were being paid in cocaine. When I demanded cold hard cash instead, Hi-Hat Eddie and I parted ways.

Though we hadn't spoken in months, I was desperate enough to hope he might be willing to help me. I pasted a shit-eating grin on my face.

"You're The Man in this neighborhood," I said, flattering him shamelessly. "You always know what's going on. An expensive trumpet was stolen from the Institute last night. They're offering a big reward for its safe return, no questions asked." I had no idea if the part about the reward was really true, but it sounded good. "If anybody in Boston knows what might have happened to this stolen trumpet, it's *you*. Have you heard anything?"

Hi-Hat Eddie shot me a pitying look. "You're talking about a dark blue trumpet engraved with the moon and stars with Miles's name written on the bell," he said, as if explaining the ABCs to a five-year-old. "The minute that trumpet shows up anywhere, everyone will know it's stolen. No self-respecting fence is gonna touch it, and no music dealer in his right mind is gonna buy it. The only guy with enough juice to handle something like this is Donny Byrnes."

"The mob boss?"

Hi-Hat Eddie nodded. "That's right. The guy's a big jazz fan. Hangs out in the clubs along Revere Beach. Gave me a hundred dollar tip the night my band played at the Seashore Club." He swallowed the last of his drink and looked at me thoughtfully. "Doesn't his son go to that jive-ass college of yours?"

I nodded slowly. Donny Byrnes, Jr., was about to graduate in the spring. The boy didn't have a lot of talent, but he was enthusiastic and worked hard, spending hours blowing long tones on his trumpet in a vain attempt to improve his thin, squeaky sound.

"The kid is nothing like his father," I said. "Far as I know, he's straight as an arrow. He's an excellent student. On the dean's list, if I'm not mistaken."

"The apple doesn't fall far from the tree," Hi-Hat replied with a wicked grin. "That boy is your thief. I'd stake money on it."

I said goodbye to Hi-Hat Eddie and headed back to campus. Donny Byrnes, Jr., wasn't much of a suspect, but he was all I had at the moment. Donny and I had always gotten along. On several occasions, I'd turned a blind eye when I found him practicing in the basement after closing time. The last time I caught him down there, I'd even given the kid a few tips to improve his breathing technique. Come to think of it, I'd spotted him hanging around the library archive a lot since the Moon and Stars trumpet arrived last week. I'd thought nothing of it at the time, but now, I couldn't help wondering. Was it possible Donny Jr. had been casing the joint?

When I returned to campus, I found a long line of students waiting to get into the auditorium. I asked a tiny Japanese girl with spiked pink hair and a ring in her nose what was going on. "The master class, of course," she said, looking at me as though I was the dumbest human on the planet. "Jet Sampson and Professor Taylor are going to talk about Miles Davis and then play a duet. They haven't played together since Jet was a student here five years ago. It's the Young Lion vs. the Old Master," she said with a grin. "Totally fuckin' rad."

I thanked the girl and pushed my way inside.

Donny Byrnes, Jr., was sure to be among the excited students milling around the auditorium. With any luck, I could take the boy aside and ask him a few questions. The boy's mobster father was known to be a jazz fan and a collector of fine things. The Moon and Stars trumpet would make a hell of a Christmas present for a guy like that.

The auditorium was packed. Students with guitars wrapped in soft black cases strapped to their backs jostled for space with students carrying hard cases containing trumpets and saxophones. Excited faculty members patrolled the crowd, trying to catch a glimpse of Jet Sampson before the show to remind him that they "knew him when," and, with poorly concealed envy, congratulate him on his meteoric success.

At exactly two o'clock, Dr. Randolph stepped out from the wings to the center of the stage. "It is my great honor and pleasure to present one of the Institute's most well-known graduates," he said. "He is the winner of the 1990 Downbeat Award for Best Trumpet Soloist. He's performed in Carnegie Hall, the Royal Albert Hall, and Jazz at Lincoln Center. His latest album *A Tribute to Miles Davis* has been nominated for a Grammy award. Please give a warm welcome to our very own Jet Sampson."

The assembled students, staff, and faculty leapt to their feet, shouting, clapping, and whistling in acclaim. One of their own had beaten the odds. One of their own had defied the pundits who said it couldn't be done, that you couldn't make a living playing jazz, that it was too low-budget, too intellectual a music to ever become popular. Jet Sampson was the walking exemplar of possibility, the one every student in the room could point to when he made the case to Mom and Dad that there *was* a value in going to music school after all. If Jet Sampson could become a success, why not one of them?

As Jet emerged from the wings, I spotted Donny Byrnes, Jr., sitting in the second row, his face glowing with excitement. Wild horses would not be able to drag that kid out of the auditorium now. I'd have to catch him as he was leaving the master class. I found a place to stand against the wall near the front of the stage where I could watch the show while keeping an eye on the boy.

"Due to circumstances beyond my control, I will not be playing Miles's Moon and Stars trumpet this afternoon," Jet told the crowd. "But I can still make some noise. I'm gonna play a tune I wrote called *The Ivy Tower*. It's about my time as a student here at the Institute. I've invited my old teacher, Professor Lewis Taylor, to play it with me. We haven't played together in years. Let's find out whether he's been keeping his chops up."

As the audience tittered nervously, I shook my head in disbelief. Professor Taylor had taught Jet everything he knew. He'd even gotten Jet his first gigs in New York City. It was beyond ridiculous, Jet dissing his old mentor like that.

After giving the audience a broad wink, Jet Sampson waved toward the wings. "Come on out here, Prof. Show the folks what ya got."

Professor Taylor's spine was ramrod straight as he walked onto the stage. His brown face was unsmiling as he nodded to Jet and bowed to the audience. "Let's do it," he said curtly.

Jet turned to face his backup band, four advanced students from the Institute selected for this honor by Dr. Randolph. When Jet snapped his fingers to indicate how fast the tune would be played, the students stared at him nervously. The speed Jet had indicated was a ruthless, take-no-prisoners breakneck tempo, one that would be out of reach of all but the most expert musicians.

As the band began the introduction, Jet and Professor Taylor picked up their horns and began to play. Jet's composition had a twisting, looping melody and intense, unexpected harmonies. It was meant to be performed at a fiendishly difficult tempo. Two minutes into the tune, the drummer broke a sweat, his round face twisted in intense concentration. The tiny Chinese pianist hunched over her instrument, drawing forth massive clusters of sound that punctuated Jet's frantic improvisation in all the right places.

After a lengthy and acrobatic solo, the musical equivalent of a man turning summersaults on a balance beam, Jet blew a final high C. Then, with a cocky grin, he nodded for Professor Taylor to play.

I felt a small twinge of sadness as Professor Taylor stepped up to the microphone. *Jet should have cut his former mentor some slack*, I thought. There was no way Professor Taylor was going to be able to follow that tour de force and Jet knew it. Taylor was a good musician, sure. He'd hung out with Miles Davis and played on John Coltrane's legendary *Africa Brass* album. To generations of aspiring trumpet players, Professor Taylor was a god. But Jet Sampson had just put on a pyrotechnic display— brilliant technique, flawlessly delivered with impeccable showmanship and flair. Jet was a man on the rise, the future of jazz. Professor Taylor, no matter how solid his achievements, was a man of the past. It had been nearly a decade since he'd been on the road with anyone significant.

I watched an eerie calm settle over the professor's face as he lifted his horn. What came out of his horn was a complete surprise. A rich, golden long note that seemed to float above the frenzied playing of the accompanying musicians and suspend itself over the audience like a cloud. The tone was deep and round and compelling in a way that made me hold my breath. To be honest, it was not Professor Taylor's usual sound at all. If I didn't know better, I would have said Miles Davis himself was playing. Where Jet had bombarded us with sheets of virtuosity, Professor Taylor's plaintive music caressed us, seduced us, and forced us to sit up and listen. On and on he blew, building a story that drew us all in—even Jet stood off to the side, listening in amazement to the dark, haunting tones that flowed out of Professor Taylor's horn. When he finally finished, the band wound the tune down, slowing the tempo until they fell silent. When the song ended, you could have heard a pin drop. Then the crowd leapt to its feet, shouting, clapping, and whistling in acclaim.

Professor Lewis Taylor, an enigmatic smile playing on his lips, held his horn in one hand as he took a bow. As he did so, the gold finish on the rim of his mouthpiece glinted in the spotlight. In all the years I'd known him, the professor had always used a silver mouthpiece. Maybe if I weren't a horn player myself I would have missed it. After all, I only saw it for a second, but that gold rim and the uncharacteristic warmth of his sound had got me thinking. Before I questioned Donny Byrnes, Jr., about the missing trumpet, I needed to speak with Professor Taylor.

I hurried backstage and found Professor Taylor putting his trumpet back in its case. "Nice solo," I said. "You had such a warm, plaintive sound. Richer and fuller than your usual tone. It felt like Miles himself was playing."

Professor Taylor smiled, then closed his case emphatically. "Yeah. Well. Miles Davis was a mentor to me, Amby."

"I know," I said softly. "That's why you took his trumpet, isn't it?"

"What the hell are you talking about?" Professor Taylor blustered. "Have you lost your natural mind?"

"It's no use. I *know*. To prove it, all I have to do is look at that mouthpiece you have in your pocket—the antique gold-plated Conn 5C with MD engraved on the cup. It's the same mouthpiece that was in the Moon and Stars trumpet when you took it."

"You must be on crack," Professor Taylor said, and backed away from me.

I shook my head. "I've been studying your music ever since I bought my first trumpet. I've memorized nearly every solo you ever recorded. You've *never* sounded the way you sounded tonight. Ever."

Professor Taylor turned pale as a ghost and looked at me with a foolish expression on his face. I could tell part of him still wanted to bluff his way out of the situation, but another part of him knew it was hopeless.

"You knew Jet would try to embarrass you tonight," I continued. "He wanted to make you look like a washed-up has-been. You just couldn't let that happen."

The professor looked at me for a long minute without speaking.

"Was it that obvious?" he said.

"Only to me," I replied. "When you stole that trumpet, you intended to keep it just for yourself, never let anyone know you had it, not even your family. But the mouthpiece that came with it? That was another matter. One mouthpiece looks just like another to most people. Who would even notice you'd switched the gold-plated one from the Moon and Stars trumpet for your regular silver one. Such a small thing. A minor substitution with a major effect on your confidence level. Using the mouthpiece Miles had played with was like channeling the man himself through your horn. You just couldn't resist the chance to show Jet Sampson and everybody else at the Institute what you were capable of."

Professor Taylor's shoulders sagged. "Miles told me he was going to give me that horn. He *promised* it to me. He said he was gonna set me up, introduce me around, help me get a record contract with ECM." He shook his head bitterly. "Instead, he sold the trumpet to some rich guy in Houston to keep himself in blow. The last time I saw Miles, he was so wasted he barely recognized me."

The professor reached into his pocket, pulled out the mouthpiece, and handed it to me. In the glint of the stage lights, I could see the worn metal, gold plated at the rim, with M.D. etched into the side. To a trumpet player, that mouthpiece was as distinctive as a fingerprint.

"So now what, Amby. Are you going to tell Dr. Randolph or shall I?"

As Professor Taylor watched me, I thought about all the times he had helped me. The way he'd gotten me the security guard gig after I dropped out of the Institute, the many times he'd encouraged me to keep my music going after my roommate was killed. He had committed a crime, for sure, but did I really want this man to go to jail?

Five years ago, I'd failed to save my roommate. I had run away without looking back, and I'd felt guilty ever since. I couldn't do anything about that now, but perhaps I could do something for a man who had been so kind to me.

Suddenly, I got an idea.

"Perhaps Dr. Randolph doesn't need to find out," I said, and told the professor what I had in mind.

Half an hour later, I "discovered" the missing trumpet and mouthpiece behind a pile of cleaning supplies in the janitor's closet and presented the instrument to Dr. Randolph just in time for Jet Sampson's PBS taping. President Randolph was so happy he forgot completely about firing me.

Two months passed before I saw Professor Taylor again. When we spoke, he said he had decided to leave the Institute. "I've been offered a record deal and six months of performances in Japan," he said. "It's time for me to get back out on the road again.

As we shook hands for the final time, neither one of us mentioned the Moon and Stars trumpet.

When I shared this news with Sankofa Edwards over dinner, she offered me a knowing smile. "Never take things at face value," she said. "Take the case of that white lady that got murdered in Mission Hill, for example. The cops tore up the neighborhood for weeks looking for the Black man her husband described as the killer. Turns out the woman's white husband shot her himself, then made up the whole story so's he could get away with murder." My landlady sipped her tea thoughtfully. "That's why you've always got to keep digging, Amby. Deeds done in the dark will always come to the light sooner or later."❖

# The House on Riverbend Road

## Susan Oleksiw

"How're your headaches now?" George Cooper asked, stopping along the gravel walk. The garden was laced with narrow paths of gravel, slate, and other surfaces designed to signal change in the gardens, from lilies to daisies to irises to wild grasses and more. In his khaki slacks and blue shirt, he looked like he belonged there, a homeowner inspecting his yard.

"Much, much better." Eleanor Branch brushed a few wisps of hair from her face. "So much better. I can appreciate color again."

"Glad to hear it." He nodded. "We're almost finished, but I suppose it doesn't matter."

"No, it doesn't. I can guess the results. No one has to spell it out." She glanced at the draft of the investigative report he'd given her earlier.

"How long has your family lived here?" He turned to look back at the property. A white clapboard house of two and a half stories rose beyond a terrace that ran the length of the back. A pergola jutted out from one end, the wisteria lacing its cross pieces with bright purple flowers.

"Goodness, at least five generations. My great-great grandfather built the house for his bride in the 1830s and we've been here ever since."

"The river must have been closer then."

"Yes, it ran right along here." She pointed to a depression over which arched a small footbridge. "The channel's dry now, but it used to fill up during the rainy season."

"Must have been pretty."

"It was. I sailed little boats in it, waded, looked for fish, though I never found any. I played in it almost every day in the summer. And so did my boys."

"Must have been magical." He gazed over one end of a vegetable garden.

"It was. To all of us."

"Your children all grown now?"

"Grown and gone." Eleanor's family didn't approve of sentiment and she lifted her chin. "All except one, of course."

"Yes, well . . . " George had nothing to say to that. "Thank you for your patience through all this."

She accompanied him to his car and watched him drive off.

*He was a nice man*, she thought. *It wasn't his fault he had to deliver bad news.* She turned back to the garden and wondered what would come into bloom this year, if anything. She hadn't done much— no motivation, she told people. Since her divorce, she hadn't seen the point. And then came the car accident. Surely breaking down in tears while driving was less horrible than driving drunk. But Melissa didn't seem to think so. Despite the damage to her car, she survived with barely a scratch, but you'd never know it from the fuss she made. She was debilitated with trauma and PTSD and god knows what else. The jury wept for her, and then proceeded to award her an amount that scrambled Eleanor's brain. Whenever she encountered the other woman now, she couldn't help thinking, *No wonder my husband dumped her.*

Eleanor shouldn't have been surprised at the way Melissa behaved. Two years ago she sued a small airlines. She was late, as usual, the last one to board, and claimed she tripped on the gap between the airway and the plane, a gap that had grown dangerously large as the attendants tried to hurry the departure. The airlines paid her to go away. And before that it was the local supermarket when she slipped in front of the meat counter and hit a freestanding display of canned pumpkin set up for Thanksgiving. Eleanor couldn't remember which lawsuit came before that. Discussing Melissa's many lawsuits had become part of the general entertainment among her friends at their monthly luncheon.

In the distance a clock chimed. Eleanor checked her watch. Startled at the time, she hurried to her car and headed to finish her errands before her meeting. Two hours later she sat down with her attorney in his office. This had been a disappointment the first time she met him. Instead of the traditional dark-paneled room with thick carpeting and Tiffany-style lamps, Martin Stoler preferred modern—a sleek desk set in front of floor-to-ceiling windows, with a seating area right out of *Modern Architecture.*

"Good to see you, Eleanor." He led her to the sofa and Eleanor fell into it happily.

"I'm glad to rest my feet."

"How've you been feeling?"

"Pretty good." She took a deep breath and looked around at the stark setting, the polar opposite of how her home had always looked—cluttered with family mementoes from almost two hundred years of living, every stick of furniture with a story, photographs everywhere. "I've been taking your advice and accepting the inevitable and preparing myself."

"Good." He was laconic but not terse, and she appreciated that. She really didn't want to have anyone comforting her. "I've spoken with Melissa's attorney again, but I didn't get anywhere. She is adamant that she wants payment now, which means the house and property. She's not willing to wait while you try to raise the cash to meet the court judgment."

"Not that I have any other assets, anyway. Just the house."

"She seems to know that."

"Yes. She was one of my husband's girlfriends before he decamped with someone else."

"You think she's still holding a grudge about that?"

"Who knows?" Now that she was facing the inevitable, she didn't feel quite as distressed as she expected. There was something to be said for letting go.

"Well, I didn't press him. I didn't suggest raising the money from the house."

"I wouldn't want to do that."

"No, I didn't think so."

Eleanor glanced at him, surprised by something in his tone.

"When we go into court tomorrow," he continued, "I have to hand over the keys, and the house will be hers at the end of the session. Your insurance is inadequate to cover the judgment against you, and she wants payment in full." Martin was watching her as he spoke, which she expected. He was like that, making sure whatever he said was heard and understood. He was probably waiting for her to have another breakdown, she thought, but she wasn't going to do that. Between George Cooper, kind though he tried to be, and Melissa Fraser, who didn't have the word *kindness* in her vocabulary, she was ready to capitulate.

Eleanor thanked Martin, and left.

Suddenly she was very tired, drained of any desire to do anything except sit down and enjoy the feeling of not having a headache. Just sit and feel normal. Free of stress and worry.

After her meeting with Martin she was supposed to go to another meeting, this one on the future of their little town, but it seemed like too much work to listen to town planners droning on about what was possible. It was always about what was possible, not what would you like to do, but what could you do under the circumstances. *Circumstances.* She was coming to hate that word. Better to skip the whole thing and get a good night's sleep. She wanted to look her best in court tomorrow. Let people look at her and think, "That Ben Branch sure was a fool to leave a beautiful woman like that and that beautiful historic house. No one else in town has all that history right in their own home." Just thinking about it made her feel better and she marched off to her car, reinvigorated.

Determined to maintain her dignity, Eleanor arrived at the courthouse in a navy-blue suit, white blouse, and antique gold jewelry. Her fantasy of people seeing her and wondering how Ben could have been so crazy didn't clash with reality as she feared it would. There, filling every row, were her friends and cousins and other relatives, people she had known for most of her life who had come to support her. It almost brought tears to her eyes. She couldn't help smiling, but she knew that wouldn't look good, so she composed herself and walked in with an expression of professional duty. She was good at that one. It was the story of her life, from joining every committee that asked her to help to anticipating possible problems before the verdict was in, so to speak. She took her seat next to Martin. He reached over and squeezed her hand.

Across from her was Gerald Taransky, Melissa's attorney. He merely glanced at her and returned to his notes.

"What happens at the end, when she takes the keys?"

"The judge enters an order, and it's going to be almost like a sale. Gerry's going to take that judgment and go straight to the Registry of Deeds and reregister your property. It will be hers before the clock strikes midnight."

Startled by Martin's only ever turn of phrase that suggested an imagination, Eleanor looked at him, wondering why his eyebrow was coyly arched. He was twenty years younger than she was and married, so it couldn't be romantic or sexual in any way. She forced a tight smile. She'd be glad when the whole thing was over.

"Where are you staying?" he asked.

"I have a small apartment in town."

"Not buying?"

She glanced at him. "No, definitely not buying."

The judge entered, everyone rose, and the case began. It went quickly. Melissa took the keys from her attorney and tossed them once in her palm, then leaned back in her chair, better to see past Gerald, and nodded to Eleanor, as though they were pals and this was just a friendly competition. She strutted out of the courtroom while her attorney stopped to shake hands with Martin.

"That went smoothly. Thanks," Gerald Taransky said.

Martin nodded.

"You missed the Board of Selectmen meeting last night," Martin said when he and Eleanor were alone.

Eleanor eyed him, wondering where this was going. "Yes, I did."

"You might have enjoyed it."

"How so?" She noticed for the first time the wild pink handkerchief in his suit-coat pocket. She wondered if it was something he wore for luck, since it didn't seem to go with the rest of his apparel.

"George Cooper's office is on the floor below mine."

"Oh?" Eleanor wasn't sure if she should deny everything or just run as fast as she could.

"Enviro Corp gave a preliminary review of its testing of various properties abutting the river, and its estimate for land reclamation. The company made a proposal that the town take on the responsibility for paying for the work, since the company that originally polluted the river with toxic waste has long since disappeared and no longer exists in any form."

"And the board voted how?"

"How do you think seven crusty New Englanders are going to vote?"

"After two hours of discussion, shoot it down in a majority vote in thirty minutes?" Eleanor squinted at him, trying not to grin.

"Down in five. Unanimous. Owners face mandatory reclamation costs."

"And was a certain person there?" Eleanor was almost afraid to ask but she had to know.

"If it's one thing I've learned through this case it's that neither Melissa nor Gerry follow local issues."

"How much do you think the mandatory clean-up will cost?" Eleanor inched closer to her attorney; she was practically whispering in his ear she was so afraid yet eager to learn the results.

"Enviro Corp will be sending out the final report in about a month, with the estimated costs to each homeowner along the path of the river. The cost for the reclamation of the land attached to your former home is estimated at three times the value of the house and its contents." Martin took a step back and extended his hand. Eleanor took it.

"Well done, Mrs. Branch."

"And the same to you, Mr. Stoler." ❖

# Contributors' Notes

**Jason Allison**, a Bronx native, spent two decades with the New York City Police Department. He won the 2022 Al Blanchard award for crime fiction, and his work has been featured in the lit-noir journal *Rock and a Hard Place* and *Deadly Nightshade: Best New England Crime Stories 2022*. He has consulted for authors and screenwriters and presented to members of the Mystery Writers of America and attendees of ThrillerFest. He lives in New England with his wife and their Golden Retriever. He can be reached at jason-allison.com or on Instagram @jasonallison76.

**Christine Bagley** publishes her short stories in both crime anthologies and literary journals. With an MFA in Creative Writing from Lesley University, she was a fiction contributor to the Bread Loaf Writer's Conference, and taught writing and presentation skills to Harvard Medical School foreign national scientists and physicians from 2011 to 2019. Short-listed for the Al Blanchard Award, her stories have appeared in *Briar Cliff Review*, *Bryant Literary Review*, *Untoward Magazine*, *Fiction on the Web, UK*, and she is a regular contributor to *Best New England Crime Stories*. When she has time, she enjoys writing Amazon book reviews.
www.christinebagley.com

**Brenda Buchanan**'s crime fiction reflects her experience as a journalist and lawyer. Her three-book Joe Gale mystery series—*Quick Pivot, Cover Story,* and *Truth Beat*—feature a Maine newspaper reporter covering the crime and courts beat. Her short story, "Means, Motive, and Opportunity," published two years ago in *Bloodroot*, made the list of Other Distinguished Stories in *Best American Mystery and Suspense 2022*. Brenda serves on the organizing committee for the New England Crime Bake and the Maine Crime Wave conferences. You can find her on the web at https://brendabuchananwrites.com

**Christine H. Chen** was born in Hong Kong and grew up in Madagascar before settling in Boston, where she worked as a research chemist. Her fiction has been published in *The Pinch*, *Hobart*, *Bending Genres, SmokeLong Quarterly, Atticus Review*, and other literary journals. This is her first publication of a short mystery story. She is a recipient of the 2022 Mass Cultural Council Artist Fellowship and the co-translator from French of the novel *My Lemon Tree* (Spuyten Duyvil, late 2023). Her publications can be found at www.christinehchen.com

**Bruce Robert Coffin** is the award-winning author of the Detective Byron Mysteries. A former detective sergeant with more than twenty-seven years in law enforcement, he is the winner of Killer Nashville's Silver Falchion Awards for Best Procedural, and Best Investigator, and the Maine Literary Award for Best Crime Fiction Novel. Bruce was also a finalist for the Agatha Award for Best Contemporary Novel. His Anthony Award nominated short fiction appears in a number of anthologies, including *Best American Mystery Stories 2016*.

**Michael Ditchfield** is a writer of novels, plays, haiku, essays, and short stories. A quarter-century of practicing social work taught him that life is fragile, life is dangerous, everyone is wounded, yet people do heroic, selfless, and beautiful things. He tries to capture that spirit in his writing. He won the William Faulkner–William Wisdom Writing Contest for his essay "Zen and the Art of Dementia," about caring for his mother who had Alzheimer's Disease. He also won the Stonecoast Writers' Conference Humor Award. But his first literary love is crime fiction. He's thrilled to be included in *Wolfsbane*.

**Judith Green** is the sixth generation of her family to live on her hillside in rural western Maine, with the seventh and eighth generations living nearby. As Adult Education Director for her eleven-town school district, she wrote twenty-five high-interest/low-level books for adult students for several publishers. Her mystery stories and poems have appeared in multiple magazines and anthologies. "A Good, Safe Place," published in Level Best's *Thin Ice*, was nominated for an Edgar.

**Connie Johnson Hambley's** short stories appear in *Mystery Magazine, Running Wild Collection,* and the Anthony Award— nominated Mystery Writers of America anthology *Crime Hits Home.* Her writing also appears in *Bloomberg BusinessWeek, Financial Advisor,* and *Nature.* Connie is co-chair of New England Crime Bake, a past president of Sisters in Crime New England, and a passionate fan of (fictional) crime. Learn more about Connie's award-winning novels—where family secrets link a world-class equestrian to a Boston-based terrorist cell—at www.conniejohnsonhambley.com and follow her on Twitter @ConnieHambley.

**Sean Harding** spent over two decades as a clinical social worker working with people in the Massachusetts criminal justice system. Lately, he has devoted time to writing crime fiction. This is his first published story. Sean is a lifelong resident of Massachusetts. He currently lives in a metro west suburb of Boston and is the proud father of an adult daughter.

**Eleanor Ingbretson**, a Northern New Hampshirite, busies herself with family, church, gardening, reading, and writing short stories, though not necessarily in that order. "Rodrigo's Revenge" was published last year in *I Found Happiness and Tragedy*, a Literary Taxidermy publication. "The Tabac Man" was published in 2022 in *An Element of Mystery,* a Bethlehem Writers Group publication, as the first-place winner and subsequently nominated for a Derringer Award. "Seven Women," which appears in *Wolfsbane: Best New England Crime Stories 2023,* is linked to, and follows "The Tabac Man" chronologically. The author is continuing the series.

**Zakariah Johnson** plucks banjos and pens horror, thriller, and crime fiction on the banks of the Piscataqua. He is the author of the collection *Egg on Her Face: Stories of Crime, Horror, and the Space in Between* (2022) and of the 1990s ecoterrorism crime-horror novel *Mink: Skinning Time in Wisconsin* (2023). Follow him @pteratorn (it's a bird!)

**Paula Messina**, who can name the capitals of the six New England states, has a great sense of direction and rarely gets lost. When she isn't strolling the first public beach in the Unites States, she writes short stories and essays. She's working on a novel set in Boston during 1944. Her work has appeared in various publications, including *The Boston Herald, The Cambridge Chronicle, THEMA Literary Journal, Ekphrastic Review,* and *Indelible Art and Literary Journal.* An award-winning public speaker, she records works in the public domain for librivox.org.

**Susan Oleksiw** is the author of three mystery series. The Pioneer Valley Mystery series features Felicity O'Brien, farmer and healer (*Below the Tree Line*). Anita Ray, Indian American photographer living in her aunt's tourist hotel, uncovers murder in South India, (*Under the Eye of Kali*). The Mellingham series features Chief of Police Joe Silva, in a coastal New England town (*Murder in Mellingham*). Susan's short stories have appeared in *Alfred Hitchcock Mystery Magazine* and other magazines and anthologies. She co-founded Crime Spell Books, with Leslie Wheeler and Ang Pompano. Susan is a member of Sisters in Crime, and currently vice-president of the New England chapter. She is also a member of Mystery Writers of America and The Authors Guild. https://www.susanoleksiw.com

**Robin Hazard Ray** is a crime fiction writer, historian, and essayist. She leads tours at historic Mount Auburn Cemetery in Cambridge. The cemetery provides the setting of her Murder in the Cemetery novels

*The Strangers' Tomb* and *The Soldiers' Rest*. Her story "Clay" appeared in *Deadly Nightshade: Best New England Crime Stories of 2022*. In her spare time she helps tend the courtyard garden at the Isabella Stewart Gardner Museum and makes quilts. She lives in Somerville, MA, with her husband David and two black cats.

**Ray Salemi** (as Ray Daniel) is the award-winning author of Boston-based crime fiction. His short story "Give Me a Dollar" won a 2014 Derringer Award for short fiction, and "Driving Miss Rachel" was chosen as a 2013 distinguished short story by Otto Penzler, editor of *The Best American Mystery Stories 2013*. Salemi's work has been published in the Level Best Books anthologies *Thin Ice, Blood Moon*, and *Stone Cold. Terminated* is his first of three novels featuring series character Tucker.

**Lauren Sheridan**, when not collapsing under the weight of mounds of Japanese-to-English translation, enjoys the classic mysteries of Agatha Christie, Louise Penny, and Anthony Horowitz. She has an irrational fear that her internet search history on poisonous concoctions will land her on the FBI's most-wanted list. In addition to writing, she enjoys photography and therapeutic watercolor painting. Her niece enjoys guessing what the paintings are. Lauren enjoys the 70% success rate.

**Bonnar Spring** writes eclectic international thrillers. A nomad at heart, she hitchhiked across Europe at sixteen and joined the Peace Corps after college. After living and teaching overseas, Bonnar returned to the U.S. where she earned an M.Ed. from Harvard and taught ESL for many years. Bonnar recently trekked to Macchu Picchu for a significant birthday. Her award-winning debut, *Toward the Light*, is set in Guatemala, and the newly-released *Disappeared* takes place in Morocco.

**Gabriela Stiteler** is a writer and educator based in Portland, Maine. She grew up in Northwestern Pennsylvania on a steady diet of paperback books from the Golden Age of detective fiction and classic noir films. She's partial to twisty plots and classic tropes reimagined. Lately, she's been thinking about what might cause a good person to do bad things. Her debut short story, "Two Hours West of Nowhere," was published in *Ellery Queen Mystery Magazine* earlier this year.

**Frances Stratford** writes historical mysteries featuring unusual sleuths, colorful places, and all kinds of political treachery. Frances has published several historical short mysteries and is working on a mystery novel featuring Anne of Cleves, Henry VIII's fourth wife. Before she started writing historical fiction, Frances earned a Ph.D. in English Literature from the University of Massachusetts. She's currently a recovering academic who dreams of writing fiction full time. You can find her hiking with her dog, teaching Chaucer, and at FrancesStratford.com

**Leslie Wheeler** is the award-winning author of two mystery series: the Berkshire Hilltown Mysteries and the Miranda Lewis Living History Mysteries. Her short crime fiction has appeared in numerous anthologies including the Best New England Crime Stories anthologies, published by Level Best Books, where she was a co-editor/publisher for six years, and now by Crime Spell Books, where she holds the same position. A member of Mystery Writers of America and Sisters in Crime, she serves as Speakers Bureau Coordinator for the New England chapter. She divides her time between Cambridge, Massachusetts, and the Berkshires, where she writes in a house overlooking a pond.

**Carolyn Marie Wilkins** is the author of *Death at a Séance, Melody for Murder, Mojo for Murder, Damn Near White,* and *They Raised Me Up.* She is a psychic medium, a Reiki Master, and a priestess of Yemaya, the African goddess of motherhood. A professor at Berklee College of Music Online,

Carolyn has performed with the Pittsburgh Symphony and toured as a Jazz Ambassador for the U.S. State Department.

*Wolfsbane*

Made in the USA
Middletown, DE
10 October 2023